THE
DEFENDER

BOOK ONE OF THE GATLIN SERIES

LARISSA SOEHN

Tellwell Talent
www.tellwell.ca

ISBN
978-0-2288-6604-6 (Hardcover)
978-0-2288-6603-9 (Paperback)
978-0-2288-6605-3 (eBook)

This book is dedicated to my husband.
He is the strength behind my creativity.
Without him, this book would not have been possible.
I love you, Kyle.

Galaxy of Gatlin

Muskoux

Alars
(Planet of Knowledge)

Lillon
(Planet of Entertainment)

Zeya
(Planet of Transportation)

Trayton
(Planet of Resources)

Solax
(Home of the Planetary
Peace Council)

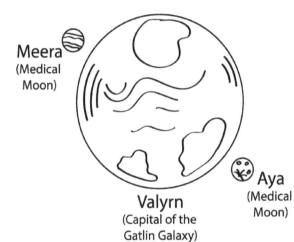

Meera
(Medical
Moon)

Valyrn
(Capital of the
Gatlin Galaxy)

Aya
(Medical
Moon)

Barter
(Prison Planet)

PROLOGUE

His hands drip with thick green blood. His fingers slide around inside the creature's body, pulling, pushing, prodding. Finally, he finds what he is looking for, and with a sharp pull, he takes out the small object. He stares down at the tiny orb and marvels at it.

This will be the thing that ends them, rendering them powerless. The thought is vicious, but he has no time for kindness. Not now.

Quickly he turns and gently places the soft ball under a microscope. Staring into the lens, and using advanced medical tools, he prods at the centre of the ball, peeling away the outer shell. Inside is a thick, hard stone-like substance. Carefully he pulls it out. Cold radiates from it as if it could snatch all of the heat out of the room.

Careful to not drop or touch the substance, he swivels around and walks past the dead creature while moving to the second table.

Strapped here is a creature of nightmares. A long, lean body that will tower over all that it meets. Pincers adorn each appendage that will cut through anything it desires, and a face to leave the beings of the societies wetting themselves in fear.

He laughs lightly, looking over his creation with manic fondness. Carefully, he inserts the rocky substance into the cavity that has been carved open to receive the powerful object. The creature's chest rises and falls lightly, supported by the machines that whir next to the table.

Stitching up the creature, he flicks a switch that pumps adrenalin into its massive system. It takes a few seconds, but the creature's eyes fly open and look around aggressively. The eyes looking back are human, but everything else is alien. The strongest parts of many species, all stitched together into one beautiful destroyer.

With one wild whoop, the creature activates its newest power, sucking all the heat from the room. The creator shivers and lunges for the control button. As the room starts to frost over and the air freezes, he presses the button, his fingers creaking as they bend against the cold that suddenly engulfs him.

With a violent spasm, the creature jerks madly on the table and is rendered temporarily useless. He smiles grimly. This is it; this will kill them all.

CHAPTER

Her heart races and her lungs burn while yearning for oxygen. Blood rushes through her veins, thumping past her ears. She pushes herself, urging her legs to move faster. Glancing around, she makes a last-minute decision and veers left, pushing her body across the long field. The grass is damp with morning dew, and it compresses under her feet, barely leaving any indication that she was there.

Alexia Harmon breathes deeply, feeding her tiring body with the fuel that it so desperately craves. Finally, she slows to a jog and rounds the corner of the park. The sun rises over the edge of the houses, winking at her.

Allowing her steady breathing to return, she moves at a slower pace. Her lean muscles rejoice at the chance to recover from the fast push.

Her busy mind suddenly floods with anxious thoughts; the frantic workday she has ahead of her, the meals she has to make to feed her family, the shopping she needs to get done. The list goes on and on. Her breathing becomes rapid once more as anxiety pulls at her and threatens to spill over.

Alex's feet stop suddenly, seemingly unable to move another step. Her chest rises and falls rapidly, moving faster than it did when she was running. Anxiety washes over her, and she doubles over. Resting her hands on her knees, she tries to catch her breath and loosen the tightening feeling in her chest. Long moments pass with her standing motionless, her body paralyzed by her anxiety.

Finally, she draws her thoughts to the edges of her mind and digs for something positive. She reaches for the happiest part of her life. As thoughts of her family trickle in, her angst starts to ebb slightly. Images of her sweet little girl float through her mind, and a slight grin spreads across Alex's face. Next, her husband dances into her mind, literally. The image of him smiling and dancing pops into her head, and she chuckles lightly. She takes another deep breath and allows her family to bring her back from the brink of a panic attack.

Continuing to focus on her breath, she thinks of the truly important things in her life — family over everything.

Breathe, Alex, breathe. You are strong, you are independent, and you are worthy. The mantra runs through her mind. She repeats it until the worry that incapacitated her starts to subside, and she can force her feet to step forward once more.

Rounding the corner to her home, a harsh barking disrupts her moment of mindfulness. Pulling her attention back to her surroundings, her eyes find the aggressive little dog in the neighbour's yard. "Shush," she scolds the small dog, "must we do this every day?" Despite her efforts to silence the little yapper, he continues to bark regardless. Alex sighs.

Passing by the grumpy dog, she tilts her head up to the sky and works to tune him out. The brightening sky overhead forces her eyes to squint against the harsh light. The sun beats against the overhead clouds, and a few errant rays peak their way through. *It's going to be a nice day,* she thinks to herself, and a moment of thankfulness pushes into her head.

Reaching the edge of her home, Alex stops in the driveway and moves into a deep lunge. She feels the deep ache that comes with her morning workouts, a feeling that is enhanced by the push of her final sprint across the field. Deliberately taking care to target each muscle, she moves through a series of stretches.

Her lean legs, clad in black jogging capris, sweep out in front of her. Long blonde hair falls over one shoulder as she uses her arms to pull herself forward. Letting out a deep sigh, she works to slow her mind even further. Straightening up, she pulls down on her pink tank top in a nervous motion. Her fingers tremble as she imagines the wrinkles of her mind smoothing out the way the shirt does.

Why am I like this? The thought bounces into her head, along with a million other negative feelings. *I am weak; I am useless; I am unlikeable.* Tears well in her eyes as the depression sneaks up inside of her and forces cruel thoughts into her head. *Stop!* Shouting the thought to herself, she pulls back on her mantra, *you are strong, you are independent, and you are worthy. Not today, depression.*

She moves to a seated position and, with a deep breath, crosses her legs and rests her hands in her lap. She sometimes laughs at what her neighbours must-see; her seated in her driveway in what must appear to be a trance. Regardless of what they may think, she turns her mind inwards and works to tune out the noise of the moving world around her. The sound of laughing children and moving cars pulls at the edge of her attention, but she focuses on her inner self, picturing her happy place in her mind. She sits like this for several minutes, breathing steadily in and out and counting her breaths as they pass through her lips.

The feeling of peace washes over her, and she lets her eyes drift open and pulls her body up to standing. Shaking out her arms, she looks around, squinting as her eyes adjust to the light once more. With effort, she moves her stiff muscles forward and climbs the steps to her home.

She enters the code into the front door with quiet motions and winces as the lock slides back with a loud clunk. *Shh...* Cautious of her still-sleeping family, she creeps inside the modest home and shuts the door behind her. It clicks closed, and she slides the lock back into place.

Kicking off each shoe, she nudges them onto the shoe rack with her toes and peels off her sweaty jacket, throwing it onto the stair railing, *something to deal with later.*

She steps further into the home on soft feet and glides through the living area, careful to avoid stepping on any of the noisy toys that are strewn about haphazardly. Entering the kitchen, she reaches over the top of the stove and pulls down a small wooden chest.

Gently she sets it down on the counter and removes the lock securing it shut. With sure fingers, Alex reaches into the chest and rummages through the assortment of pill bottles. Reading the labels carefully, she continues to push each bottle aside until she finds the one she is looking for, Xanax. Sighing with relief, she pops the lid open and takes out two pills. With a quick movement, Alex swallows the pills and leans against the countertop, allowing the soothing feeling of relief to run down her throat and into her stomach. She knows that she will soon feel the comfort of the medicine wash over her, and she will be able to continue with her day.

The house is still. Alex revels in the sound of silence that floats around her, only broken by the hum of the household electronics. In mere moments her family will wake. The house will again fill with light and love, but for now, it is full of peace and serenity.

Pushing away from the counter, Alex walks across the kitchen and moves to her favorite piece of technology, the coffee maker. Clicking it on, she listens as it purrs to life and begins its process of heating the water.

While she waits, she turns and looks out the window that faces her backyard. The stillness that she feels inside the home is matched by the calm that radiates from outside. The sun peaks through even more and casts long shadows on the grass. Alex smiles as the light wind picks up the bright green leaves, making them dance.

Smiling and looking out over the yard that she has become so proud of, a sudden flash of light blinds her. Slamming her eyes shut, she winces back as a loud pop echoes from the backyard. It takes Alex a few moments to gather her senses; it happened so quickly that she isn't even sure it happened at all.

Standing in stunned silence, she first listens for the sounds of her family. *Did they hear that? Did it wake Harley? God, I hope not; she will be so cranky.* Alex loses herself momentarily at the thought of her angry child. Remembering the blinding light and the noise, she allows her curiosity to creep back up.

Moving away from the coffee machine, she walks to the double doors that lead to her yard. Gently turning the handle, she pushes the door open and steps out onto the deck. The yard sprawls out in front of her, wrapping around the side of the house. At first glance, everything appears normal. The garden looks undisturbed. The lawn looks pristine. The deck, while needing some paint, looks just as she left it.

Alex starts to think that it was in her imagination and turns to go back inside. Turning on her heel, she draws to a halt as a slight breeze kicks up and the smell of something metallic wafts through the air toward her. As she turns to investigate, she catches a glint of something in a nearby tree. Light bounces off it in a mesmerizing way, urging her to investigate. Alex moves closer to it, and with each step, the metallic smell gets more substantial, and a faint humming noise thrums through the air, pricking at her ears.

Nestled against the tree are two foreign-looking objects. The first object is a perfectly round orb. Light bounces off it easily, reflecting the sun in a dazzling display. The material it is made of isn't one that Alex recognizes. The orb looks silver, but the way it amplifies the light is unlike anything she has seen before. The second item is propped on a lower branch and appears to be made of the same metal-like material, but it does not amplify the light. Instead, it seems to absorb it, taking in the dancing colours from the orb and swirling them around inside like a jubilant cocktail. The object is so bright and vibrant that she can't quite make out its shape.

Both objects hum loudly, each with their own frequency. Alex reaches out to pick up the orb, her hand shaking with anticipation. Grabbing the orb, she finds it slides easily into the palm of her hand, leaving her with a cooling feeling. As she moves it away from the other object, the humming grows fainter, and the light reflected from the orb seems to dull.

She gracefully turns it over in her hand, taking in the incredibly smooth texture, a perfect orb. As she rotates the orb fully, she feels the surface start to shift, and the once smooth material now has slight bumps, the places her fingers grazed only seconds ago now have very faint etchings on the surface. She runs her fingers over them again to feel the ridges of the markings. As she touches them, the edges become more defined, and the markings begin to deepen in color, standing out against the shiny metal material. Alex stares in amazement, grappling to try and understand how the orb is morphing before her eyes, as if it is reacting to her touch. Continuing to stare, she gets the impression that the etchings form a word, but it is not a language she recognizes. Her mind struggles to find the pattern, trying to piece together what it might say.

Alex's curiosity is at an all-time high. After a few moments, the orb stops changing, and Alex begins to feel the cold radiate up her arm. She reaches for the other item with her other hand. Fingers trembling, she makes contact with the second item, her fingers gliding smoothly over the surface.

While her eyes are still blind to the exact composition, her fingers determine the shape to be a small rectangle with beveled edges. She gingerly rubs her fingers around the edges before picking it up fully. At first, all she feels is heat. It pulses in her hand, leaving her with a feeling of burning, as if her hand may burst into flames. She frantically opens her clenched fingers in an attempt to drop the hot object, but it holds firmly to her hand, burning into her skin. The orb in her other hand starts to react similarly, except it radiates with a cold that leaves her with a frostbite feeling in her hand.

The two sensations run up her arms, meeting in the centre of her chest. She feels herself being simultaneously burned and frozen. Her hands scream with pain unparalleled to anything she has felt before. The dualling sensations meet in her chest, splitting her between intense hot and cold. She struggles for breath, trying to shake her hands free, but the items stick firmly as if superglued in place. Alex's vision begins to blur, and her body threatens to lose consciousness. Suddenly she hears the faint humming of the objects. They hum louder and louder until their frequencies match, and they reach an ear-splitting pitch. Light starts to emit from the orb and bounces over to the rectangle. The rectangle drinks the light in hungrily, absorbing it and then shooting it back out into the world.

Alex feels a huge pull inside her body as the items give her one final burst of energy. The light continues to intensify around her until she is blind. With one loud whoosh, Alex loses consciousness.

CHAPTER

2

lex lies on the cold ground, her mind trying to shake off the fuzziness that comes with fainting. The pain in her body that she felt only moments ago is gone. She clenches her hands together and squeezes her fingers painfully, trying to pull herself back into reality.

The light that blinded her has faded, and the sound that deafened her is gone. She pushes her palms flat onto the dirt and moves to a crouching position. She finds that extra effort is needed to push herself up, as if she is fifty pounds heavier. She grunts in response to the extra exertion. With her eyes still clenched shut and aching from the flash of light, she does a quick internal scan of her body, searching for any feelings of injury. Overall, she feels physically fine, other than a slight burning feeling dancing over her skin. Using her senses, she tries to understand exactly what just happened. She listens for sounds but is confused to find a lack of familiar noise. *What has happened to the street noise that surrounds my home? What happened to the kids laughing at the neighbour's house? Did they all feel and hear the same thing I did? Is my own sleeping family OK?* Very slowly, she opens her eyes and looks around.

The sight before her is enough to make her lose her breath all over again. Her home and everything she knows is gone, leaving her standing on a flat patch of green dirt next to what appears to be some kind of shelter.

Alex stumbles backward on heavy feet. Her breath comes in as rapid gasps, and her body shakes. *What the hell is going on! Where the... What the... What is happening!* A million thoughts run through her mind, all of them twisting and spinning around each other, creating a massive tornado of fear and dread.

Alex frantically looks around, trying to find something that looks familiar, but all she can see for miles in any direction are the strange land and the shelter. Not believing what she is seeing, she collapses to the ground. Her fingernails dig into the soil, and she can feel the small sharp rocks press into her cuticles, threatening to cut her skin. Regardless of the pain, she cannot stop the motion that she knows is hurting her. She cannot breathe. She cannot think beyond the intense imagery that is before her. Forcing her eyes shut, she pulls her knees up into her chest and wraps her arms around them. Gently, she rocks back and forth. *I don't understand. This can't be happening. Please, someone, tell me this isn't happening.* Terror whips through her body, thrashing against her like an angry storm. *I must be dreaming.* Remembering the pain of the rocks, she sobs as she realizes that she is indeed awake.

Letting go of her legs, she moves to bury her hands in her face but pulls up short as she takes in the state of her palms. Her mouth falls open as she finds new markings burned into her hands. Holding both hands up, side by side, she stares at the symbols. The edges are an angry red, having been just freshly imprinted into her soft skin. Her mind drifts back to the intense freezing feeling she felt from the orb. Looking closely, she stares in shock as her eyes scan the faint outline of a foreign language etched into the palm of her hands. The two objects responsible for these markings are nowhere to be seen.

With a quiet sob, she lets her hands drop back to her knees and looks around. She starts to cry harder. Fear roots her in place. *Even if I wasn't terrified, what would I do?* The thought is frightening. She feels completely out of power, like all the things that she can control have been ripped away from her and she is at the mercy of someone, or something, else. Continuing to cry dramatically, she goes back to her mantra: *you are strong, you are independent, and you are worthy.* Again and again, she says this to herself, willing herself to believe it but struggling to keep herself together. On the fifth repeat, something in her is put back into place, and she looks up and around. *I am strong. I am strong! Get up! Prove it!* Finding her resolve, Alex stands up and looks around, a new determination on her face. *I won't just sit here and accept this. I will do something about it. I am in control!*

There are a few things she immediately notices as strange. First, the soil she found herself lying in is a deep green rather than the brown she would expect. Second, it is very dim, not necessarily dark, but fainter than she would expect, considering she was just recently looking up at a cloudy sky.

As she thinks of the sky, she looks upward and notices a lack of clouds and, even more shockingly, a distinct lack of sun. It's not as if the sun has gone down for the night, but more like the sun doesn't exist at all or is much further away than it would typically be. There is nothing to see for miles, just green dirt that stretches out in every direction. The only structure in sight is the small shelter behind Alex.

With a shaky breath, and the panic attack threatening her, she closes her eyes again and wishes for this dream to be over. Peeking out past her eyelids, she exhales loudly and is disappointed to find herself standing in the same spot. With a hard feeling in her chest and tears drying on her cheeks, she walks with slow, heavy steps back towards the shelter and stops in front of it. The shelter closely resembles a bus stop she would find at home. Four brown walls, three of which appear to be made of a solid foreign-looking metal, and the fourth is made of a transparent plastic-like material. Small windows outline the space between the roof and the walls to allow what little ambient light there is to filter in. Inside the shelter is a small bench placed next to the clear wall. Alex moves inside to sit down, her body falling heavily and faster than she is used to. *Has the gravity increased? Why do I feel like a sack of potatoes?* She thinks to herself.

Looking around, she notices a sign in front of her that is written in another strange language. She stares at the sign for a few minutes, but there is no way to read what the message says. Next to the message is an image that looks an awful lot like a floating bus.

Sitting down, she does a quick inventory of what she has with her, and with a sudden gasp, realizes that she still has her cell phone. It, along with her house key, was in her pocket after her run and has somehow travelled all this way with her. She pulls it out and is both happy to see the full battery and devastated to see that she has no service. Wherever she is, it's far enough from home to take her out of the cell phone range.

"Oh, that can't be good," Alex says to herself with a small sigh.

Quickly, she takes a picture of the foreign sign and hoists herself to stand, groaning with the effort. She steps outside to take a photo of the shelter. The way she sees it, she will need photo evidence to show all the doctors when she is put in a mental ward later. Something to prove she is not crazy. That's what she hopes anyway.

As she looks at her camera, she hears something approaching from the distance, and a low rumble carries across the vast plain of the barren surface. Quickly she scans the area and sees a shuttle, similar to the one pictured on the sign inside the shack, approaching over the horizon. With a quick motion, she dives behind the shelter and hides from view.

Fear strikes through her as the shuttle approaches. Instead of travelling on wheels, the shuttle hovers eight inches above the ground and moves at a rapid speed, faster than anything she has ever seen back home. The shuttle draws near the shelter and pulls to an abrupt halt. After a moment of idling, a set of doors open at the front of the shuttle, and a small purple alien steps out holding a little bag. The alien has a series of huge eyes on its large, oval head. Two antennas poke out from the tip of its head, falling to the sides. The small nose of the creature is dwarfed by bulbous eyes and a large round mouth.

Alex works to stifle a scream as her mind races with a thousand scenarios. Is *it really possible that I am on an alien planet? What the hell is going on?*

As she stares out from her hidden spot, she starts to waver on her feet, her nerves getting the best of her. Alex grips the edge of the shelter a bit tighter to keep from passing out. The alien steps away from the shuttle, and the door closes behind it. Alex starts as the shuttles roars to life and speeds off, leaving Alex alone with the alien. The alien straightens its plain white robe and moves into the shelter, stepping out of Alex's view. Anxious by having lost sight of the alien, Alex moves silently around the outside of the shelter. Her body feels like lead, each step feeling heavy and exaggerated. She peers through the transparent wall, her body shaking with anticipation and fear. In front of her, the alien stands facing the opposite wall with its back turned to her. The creature has a small bald head that shines as if it was recently oiled. The robe the alien wears is thin and baggy, covering the overall shape of the creature, leaving Alex to imagine what the form of its body is.

Alex leans onto the wall, and with a soft click, the panel shifts slightly, but the noise and movement are enough to make the tightly wound Alex jump dramatically into the air. Her feet kick out and contact the side of the shelter, creating a loud thump.

The small alien whips around and stares at her. The look of panic in its eyes matches the racing feeling inside of her. Quickly she turns and runs, dashing as quickly as she can in the opposite direction. She can hear the alien calling something out to her, but she does not stop.

Her feet rush forwards as she tries to put as much space between herself and the alien as possible. With a sudden lunge, Alex is pitched forward as her foot comes in contact with an errant rock. She flips uncontrolled through the air and lands hard on the ground. Stars dance overhead, and her vision blurs. Unable to move, Alex lies on the ground and panics as she catches sight of the small alien moving towards her. Terror forces her to roll over and push herself up to a stand. As she places weight on her ankle, pain seers up her leg, and she cries out. Dropping back down to her knees, she starts to crawl away, desperate to avoid the alien that grows closer and closer.

"Please, don't hurt me!" She screams at the alien, but it does not slow its approach.

"⚶□■⸫◆ ♌︎♏︎ ☞⚹□☞⚸⚹♍︎☞ ✋ ◆⚷●● ■□◆ ♒︎◆□◆ ⊠□◆◆." The alien holds its hands up in front of it, and Alex recognizes what she hopes is a sign of peace. Unable to crawl further, she stops shuffling and turns to stare at it.

"Please, I don't know what's going on, don't hurt me." Her words come out as sobs. Her hands and knees bleed freely from crawling across the rough gravel. Her ankle has swollen to nearly twice its normal size, and her head aches from her fall. Alex stares at the alien as it moves a few steps forward and then stops. Alex starts crying, and the small alien seems to take pity on her. It kneels before her and reaches into his bag.

Imagining the worst, Alex begins to back away again, but she does not make it far. Her body aches, and the pain from her ankle threatens to pull her into unconsciousness. The alien, moving slowly and trying not to startle her, pulls out a small vial from its bag. Holding it up, it gingerly offers it to her.

Not understanding, Alex shakes her head and inches back further.

The alien gestures to her ankle and her bleeding hands and then offers the vial again. Starting to understand that the alien is offering aid for her injuries, she tentatively reaches out and takes the vial. The small circular tube slides into her hand, and she finds that it is secured closed with a tight-fitting lid. Keeping an eye on the alien, who now stands a few feet further away from her, Alex shakes the vial. Hearing nothing, she becomes slightly disappointed that it's not pills. The longer she sits on the ground, the worse the pain grows; *I think I broke something.* Glancing down, she looks at the limp way her foot hangs and how it lolls awkwardly off to the side; *yes, definitely broken.* New tears form, and she is pulled into a pile of self-pity and pain.

"Will this help me?" She asks the alien, but it does not respond with words. Instead, it motions for her to open the vial.

Not seeing much else for choices and desperately wanting some relief from her pain, she pops the lid open. Immediately her senses are overcome with a fragrant but pungent smell. Her eyes water as the vapours waft up and flood over her face. The moment she inhales, she knows she has made a mistake. The space around her starts to fade. No longer able to support her own weight, she flops backward onto the ground. As she lays there, unable to move, she watches the alien steps closer and mutters something. Her mind panics as it reaches out for her and gently touches her shoulder. Unable to move, she tries to scream, but only a low moan escapes her. Blackness envelopes her, and she once again passes out.

CHAPTER

Andy happily rushes around the house, moving seamlessly between the kitchen and the dining area. "Pancakes for sale! Pancakes for sale!" He swings a hot plate of fresh pancakes comically through the air and lands them with a loud drop in the centre of the table. Harley laughs happily at her silly daddy. Alex laughs along with them.

She feels joy at being with them. Everything is once again right in her world. She watches as Harley giggles along with her daddy. When Harley is fully distracted with her pancakes, Alex pulls Andy into a soft kiss and gives his butt a squeeze. He gives her a small wink and then turns back to his daughter, always the doting father.

"Are you excited for the day, dolly?" Alex asks her daughter, watching as the small girl pulls a huge piece of pancake towards her mouth.

But something isn't right. They don't hear her.

Suddenly Alex is standing outside the house, staring in through the window. She presses her hands against the glass and knocks against it, but they don't hear her. She starts to panic as she watches the happy family bustle around without her. She calls, "Andy! Harley!" But they do not respond. Alex lightly knocks against the glass, trying to get their attention. She does not understand why she cannot get back inside. Growing nervous, she begins pounding harder against the glass. She watches as the frame ripples under the pressure. With one final scream, her fists push against the glass, and it shatters into a million pieces. The images of Harley and Andy fall with it, and she is left staring into a dark house. The lights are out, and there is no noise to be heard. Alex steps through the broken glass and winces as the jagged pieces cut into her feet. As she steps into the house, her feet leave bloody streaks behind her, the blood standing out as a vibrant red against the blackness of the home. She shouts again, "Andy! Harley!" No answer.

Sliding around on the thin pool of blood that has formed under her, she steps over to the dark staircase and begins the climb. Everything that made this house feel like a home is gone. There is no love or light. It feels like something has devoured all that she cherished and left nothing in its place. The walls echo her sound back to her, enhancing the feeling of desolation.

Stepping up to the doorway that leads into the master bedroom, Alex becomes aware of a harsh cold that leaches from under the bottom of the door. The toes of her bloodied feet curl under, trying to protect themselves against the frozen air. Her hands tremble as she reaches for the handle, but as she pushes her fingers forward, she watches the door handle inch away. Alex stares in bewilderment before she realizes that something is pulling her from behind. Not seeing anything, she fights against the mysterious force and reaches further, only to be drawn back even more. Despite all her effort, the door handle remains out of her reach.

Suddenly, where there was once nothing, she feels the firm grip of something wrap around her waist. Looking down, she sees the tentacle of a monster wrapping itself around her. Terrified of the creature, she thrashes violently and tries to scream, but no noise escapes her lips. The creature behind the tentacles eyes her hungrily. The grip it has on her starts to tighten, and her ability to breathe becomes restricted.

With a gasping jolt, Alexia wakes up and finds herself strapped to a bed. All around her, aliens shuffle about, moving around her small bed frame, all on a mission of their own. Alex's eyes go wide, and she screams bloody murder, but the noise that escapes her comes out muffled. Realizing that she is wearing a muzzle, she pulls aggressively against her restraints and thrashes around.

A passing alien stops beside her and mutters something in an alien language. Without much consideration for her, he pulls out another vial from his pocket, places it under her nose, and pops it open. In a second, Alex is pushed back into her horrible nightmare.

* * *

This time when Alex wakes up, she works hard not to freak out as she recalls how they sedated her the last time she panicked. She does have to admit that after some medically induced sleep, she does feel better. *I haven't slept like that in years!* The moment of glee is short-lived as she once again finds herself in the middle of what appears to be an alien hospital.

Still strapped to the bed, Alex grunts and wiggles lightly until an alien passing by stops. It appears to take pity on her and removes her muzzle. "Please! Where am I? I don't understand." She immediately calls out.

Aliens all around look over to her, but the one standing before her responds,

"⬡□◆ ⬡◌⦿ ⵋ■ ⬧⬡⬟⬠□⬚ ⬡□◆ ◆⦿⦿ ◆□⬡ ■◆□□□◆⦿⬩ ⬧⦿⦿ ⵌ⬡ ◆⬧⦿ ⬡◌ⵋ ⦿■ ◆⬧⬡◆ ⵋ□◆■⬩ ⬡□◆ □■ ◆⬧⦿ □◆◆◌⬒ⵋ◆◆⬒ ⬢⦿ ⬡◌⦿ ⬧⦿□⦿ ◆□ ◆□⦿⬡◆ ⬡□◆□ ◆□◆□■⬩◆."

Alex gawps at him as she struggles to understand what he is saying. "English?" she says with a squeaky voice.

"Nglsh?" The alien awkwardly tries to repeat her word back to her.

"ⵌ□⬚ ⵖ ⵍ⬡⬡■■□◆ ◆□⦿⬡⬒ ◆⬧⬡◆ ⦿⬡■⵾◆⬡⵾⦿⬚ ⵋ◆◆ ⵖ ◆ⵋ⬟⬟ ⬭ⵋ■⬩ ⬡□◆ ◆□ □⦿□■⦿ ◆⬧□ ⵍ⬡■." Abruptly the alien turns and leaves. Alex is grateful that he did not put the muzzle back on, but she is terrified to find herself still strapped to the bed. All around her, aliens lay on similar beds, but Alex's heart falls as she realizes that none of them are strapped down. She pulls lightly against the restraints again. *Damn, they are tight.* Resigning to the fact that she is stuck here until someone releases her, she lays her head back down and lets her depression wash over her. *My life is over; my family is gone; who knows what has happened to them. What if they are dead? What happens if these beings torture me?* So many terrible thoughts run through her head, and even her mantra is not strong enough to pull her from her trance.

Lying still and crying, her mind has plenty of time to contemplate every terrible scenario, all of which end with her death. *I definitely won't survive this. Whatever is happening, I won't survive.* Stealing herself to that fact, she looks around the medical space and spots the same Doctor that removed her muzzle coming back to her. This time he has another alien in tow. *Here we go. This is when the torture begins.*

The two aliens come to stand in front of her. The first alien Doctor has grey skin with speckled cheeks. Its head is rounded with a healthy head of feathered hair and fine facial features. Its face reminds Alex of a monkey. The other is a small green individual. The creature only comes up to her shoulders and has a small body frame. Its round head showcases thin lips that mirror her own, as well as two deep-set eyes that hide a depth of knowledge. From what she can tell, the creature is not built for manual labour, its frail-looking body seeming to shake under the slight gusts of atmosphere that filter in through some unseen door.

The green alien looks at her as they approach and gives her a thin-lipped smile that doesn't meet the being's eyes.

Continuing the intense effort of keeping her mouth from hanging open, Alex attempts to stutter out the words to ask where she is. But before she can speak, the small alien starts talking.

"⟡♏●♏♍□○♍ ◆□ ♫⟡◆●♓■ ♒ ♌□ ■□◆
□♍♍□♌♓■♓♍ ⬜□◆□ ◆□♍♍♓♍◆⌨ ◆♒♓ ♍♒♒
□●♫■♍◆♫□⬜ ♌♓◆♓♍♍♏◆ ♫□♍ ⬜□◆ ♐□□○♋"

Unfortunately, all she hears is a low, muffled sound that means nothing to her. The alien continues to stare at her with a fake smile on its lips. When she fails to respond, the alien tries again, this time in what sounds like a different dialect.

"Ωελχομε το Γατλιν! Ι δο νοτ ρεχογνιζε ψουρ σπεχιεσ; ωηιχη πλανεταρψ διστριχτ αρε ψου φρομ?"

Again, unable to understand the small, thin creature, Alex manages to squeak out a single word. "English…?"

The alien's face takes on one of confusion and uncertainty. Alex worries that she will never be able to communicate with these beings. Just as she starts to pull harder against her restraints, the alien smiles once more and repeats her word. "English. English!" It says. The alien grows overly excited, a genuine smile spreading across its face as it pulls out a book that was hidden somewhere in its baggy clothes. It flips through the pages, and Alex catches a glimpse of what appears to be multiple alien languages, until suddenly the creature lands on one that she recognizes, English!

The alien takes a quick read through the contents, its large eyes moving rapidly over the page, seemingly absorbing the content more quickly than Alex ever thought possible. With a slight throat-clearing sound, the alien says, "Welcome to Gatlin! I do not recognize your species. Which planetary district are you from?"

Alex shifts uncomfortably on the bed. *How could anyone learn a new language so quickly?* With a deep breath, she manages to string together a few words. "I am human... from Earth?" The statement comes out as a question. She has never had to explain her galactic origins before. With her mind still struggling to keep from collapsing in on itself, she stutters out a more important question, "Are you going to hurt me?"

The alien gives her an appalled look, "No, we are not going to hurt you. We are not barbarians. You are on the planet Meera, which is the main hospital moon for the Galaxy of Gatlin. Tell me, how did you get to Gatlin?"

Alex looks at the being, trying to keep up with what the creature is saying to her. Her mind works to form an intelligent response, but all that comes out is, "Gatlin?"

"Yes, we are in one of the thousands of inhabited galaxies, all thanks to the Stone Set Holders." The being's tone remains pleasant, but its face starts to show some annoyance at her lack of understanding. "How did you get to this galaxy?"

"What are Stone Set Holders?" Alex continues to stare at it. She doesn't mean to dodge the being's question, but her mind simply cannot process all that it is telling her.

Sighing, the smile drops off the alien's face. "The Stone Sets are the...You know what, now isn't the time. How did you get here?" The alien's question is no longer pleasant.

"I was in my backyard on Earth, and these two objects appeared out of nowhere. When I touched them, they took me to a weird shelter in the middle of nowhere." Alex looks at the alien desperately. "Then I was attacked and woke up here!"

The Doctor chimes in, seemingly having learned English just as fast as the other alien, "You were not attacked. You were discovered by one of our medical staff who was on her way to work. You were lucky to have been found by someone so kind. She certainly didn't have to help you and transport you here." The Doctor's nasally voice is indignant.

Alex rolls her eyes, "Whatever, it sure felt like an assault to me." She awkwardly motions down to her broken ankle. But as she does, she realizes that it no longer throbs. Tentatively, she flexes the foot back and forth and finds that there is no pain at all.

"We fixed that for you," the Doctor huffs, "no need to say thank you." With that, he turns on his heels and stalks away.

The remaining alien stares at her, eyeing her up and down. A long moment of silence stretches between them before the being finally speaks. "So, you travelled via Stone Set? How strange." He turns to pull out another object from inside his clothes. This time he produces a small computer-looking device. With the click of a button, a hologram flashes up before his eyes. "I don't see any new Stone Set Holders Catalogued here, nor do I see any registered deaths. Tell me, human, what is your name, and how did you come to possess the Stone Set?"

Alex glances around and notices that other beings nearby have perked up at the mention of human and are listening intently.

"My name is Alexia," she replies, "and like I just told you, I was in my yard on Earth when these objects, a Stone Set as you called them, appeared out of nowhere. I picked them up and found myself in the middle of nowhere," she continues, angry that she has to repeat herself. "Now it's my turn to ask a question again. If you aren't planning on torturing me, then tell me how to get home!" Her question quickly turned into a demand.

The alien looks her up and down, this time more tentatively. "So, you did not receive instructions or training with the Stone Set. Hmm, that is a problem." The alien takes a moment to form a response. "Where is the Stone Set now? Can I see them?"

Alex looks around hesitantly; something in her is telling her to keep the information about the Stone Set a secret, like a small voice in the back of her mind, one that she isn't entirely sure belongs to her. Tentatively, Alex responds, "When I arrived here, on this planet, the Stone Set was gone, leaving only these marks behind." The voice in the back of her mind makes her feel as if she has revealed too much.

But Alex doesn't have time for mysterious feelings or voices. She can barely process the ones she already has bouncing around in her head. Besides, she is getting very annoyed with this little alien. Why won't it tell her how to get home? Why does it care about this Stone Set so much?

Easy Alex, she says to herself, *you're on a foreign planet, for crying out loud. Take a breath and let the alien speak.* With a small, strangled giggle that makes her feel like she is going crazy, she turns her attention back to the alien.

The alien glances at her hands, and Alex realizes she is still holding them face up for the alien to see. The marks on her palms are a bright red, standing out vibrantly against her pale skin. The alien makes a slight sound of discontent. Quickly, it moves around to the side of her bed. Despite her hands and feet still being bound, Alex pulls as far away from the alien as she can. A look of terror comes over her face as the alien reaches for her. Its hands fall impatiently to its sides, "Oh, relax! I am just going to undo your restraints… Unless you are going to do something stupid?"

Alex shakes her head and relaxes only slightly as the alien undoes the series of clasps. Sitting up, she rubs her wrists. "Thanks." The idea of simply running away crosses her mind, but then she realizes that she has nowhere to go.

From her new vantage point, she can fully take in the oddness that is this being before her. Unlike her traditional human body, this being has three legs and four arms. The alien is outfitted in a sizeable beige suit that hangs loosely over the variety of limbs. Alex makes a note of the arrangement of pockets in the shirt, impressed by the amount it must be able to carry. *I wish my clothes had that many pockets.* The thought makes her giggle, *I'm losing my mind.*

The alien looks at her warily, grabs its translator book, and motions for her to follow it. She hesitantly steps forward, unsure of what other actions to take. "My name is Androx, I hail from the planet Lillon, but I work for the Embassy on Valyrn." Androx rattles on about Valyrn and Gatlin, but Alex was lost from the beginning, barely registering that Androx was a name, not a place. He continues to talk as they wind their way through the medical space. "We are going to be travelling by transport station to the heart of Valyrn, which is the capital planet for Gatlin. As I said before, we are currently on Meera." Androx explains.

Androx leads a nervous Alex from the main room of the hospital and takes her into a long, narrow hallway that extends as far as she can see in either direction. "This way Alexia." He pauses, "Just to confirm again, you are *not* going to run away screaming and crying, are you?"

Alex wonders if the alien is subtly referring to her first interaction with an alien but brushes it off as a coincidence. "No, I have nowhere to go until you tell me how to get home." The words are simple and true, but to Alex, they sound like a nail in a coffin. She is stuck here and at the mercy of these aliens, whether she likes it or not.

Alex shuffles her feet along, noticing that her ankle now makes a slight clicking noise when she walks. With a bit of happy insight, she realizes that she is still in her jogging clothes. Thankful that the aliens didn't see fit to undress her, she sighs. Her hand lightly brushes against her pocket, where she feels the bulge of her cell phone.

Androx leads her down the hallway and past a series of doors. Pausing at one, he pushes the large door open, and they enter a large white room. Aliens bustle around, making Alex's brain want to explode. She stares with a tangle of terror and awe at the mixture of races before her.

As she stares, she finds yet another thing to be mystified by. The aliens in this room seem to appear out of thin air, and then disappear just as easily. Androx looks to her, "Transport stations. They will carry you to any of our inhabited planets in Gatlin."

Despite her best efforts, Alex's mouth hangs open; this is too much for her. As a large yellow alien lumbers towards her, she presses herself back against the wall and stares with horror. The yellow alien, who is headed for the door next to Alex, stops briefly and takes in the terrified look on her face, "☼◆♎♏," it says and then pushes past her.

Androx chuckles, clearly he thinks that whatever the alien said was funny, but Alex highly doubts she would agree.

"I can't do this. Just send me back to Earth. Please." Tears start to roll from her eyes as her breathing becomes laboured, and a panic attack forces her to squat down against the wall.

Looking embarrassed, Androx comes to stand before her, "Alexia, this is not the place, nor the time. I cannot send you home. You must get up so we can take you to the Embassy of Valryn. I will be able to explain more to you there." He is impatient with her, but he doesn't understand that his impatience only adds to her anxious state.

Sinking deeper into her legs, she wraps her arms around her head and cries deeply. Her arms act as a shield to block out the sights and sounds of the room.

Above it all, she can still hear Androx sigh, "This is ridiculous," he mutters to himself. Alex can hear him shuffling through one of his many pockets. Lifting her head slightly, she catches sight of another vial.

Quickly she stands up and skirts around him so that her back is facing the room. "You will not use that on me!" She yells, drawing more unwanted attention to herself.

"Relax, this one isn't a sedative. It's a relaxing agent. It will help you cope, unless you would prefer to stay here and cry?"

Alex thinks about his offer. She desperately misses her Xanax back at home. Making an irrational decision based solely on the fact that she yearns for medication to help control her increasing panic attacks, she reaches out and takes the vial. It looks the same as the one that knocked her out twice. Hoping not to be a fool that is tricked three times, she looks at Androx, "Promise this won't put me to sleep?"

He rolls his eyes, "I promise, can you just get on with it? I have other business to attend to today."

Resenting him for his lack of compassion, she pops the lid of the vial and inhales deeply. She is pleased to find that the smell wafting out is indeed different than that of the sedative. This one smells acidic with hints of sweetness. Images of oranges flash through her mind.

"Wow, that stuff is amazing!" Immediately, Alex feels her body relax, and her mind move to a fuzzy state. Her worries and fears subside, and she is left with nothing but open curiosity for the space she is in.

"You aren't the only being to suffer from anxiety, now, come." He leads her to the edge of the room, where a stand holds a panel of buttons. Alex recognizes them as being similar to the ones she found in the strange shelter when she first arrived. Her fingers reach out, almost as if they are out of her control, and hover dangerously above a button. Androx slaps her hands back. "Don't touch that one. We are going to Valyrn," he points to another button, "this one. Once you press it, you will be transported to a transport station directly outside of the Embassy. I will be right behind you. Just wait for me, OK?"

Alex nods, the relaxant in her system working fully. She is excited. Taking a numb finger, she pushes the button. A light pinching sensation washes over her body, and a whooshing sound echoes around her ears. For a brief moment, the world goes black, and then light erupts once more. The white space she was standing in is now gone, and a brightly coloured outdoor space has replaced it.

Quickly closing her eyes and reopening them, she finds herself thrown into the middle of what she can only assume is a high-functioning alien society. Alex finds herself inside a small shelter, one that mirrors the first one she saw. Cautiously, she steps just outside of the doorway and finds the space opens up into the centre of a busy pedestrian roadway.

All around her, life bustles as creatures move around with an unknown purpose. Tall, vibrant blue buildings shoot up out of the ground toward the skyline. They are taller than anything she has ever seen back on Earth. They arch over the top of the streets to make contact in the middle, repeating this pattern for as far as her eyes can see. It's as if there are layers upon layers to this civilization, each bringing something new to marvel at. It reminds her fondly of a rainbow, minus the varying colours.

The infrastructure around her is a stunning mix of shapes and colours. Bright lights dance across all the surfaces, reflecting off the tall buildings around her. Looking for the source, Alex's eyes land on what she can only assume is a makeshift sun stationed high above the buildings.

The large ball of light in the sky is similar to the sun she would find on Earth, powerful enough to cast light across an entire alien city. Cords can be seen running from it, powering the orb to give off light. It throws light over the city with a bright but eery, yellow tint. A large pole runs up the back of the light, holding it firmly in place.

Wind blows through the air around her, lifting her hair off her shoulders. Alex realizes with a startling notion that she can breathe the atmosphere here. Looking around frantically, she finds that all the varying species around her seem to be breathing without difficulties. *How strange. There is no way we all need the same oxygen to breathe. How are we all still alive?* The thought is chilling.

Looking around for an answer, she follows the direction of the incoming wind and finds a large air conditioner-looking machine with a series of bright lights lining the top. Each light flashes on and off, cycling through in some rhythm that Alex can't detect. The machine is positioned next to the large light bulb and blows something over the city. Alex can't begin to comprehend what it is blowing at them, but whatever it is, it supports all of them. Alex stares in awe.

Looking back down to her feet, she finds black streets wrap around the brown shelter in varying directions, seemingly moving any way they feel.

Alex watches as alien pedestrians move on foot throughout the streets, milling around in organized chaos. Violet trees thrust into the sky around her, closely resembling palm trees, but their leaves point upwards rather than down. Small orange bushes line the edges of the streets, breaking up the travel paths of the aliens, guiding them towards popular destinations. There are two other brown shelters near her. Aliens whoosh in and out of them, coming and going in a steady stream.

Clamping her eyes shut again, she looks down to the ground and forces herself to breathe. Even with the help of the relaxant, the dramatic scenery is more than she can handle. Her anxiety is slamming against the inside of her mind, barely held in control. It threatens to drop her to her knees and leave her feeling empty, lost, and out of control. *You are strong, you are independent, and you are worthy. Say it again.* The mantra pulls her clear of the panic attack.

Opening her eyes once more, she looks around, and her eyes dart across the street in front of her. All around her are aliens of varying shapes, sizes, and colors. Their clothes are all very neutral coloured, as if it is the colour of their skin that makes them stand apart from each other, not the clothes they wear on their bodies. All of them are going about their daily business, shuffling around on any number of legs. Thankfully, none of them are taking any notice of her.

As she stands rooted in place, another alien appears in the shelter behind her. With a rude push, the small fuzzy creature jars her body to the side so it can exit the shelter and carry on its way. Bringing her gaze down to the being that shoved her, she makes a conscious effort to close her mouth, which she now realizes has been hanging open since she arrived in the strange place. Shuffling her feet, she moves further away from the shelter. *Where is Androx?* As if on queue, the slight alien appears from one of the shelters and strides towards her.

"Quickly, quickly, there is much to do, Alexia."

He leads her away from the shelters and toward a large set of stairs across from them. From what she can see, everyone here is travelling on foot; there are no cars in this area of the city.

Reaching the stairs, she stops again to take in her surroundings. The building at the top of the stairs is a massive structure. With large silver pillars holding up a panoramic roof, alien statues border the edges of the walls, and wide doors stretch across the opening. Above the door is a sign written in an alien language. One door is propped open, and inside, Alex can see a row of aliens working on high-tech computers. Alex follows after Androx, who happily climbs the stairs. Alex has to be more careful. Her body feels heavy under the increased gravity, and she has to work harder than normal not to stumble. She walks toward the open door and follows Androx inside.

All around her, aliens continue to work, none of them lifting their heads to acknowledge her entrance.

Feeling unnoticed and thankful for it, they continue to walk deeper into the building. As they walk past dozens of aliens, Alex's eyes land on one being who moves its arms rapidly in front of its face, seemingly swiping at bugs that are not there. "What is it doing?" Alex asks, mesmerized by its fast-moving arms.

Androx follows her gaze, "Not it, she. We identify as male and female here. I am a male, not an 'it.'" He seems annoyed with her and ignores her question, ushering her forward, past the being with the quick-moving arms.

Alex has a tough time grasping the idea of an entirely different planet existing in this foreign galaxy, one that is occupied with more aliens. Her mind is having a hard time grasping at anything right now. The best she can do is keep her feet moving, one in front of the other.

Quickly, Androx leads her past the row of desks and toward the back portion of the building. On the desks of the quietly working aliens, Alex can make out various signs, all seemingly in different languages. Every sign she passes makes her really wish she had a translator like Androx and that her mind could process the information as his did. It's very strange not being able to make out any words. Even when she travelled abroad, she could always make out some of the local languages, but here, she is at a total loss, which plays havoc with her anxiety.

Androx leads her through a set of double doors and into a long hallway. The hallway is lined with doors that lead to offices which house more working aliens. Here, Alex can make out alien-looking cars whizzing around.

Quickly, they move toward a corner office with a large window facing the streets of the civilization.

As they step into the office, Alex's eyes land on a tall purple alien seated behind a large desk. The creature has a single small eye in the centre of a large square head and a small round mouth. Its strange alien hands host two extra fingers and fly rapidly over a hologram on the desk.

With a disgruntled noise, the alien looks up at Androx, clearly displeased at being interrupted. "⸸≋☺ ⵋ⬧ ⵋ⬧⬛ ⸙■⬥⬜⬜⌧?"

Unable to understand, Alex waits for the beings to exchange their words. As Androx speaks, the alien behind the desk slowly turns its head to face her, eyeing her with interest. When Androx is finished, the alien behind the desk motions for Androx to hand over his book. With the same speed that Androx had, the purple alien absorbs the basics of the English language. Finishing in just a few moments, the alien hands the book back to Androx. It stands and moves around the desk, coming to stand in front of Alex. The being towers over her in height but is smaller than her in every other way. Its arms are thin and spindly, legs long and lean. Its clothes are made of a striking black material that reflects light as it moves. The creature looks to Androx and whispers one final thing in their native tongue. When Androx responds, both creatures turn to look at her.

Suddenly, Androx smiles and says, "Alexia, this is Stellie. She is going to join us. Please come this way Alexia, we need to take you for Stone Set Cataloguing."

She follows Androx out of the office, leaving Stellie behind to shuffle through her desk. Together, they move deeper into the building to a small room with a single chair and a small table. The room is no bigger than her office space back on Earth, but here, the walls are decorated with strange images of scenic views. Alex can only assume that these are pictures of other locations on Valyrn or possibly other planets. As she browses the pictures, one catches her eye. Nestled in the corner of the room is a picture of a small lighthouse on a rocky cliff.

She excitedly turns to Androx, "I have seen this lighthouse before. This is on Earth! Has your species been there recently?" She eyes him suspiciously. "For you to have this picture, there must have been aliens on Earth or humans here. How did you get this picture?" She looks at Androx, her mind combing through everything the alien has said, her anxiety putting new tones into the conversation, looking for areas of deception. She feels as if he is holding something back. She knew he acted differently after discovering she was a human but is there more to it? Surely, they must be used to different species in a place that is the home to intergalactic space travel, whatever that means.

Androx looks at her impatiently. He mumbles something under his breath about "newbies" and puts the fake smile back on his face. "The Stone Sets are passed down from generation to generation, and the Holders of the Sets make up the Planetary Peace Council, commonly referred to as the PPC. The Stones allow the PPC members to travel to various places around the galaxies."

"Normally," he says the word with an over-exaggeration, as if she falls outside the normal he is referring to, "to receive a Stone Set, the current Holder of the Set, upon retirement, will select whom they hand the Set down to. Typically, it stays within the family and is formally handed over. There is a large ceremony and then a lot of training for the new recipient." Androx's face grows concerned once more.

"However, in rare cases when a Council member dies unexpectedly, the Stone Set will find its new owner independently. That is what has happened in your case. If you were not gifted the Stone Set from a previous Holder, then a former Holder must have died, allowing the Stones to choose you. Because there are no deaths registered in the system, that means all the PPC members are alive and well. This tells me that you are the newest Holder of an unregistered set, a set that we did not know about."

"You see, the Stone Sets are intelligent beings in themselves. They can sense power and authority in any species and align themselves with what they need most. At least that is how we understand them to function."

"While they may appear to be simple objects, they most certainly are not. They are the balance to our intergalactic peace; they are the key to our complex system. Without them, our societies would surely fall. And should they find themselves in the wrong hands, the results could be catastrophic. When humans first appeared on Earth, they were deemed erratic and violent. The Council at the time determined that the human species was not fit to participate in the Council. They deemed that humans would not be capable of safely managing the Stones, nor could they adapt to the new ways of the fast-emerging, highly advanced societies of the other Galaxies."

"For thousands of years, the PPC has existed without a member from Earth. Periodically, a member of the PPC will check in on Earth to determine its vitality and if it is ready to participate in the PPC once more. Each time, the collective decision has been made to leave Earth as it was, a silo to stand apart from the more sophisticated societies. The PPC always knew there were lingering Stone Sets on Earth, but from what I understand, they were unable to locate them, despite their best efforts. Hence, the existence of unregistered Sets. Now that you are here, and you have returned with one of the presumably missing and unregistered Sets, it's time to have you registered."

CHAPTER

After Androx briefly explained the Stone Sets and their purpose, he left the room, leaving Alex with more questions than answers. Her mind is a vortex of worry and fears. Her breath is coming in fast and uneven, her anxiety spiking through the roof. She desperately wants to curl up into a ball on the floor and fall asleep, hoping to wake up back at home with her daughter and husband. *Where are they now? Have they noticed I am missing yet? What terrible things must they be feeling right now?* Her mind is a speeding trap, threatening to slam her into a wall and leave her struggling for breath.

Just as her thoughts start to get the best of her, the door to the small room opens and the tall purple being from the office enters. Stellie has to duck slightly to avoid hitting her head on the door frame. She postures herself in a straight-backed stance and in a high-pitched voice launches into a rehearsed speech. "Valued Stone Set Holder, welcome to Valyrn. As part of the Planetary Peace Council requirements, all new Holders must be Catalogued to ensure laws are followed and the high standards of our society are upheld. This process will be efficient, and your species rights will be maintained at all times. Do we have your consent to continue?"

With a tight throat, Alex gives a curt nod to the purple being.

Stellie looks at her and rolls her eye, pointing to the device in the top corner of the room.

"Out loud," she says in a bored tone.

Alex clears her throat and manages a clear answer, "Yes, I give consent".

Back on track, the purple being straightens again and continues. "Thank you for your consent. This session is being recorded using our high-tech recording system. This system is secure, and all your personal information will be stored in our internal logs. This is a mandatory process for all new Stone Set Holders. As mentioned, my name is Stellie, I am a lead Cataloguer, and I will be responsible for the safety of your persons and your information throughout this process. Do you give consent to proceed with the Cataloguing?"

As Stellie works through her speech, Alex has a growing feeling of fear in her stomach. She is being asked to give consent to be Cataloged by an alien race. *Is this something I should really be doing? What happens if I say no? What happens if I say yes?* Her voice rings through her mind, but it's not the only one there. Once again, Alex feels a small voice in the back of her mind telling her to proceed with caution.

Seeing no other options, and still ignoring the voice, she replies, "Yes, I give consent to be Catalogued".

"Excellent," Stellie responds. "Here is a form for you to sign. I'm sorry, I did not have time to translate it into English. The language is so infrequently used that our computers aren't familiar with the dialect. Simply sign on the dotted line and we can continue."

Stellie hands Alex a small scroll of paper. At first, Alex is surprised by the use of such an old style of record-keeping, but as she unrolls the scroll, she is once again left puzzled. Opening the scroll Alex can see that the surface of the paper is actually an exceedingly small holo-projector. Once fully unfurled, the holoscroll locks into a flat position, and a form pops up in front of Alex's nose. Moving the scroll father from her face, Alex looks over the foreign document. Stellie was right, it is all in an alien language that she cannot understand. Alex glances up to Stellie who gives her a curt nod. With nothing to sign with, Alex lifts her finger and scrolls through the document. Once she has found the bottom of the extensive document, she uses her finger and signs her name, *Alexia G. Harmon.*

The moment the holoscroll is signed, Stellie's posture becomes more relaxed. Her face twists into a mischievous smile, and Alex gets the feeling that Stellie is very much looking forward to the next step. "Alexia, we will be having other Cataloguers and members of the PPC joining us for this process. They have already been called in and are gathering in the Cataloguing Chamber." Stellie looks overly excited to have PPC members present. "You see, you are a unique case. We haven't had a human in Valyrn for many lifetimes, and I don't think we have ever had one go through the Cataloguing process. We are all curious to see how you do during this process." Stellie's smile grows across her face, making the fear in Alex's stomach grow and spread directly into her heart.

CHAPTER

5

Stellie leads the way out of the room and down a long hallway past many identical doors. Alex can feel her heart beating in her chest and hear the blood rushing in her ears. The last thing Stellie said to her, coupled with the intense look of odd joy, has left Alex feeling wobbly and scared.

She follows Stellie down the hallway that ends with doors to an elevator. Together, the two climb into the elevator, and Stellie presses a button to take them to their next destination. Alex is left feeling weak in the knees as they rapidly ascend. Soon, a feeling of moving not only up but sideways overtakes her. As she looks at Stellie in confusion, the elevator is suddenly bathed in light from an external source. Alex finds herself positioned inside a clear tube that holds the elevator as it makes its way to the destination.

Alex stares around in amazement as her senses are once again overcome by the dazzling sights before her. She struggles to process all the information that she sees, her eyes simply taking in more than her brain can handle. She was right. They were travelling not only up but also moving horizontally through one of the archways in the buildings. They are currently above a bustling roadway, moving into a neighbouring building. From this view, Alex can see the city for miles in both directions.

Aliens of all varieties travel below, some using advanced-looking cars, some moving with high-tech shoes that look remarkably similar to hoverboards, and others simply travelling on foot, moving faster than the cars.

Alex once again finds herself staring open-mouthed at the scene around her. The buildings that she first saw from the ground when she arrived have thousands of windows, a detail that she hadn't noticed before. As she tries to peer through the windows, curious to see what other mysterious things lie inside the buildings, she is plunged back into darkness. Regaining her composure, she glances over at Stellie, who has been watching her with an amused expression.

The elevator continues to travel horizontally until it finally reaches a resting point and launches upward once more. The abrupt change in travel direction causes Alex to lose her balance, and she reaches out for something to hold onto. One hand finds the elevator railing, and the other reaches out and grabs Stellie by the arm.

With a harsh hissing sound and dramatic physical reaction, Stellie throws herself backward to wrench herself out of Alex's grip. Alex is left apologizing in one corner while Stellie regains her composure in the other.

"My apologies, Alexia, but we do not touch in this society. Touching is reserved for families and close friends; you are neither. Do not do that again, with me or with anyone, otherwise you may find yourself in a sticky situation." Stellie leaves Alex with one last disdainful glance and exits the elevator, which has come to a stop at the top floor of one of the massive buildings. Alex is afraid to even think how far off the ground they really are.

She takes a moment in the elevator to gather herself with her mind still reeling from the strange and strong reaction from Stellie. She glances down at her hand. The feeling of Stellie's skin has left a peculiar texture on her fingertips, almost like ash. With one last glance around, Alex exits the elevator, following after Stellie.

This new area is riddled with fascinating things to look at, extravagant artwork covers the walls of the hallway, and brightly colored lines dance across the floor. Alex cannot find their source, but they seem to move independently of anything she can see around her. Alex wants to stop and take in more of the beautiful sights around her, but Stellie does not slow, and she will not let Alex fall behind long enough to get a good look.

"Quickly now, your Cataloguing chamber awaits," Stellie says as she ushers Alex along.

"What should I be expecting in this chamber? What does the Cataloguing consist of exactly?" Alex tries to question Stellie as they walk along but is met with stony silence.

"Please!" Alex begs.

With a sigh of someone that is giving in, Stellie stops walking and turns to Alex. "The Cataloguing process is a requirement of the PPC to ensure all Stone Set Holders are worthy and that they are capable of upholding the laws of our society. Each new Holder must undergo a series of tests to determine their weaknesses and their strengths. These tests are based on a being's strongest traits. They function similar to the Stone Sets you so curiously found yourself in possession of. The tests have the ability to morph themselves into what will best measure your abilities." Stellie stops talking and glances down at the very perplexed Alex. "Confused? Yes, your species was noted as often being confused."

"I don't understand, I'm not a Stone Set Holder, I grabbed them one time and was transported to this place. I didn't choose this; I don't want to be Catalogued as a Stone Set Holder!" The tone of her voice comes out a lot whinier than she originally intended, but it's true, she doesn't want this, she just wants to go home.

Stellie gives another heavy sigh and then continues, "All new Stone Set Holders must undergo these tests, and whether you like it or not, you are a Holder. Those marks on your hands, that is the Stone Sets way of branding you, claiming you as their chosen one. You have a strong bond with your Set, and that is final. They are a part of you now, just as you are a part of them."

"What do you mean 'claiming me'?" Alex asks, already wary of the answer.

"The Stones have marked you, chosen you. This level of bonding is fairly rare amongst Holders. When Stone

Sets are passed down, they seldom ever bond by branding. They simply choose to exist with their Holders, rather than create a full bond. But it seems you are a special case. The Stones were sure of you. All the more reason that you need to be Catalogued," replies Stellie.

"These tests, the Cataloguing, they are a rite of passage for those who have been chosen to hold the Stones, regardless of how they are chosen. Ultimately, the PPC is looking to determine the threat level of the Holder, to determine if they are fit to be a Holder and be a member of the PPC," Stellie explains in a serious tone.

"The threat level?" Alex asks. "What does that mean? Threat to what? Listen, I can't possibly be seen as a threat to anything or anyone. I can barely keep my mouth from hanging open, much less threaten anyone."

Stellie gives her a weak smile, "Oh, my dear Alexia, who are you to say what level of threat you are?"

CHAPTER

6

As Stellie and Alex enter the dimly lit Cataloguing chamber, a rush of cold crawls over Alex's skin, giving her goosebumps and the feeling of wanting to constantly shiver. She peers around the room, allowing her eyes time to adjust to the lack of light. The room is dark, not just the absence of light, but there is also a lack of colors. The floor is a stark black, almost as if it is absorbing the light and sucking it into the abyss of nothing. The walls are a deep brown, closely resembling the hue of thick mud.

Alex feels as if she has stepped into the dungeon of the building, rather than an extension of the top floor that she knows she is still on. All the brightness from the hallway is blocked out as the door swings shut behind them. Alex now understands why the space was referred to as a chamber. The room is an oval shape and resembles a stadium, only slightly smaller. Stellie and Alex have entered through the narrow end of the oval, making Alex feel like she is standing on the tip of a giant egg. The centre of the room features a wide-open space with three tables spaced far apart from each other. She can't quite make out what sits on the tables as the vast distance is too great for her eyes to cover.

The narrow end of the room, the area that Alex and Stellie now walk through, is rimmed with seats for audience members. Alex feels her trepidation grow as she stares out into the seating area. At the moment, the seats are full of aliens, all unique looking. Alex watches the crowd as she follows Stellie, her mind wondering if there are any two aliens that look the same. Still scanning the crowd, she comes to the conclusion that every alien does indeed look distinctly different.

As they step further into the chamber, the conversation dies down, and all heads turn to look at the duo, more specifically at the human. Alex's feeling of dread intensifies with each set of alien eyes that land on her. She scans the crowd and finds Androx sitting among a group of muscular blue creatures, each varying in shade and shape. He gives her a small smile and a slight wave with one of his four arms. Then he turns back to his comrades, and she sees him pointing at her and whispering in hushed tones.

Gradually, the conversation returns to the room, but Alex cannot understand any of it. Each conversation sounds like a thousand different dialects, none of which she knows. As she scans the crowd, her eyes stop on one being. His wise yet humorous eyes investigate hers, leaving her with a strange feeling, as though she recognizes him, but she knows that is not possible. She looks closer at the alien and takes in his brown skin and large body. He is rounder than a human, with his front blending into the sides and back of his body. His small, rounded head is set on top of extremely broad shoulders that extend down to thin hips and small feet. He has a similar shape to an ice cream cone. His clothes cling tightly to his odd-shaped body, the light tones highlighting the rounded lines of his frame. He stands with his arms crossed over his chest, four-fingered hands playing with his shirt creases. His shoulders slump forwards, making him look shorter than he is, at full height he would likely draw up level with Alex. Her eyes drift back up to his startlingly blue eyes, and she is once again overwhelmed with the feeling of familiarity.

Dragging her eyes away from the creature, she allows Stellie to lead her to the centre of the room.

"There will be three parts to this test—logic, combat, and basic instinct," Stellie explains, in a hushed tone that only she can hear. "I will remind you that I am in charge of your safety. This means your life will not be put in danger and if it comes to that, I will stop the tests. However, if a test is marked as incomplete, you will not be given a final score and you will be immediately transported to Barter for filing, regardless of your connection with the Stone Set."

"What is Barter?" Alex asks with a concerned tone.

"Pray you never find out, Alexia," Stellie replies with a tense smile.

Alex takes a brief moment to notice how often these aliens use her first name. It must be a customary thing here, just like the "no touching" rule. Alex makes a mental note to correct the alien and let her know that she prefers to be called Alex, but just as quickly as that idea filters into her head, it filters back out.

"You must be joking, Alex," she says quietly to herself. "You want to correct an alien race on what they should call you because it *bugs you*. Are you insane?"

"What's that?" Stellie snaps.

Alex snaps her head to look at Stellie. "Sorry, I didn't mean to say that out loud, never mind." *Smooth cover, Alex.*

Alex lets out a sigh and turns her full attention back to Stellie. "So, this first test, logic, what exactly does that mean?"

"Oh, no, Alexia, I can give you no more help or hints. You are on your own from this point on." With one last glance at Alex, Stellie moves away to join the crowd on the sidelines, leaving Alex to stand alone at the centre of the chamber. At some point, the crowds have grown immensely. The seating area that she once considered full, is now packed; the room is beginning to feel small, and Alex begins to grow anxious.

Alex's mind is a funny thing, her anxiety taking her to strange places. Is what she is wearing appropriate, how does her hair look, does she smell funny from her run this morning? *Wow, was that really just this morning?* Alex thinks to herself. Once again, her mind jumps back to her family on Earth. Surely, by now, they have realized she is missing. Just as Alex starts to lose herself to her thoughts, a loud noise calls her back to the room.

A horn blares and all conversation from the seating area stops as aliens scuttle around at the edge of the room to find their seats. The lights dim and a spotlight focuses on Stellie, who is now standing on a large podium at the far end of the chamber, near the crowding aliens. Another alien stands behind Stellie. This being has an authoritarian air floating around it. The alien has wrinkly, brown skin and a stern face. Its two round eyes are sunk deep above a nose like that of a cat and a pencil-thin mouth, all set into a thick round head. It wears a long brown robe that hides the shape of its body. Her eyes drift back up to its eyes, and the stern face makes her smile disappear. With arms crossed behind its back, the alien watches Alex with an intensity that makes her immediately uncomfortable.

"Welcome, all Cataloguers and Council Members," Stellie's high-pitched voice carries through the room as she speaks in English to address the crowd. "It is quite a special moment that gathers us all here today, and believe me, the gravity of this situation is not lost on me. I hope you all brushed up on your English before arriving, as that is the primary language we will be using today." Some aliens look around at their peers. Clearly, they did not receive the memo as they stare back at Stellie with confused looks. She carries on anyway. "It is my humble duty, and honored responsibility, to introduce you to the first human to go through the Cataloguing process in nearly two thousand years; Alexia Harmon!" The crowd eyes Alex with what can only be interpreted as an open curiosity. Some carry a look of humour, while others seem to exude a significant amount of distaste for her.

Alex swallows and continues to watch Stellie.

"Joining me today is Planetary Peace Council Member, Brookstone." Stellie motions to the alien standing behind her. Brookstone gives the audience a quick glance, extraordinarily little respect in his eyes, and returns his intense gaze to Alex. "While no one in this group, nor our ancestors before us, have ever witnessed a human move through our processes, we will treat today like any other. The tests will be conducted in the same way as they always are, and the scores will be reviewed and logged appropriately." A small smile creeps across Stellie's face, making Alex shiver all over again. Stellie seems to lose some of her formality and adds in a cheerfully menacing tone, "Now let's see what this human can do."

CHAPTER

7

With Stellie's last words still hanging in the air, the lights go out and Alex is slammed into darkness. Immediately, her mind begins to race, and she can feel the panic rising in her stomach, starting to choke her throat. Darkness has always been a weak point for her. It's the moment where she is left alone with only her thoughts to keep her company. With a strangled feeling in her chest, she manages a breath, and then another.

The darkness stretches on for longer than Alex thought possible. There is no noise from the aliens in the crowd; there is only black. The darkness begins to press in on her as if she is being compressed, her breathing becomes more rapid, and she begins to feel sweat bead on her forehead. She can feel a panic attack coming on, something she frequently experiences, but they still have the ability to leave her paralyzed, unable to make decisions or do anything to help herself.

Breathe, Alex, just breathe, she says to herself. She crouches down to place her hands on the ground and puts her head between her knees. She can feel the ground beneath her vibrate lightly, but she knows enough not to trust her senses right now. Panic attacks allow her mind to play tricks on her, altering the way her surroundings look and feel, taking everything that is real and skewing it into something negative, something scary. Her steady breathing starts to return, and the panic attack is narrowly avoided. *What is going on? Has something gone wrong with the test?* Alex thinks to herself.

Just as the thought enters her mind, a very faint light starts to appear in the far corner of the room. She stares at the light, unsure if her mind is playing tricks on her. As she stares, the light grows brighter, illuminating one of the tables she saw when she first entered the room. With a curiosity that she cannot control, she moves to a standing position and starts to take a tentative step forward. With a small step out, she is overcome with the sensation of falling, the toes of her outstretched foot slip off an unseen edge, the enhanced gravity threatening to pull her down. Her balance is thrown off by the sudden loss of surface. She pinwheels her harms and flails dramatically, working to regain her balance. Remembering the vibrating feeling of the ground, she kneels down and uses her hands to explore the space around her feet. With a small gasp, Alex finds the edge of a seemingly steep drop. She feels all around her body and realizes that somehow, in the ever-expanding darkness, the ground around her has fallen away and left her standing on a small circular pedestal with the ledge just inches from her feet. She perches herself awkwardly on the surface and tries to keep her body small, terrified that she cannot see the edge.

With great hesitation, she carefully stands back up and glances at the illuminated table once more. Now the light is brighter, shining at her like a beacon of hope. But the hope is cut short as she realizes what is on the table. Squinting her eyes, she can clearly make out what appears to be weapons. *Why do I need weapons?*

After another quick glance around, Alex comes up with a plan. It is evident to her that the test wants her to get to the table, but how? She has no idea how far down the drop is or what lies beneath her.

With a small gasp, she remembers her cell phone in her pocket. Quickly, she draws it out and uses the built-in flashlight to illuminate her surroundings. As the light spreads and illuminates the chamber around her, she is amazed to find herself standing in the middle of a maze. The drop beneath her is approximately eight feet, which is manageable for her, as long as she slides down the pillar carefully. But what catches Alex's eye is what lies within the maze.

As she directs her flashlight in various directions, she can make out something moving below her. At first, it appears to be a very large worm, but as it navigates the space of the maze, she can make out spikes on its back and razor-sharp teeth at the end that she assumes is the head.

The feeling of panic returns to her chest. *I thought this was supposed to be a safe test! There is no way I'm jumping down there with that thing.* She crouches down once more to try and centre herself and her thoughts. As she moves her feet, the worm-like creature snaps its head toward her and lets out a menacing growl. It moves quickly in her direction, but as it approaches a corner, it roughly slams into the side of the wall.

Oh, you're blind! But you also have extremely sensitive hearing. Good to know. Alex takes a deep breath and continues gathering her thoughts.

With her flashlight, she can see roughly eight feet in front of her, and within those eight feet, she can see two walls of the maze. Suddenly, an idea pops into her head. *What if I don't jump down into the maze with that nasty thing? What if I jump over it?* She lets out a small laugh, impressed with her own cleverness. The sound of her laughter echoes out around her, drawing the worm even closer. She tucks her phone into her pocket so the flashlight is still visible and turns back toward the illuminated table. She steadies herself on the platform and takes a leap toward the first wall.

With a landing that is about as graceful as a jumping cow, she finds herself perched on the edge of the wall. *I need to push harder here; the weight of the gravity pulls me down faster than normal.* There is very little foot space on the wall, and she takes a moment to thank her lucky stars that she is a fairly athletic person. She steadies herself once more, placing her feet as if she is standing on a thin tight rope, the wall no wider than the width of her foot. With a deep breath, she makes the second jump, careful to put more strength into the leap. This time she lands more gracefully.

As she moves from wall to wall, she pauses in between each jump to glance ahead of her, being careful to plan her route to limit the number of jumps she has to take. With each successful jump, she forgets about the danger below her and starts to have a little fun. *It's like being a kid at a jungle gym.*

With only a few more jumps to make, the table is getting closer and closer. She stops momentarily for a quick break, her chest heaving as she works to maintain her steady breathing. Her legs and arms ache from the exertion of jumping and stabilizing herself. She looks around once more, overall, very pleased with her progress. While her jumping has been reasonably soundless, the creature below has followed her travel path closely, using the muted landing of her feet as guidance to her location. She glances down and spots the creature only a few paces behind her, waiting eagerly for her to fall.

With a confident breath, she takes another leap, but as she does, she feels her cell phone slip from her pocket. As if in slow motion, she watches the makeshift flashlight slip from her pocket and spiral down to the ground below her, landing only a few feet in front of the worm. With a heart-breaking thud, the light from the phone goes out, and she is plunged into darkness.

CHAPTER

A terrible feeling settles over Alex, making her entire body go rigid. Without her light, she cannot continue jumping from wall to wall, and worse yet, she has lost sight of the creature below her.

With her breath rattling in her chest and her legs shaking from exertion, she steadies herself on the thin wall and tries to focus, calming her mind, settling her quivering body. *You can do this, Alex; you're so close to the end.*

Taking a moment to gather herself, she looks longingly back at the illuminated table, only twenty feet away, and then down to the space where she dropped her phone. Unsure of where the worm creature is, she refuses to jump down blindly into the maze.

Thinking through her strategy once more, she has an idea. *If I can lure the worm away, I can hop down and grab my phone. From there, I should be able to make a run for the table. But first, I need to get rid of that worm.*

With a quick breath, Alex does an inventory of what she has on her, looking for something she could use to distract the worm. She scans her pockets and finds her house key tucked away. Pulling it out, she gives it a quick kiss and tosses it as far as she can in the opposite direction of the table. She listens intently, and a few seconds later, she hears it clatter down far away. She strains her ears further and listens for the worm. A faint slithering noise drifts up to her and Alex listens as it fades, indicating the worm moving away from her.

She takes a quiet breath and crouches down on the wall, shuffling her feet sideways and bracing her hands on the ledge. Carefully, she begins to lower herself down into the maze. As quietly as possible, she drops down and lands with a soft thump. Holding her breath, she listens for the return of the worm but hears nothing. Quickly, she begins to search the ground for her phone and is pleased when her fingertips make contact with the smooth edges.

Grabbing the phone, her fingers clumsily move over the screen, and she turns the flashlight back on. With a sigh of relief, she stands back up and points the flashlight in the direction she needs to go. Taking small, quiet steps, she moves toward what she believes to be the maze exit.

Very slowly, Alex rounds the final corner and is pleased to see a set of stairs leading up to the table. As she moves to take her last steps, she hears a faint slithering noise behind her. Losing her caution for a moment, Alex quickly turns around and looks for the sound. In her haste, her phone knocks into the wall of the maze, making a loud banging sound that echoes around her.

With a gasp of horror, Alex finds herself in the direct line of the worm and its gigantic teeth. From this angle, the worm is much larger than she originally thought, and it definitely heard her. Its razor-sharp teeth are pointed directly at her. From this angle, Alex can see inside its gigantic mouth. The skin around the lips looks pale and naked, teeth pointing out in various directions. With one last breath, Alex turns away from the worm and thrusts forward into a sprint heading for the stairs. She can hear the beast approaching behind her as it starts to let out the same threatening growl as before. Running at full speed toward the stairs, she feels the worm directly behind her, its hot, sticky breath panting onto the backs of her legs. With one final leap, she lunges towards the staircase, her body passing over the bottom few steps. She dives up, landing roughly with her body splayed awkwardly on the middle stairs. Her ribs ache from the impact, and her wrists jars backward at a painful angle.

But the leap is not enough, the worm is directly behind her, and its mouth gapes open, ready to finish her. Just as it closes the final few inches, it slams against something. Alex tucks up into a small ball on the stairs and looks up at the worm, towering before her but unable to reach her. She crawls backward away from the worm, her hands fumbling and slipping as she slides up the stairs. Reaching the top two stairs, she moves to stand. The worm appears to be held back by a force field, keeping it locked in the maze just below the staircase. With careful observation, Alex can see the ripple of the shield as the worm presses against it.

Her body shakes with adrenaline, and she continues to step backward, moving away from the worm. Stumbling as she moves up the final few stairs, her eyes remain trained down at the worm. Finally, she reaches the table, her back pressing against the edge, still, she continues to focus on the staircase, cautious that the worm will suddenly reappear. After several long moments, she moves her eyes away from the stairs and turns to face the table. The surface is bathed in warm light. On the table is a series of advanced-looking weapons. *This must be for the combat portion.* As she reaches to pick up one of the weapons, a horn blares through the stadium, and the lights flare on once more.

CHAPTER

9

"Well done, Alexia!" Stellie's high-pitched voice booms out, leaving Alex feeling dazed and overwhelmed by light and sound. Alex's hand falls back down to her side, and she steps away from the weapons. "You have completed the logic portion of the Cataloguing. Your score for this section has been recorded, and we will now move to the combat portion. The testing field will be adjusted based on your performance in the first section to ensure that the methods used are in alignment with Cataloguing expectations. Good luck, Alexia." Before Alex has a chance to gather her bearings, she is plunged back into darkness, but she does catch a quick glimpse of Brookstone, still standing behind Stellie. The way the alien stares at her makes her feel as if her skin is crawling under his heavy gaze. As the lights go out, Alex is once again left with nothing but the small overhead light to illuminate her and the table. Turning back to the table, she shakes off the eerie feeling that Brookstone left her with and looks at the weapons before her.

The first is a gun that mirrors an old-fashioned pistol that could be found on Earth. She picks the weapon up and inspects the barrel. Staring at the weapon she is reminded that she is not on Earth. The weapon seems to crackle with electricity. Small bouts of energy crack out, snapping at her fingertips as she slides them along the barrel. Holding it out in front of her, she points the weapon down to the ground in front of her and fires. A small ball of electrical energy is released from the barrel of the gun, leaving a two-inch crater in the ground before her.

Alarmed, she quickly puts the gun down, mildly afraid of its power, and moves on to the next. This one is longer and features two triggers and one long, wide barrel. The triggers are positioned one in front of the other. Unsure of the inner workings, Alex tentatively picks it up and points it away from herself.

She pulls the first trigger, and a projectile is shot from the barrel, kicking her arm back with a heavy thumping sound. Giving her arm a little shake, she looks around for the residual damage but is surprised to find none. *Strange*, she tries firing the gun again, pulling the same trigger. Again, she hears the thump and feels the kickback, but nothing else happens.

Cautiously, she points the gun outward once more and pulls the second trigger. This one has a violent reaction. There are two consecutive blasts, one taking place at the first location she fired and the other taking place much closer to her. The blast knocks her backward, sending her sprawling onto the ground. Still holding the weapon firmly in her grip, it swings wildly as her arms fly around and her head smacks against the ground. Sitting up, she gingerly lifts her fingers up to the back of her head. Her fingertips come away bloody, and her ears ring from the explosions. Turning her attention back to the weapon, she examines it more closely. It appears to be an advanced grenade launcher. Moving to a standing position, she aims the weapon at the ground in front of her and pulls the first trigger, launching a grenade into the ground. She moves forward to examine it, careful to keep her finger away from the second trigger.

As she approaches the small object, she likens it more to a bomb than a grenade. She is impressed by the nature of the design; the bomb looks like a small six-legged spider. Its little legs dig firmly into the ground to hold it in place. There are no other discernible markings on the bomb to indicate its menacing nature.

Backing away cautiously to a safe distance, she pulls the second trigger and watches in amazement as the bomb detonates, giving off a blast roughly five feet wide and five feet tall.

With an appreciative sound, Alex puts the gun down on the table and turns to the final weapon. This one is a long and wide stick. At first glance, it appears to be a sword of some sort, but the edge is very dull, and the overall size of the object is too wide for it to possibly be used for anything involving combat. She reaches forward with her left hand to pick it up, but as her fingers near the handle, she is alarmed to see the sword start to vibrate. Alex pulls away, remembering the last time something reacted to her touch. She glances down at her permanently marked hands; a shudder runs through her body as she recalls the pain from the Stones.

Squaring her shoulders and bracing herself for pain, she reaches out and grabs the handle with a firm grip, hoisting the sword off the table. The sword begins to vibrate vigorously. Staring wide-eyed, she watches as the sword transforms. The metal of the handle slips up and out of her grip and slides along her inner forearm. Splitting into two pieces, a thick double-headed band molds around her forearm, securing the entire device in place. The blade starts to reduce in size, gliding towards the top of her forearm. It centres itself above her hand, now resting on the top of her hand and wrist, reaching only eight inches in front of her. The dull edges of the blade slowly start to split apart into two smaller blades with sharpened tips. The outside of each blade forms into a serrated edge while the inside thins out to the size of a razor blade. The newly formed knives take on their final shape and slide seamlessly up into the holder on the outside of her forearm.

Alex stares down at her arm in shock. While she looks at the blades, she is certain she hears a light murmuring coming from the crowd around her. This is the first time she has heard anything from the crowd at all. Alarm rings through her.

Turning her attention back to the blade, she thrusts her arm forward and watches in amazement as the blades come shooting forward, extending eight inches ahead of her fingers, narrowly missing her clenched hand. *Careful when you use this one, Alex*, she thinks to herself. *Keep your wrist flexed down, fingers in, and always point it away from your body.* Carefully, she lowers her arm, and the blades slide back into their secured position against her forearm.

Alex turns and picks up the two guns, slinging the bomb launcher over her shoulder and putting the pistol into her left hand as the two blades remain firmly attached to her left forearm. Everything here is heavier than it should be. The weight of the three weapons feels like it is compressing her spine, pulling her down. Every muscle she has works to keep her standing upright.

Unsure of her next steps, she turns away from the table, wary that whatever she has to do next has something to do with that large worm. As she steps further away from the table, the light behind her fades, and a new light begins to blossom at the far end of the room. A second table is now illuminated, revealing the next destination.

True to Stellie's word, the maze before her has adapted based on her style during the first part of the test. The walls of the maze are now topped with steep edges to prevent her from attempting to jump over the maze.

With a disappointed sigh, Alex turns to the staircase and steps down. Only this time, she does not step down into the darkness. Now, faint lights illuminate the walkways in a manner that makes her think they will help lead her from one end of the maze to the next. Descending further down the stairs, she looks around warily for the worm but is pleasantly surprised to find that it is gone. The feelings of relief are quickly replaced with a feeling of doom; *If the worm is gone, what has replaced it?*

Descending into the lowest level of the maze, she moves forward, pistol held out in front of her. She follows the lights and slowly winds her way through the maze. With each step, her heart beats louder, her breathing becomes more rapid, and her outstretched hand begins to shake. *Breathe, Alex, just breathe and focus on moving forward.*

She works to slow her mind and tune into her senses, and it's a good thing she does because something has started to move around her. She whips around and is faced with an empty corridor. She looks up and down the hallway and tells herself that the noise is just in her head. Turning back to her original direction of travel, something catches her eye. The wall just a few feet from where she stands has started to move as if something is bubbling just under the surface.

With a terrified gulp, she pulls her weapon up and levels it with the mass in the wall, and starts to back away quickly. A lump has formed under the surface and is growing larger by the second. Within ten seconds, the mass is the size of her body. With a sudden, wet sound, the wall bursts open, and a terrifying creature leaps out of the wall. The creature has more legs than she can count and is coated in what appears to be a thin gelatinous substance. Fine hairs cover the surface of its skin, giving it a spiky appearance. As it stands in front of her, it moves slightly to reveal dozens of eyes, set into a round head that is attached directly to its legs by a tall, thin neck. The eyes settle on her, and a small mouth opens in the creature's face, revealing a toothless mouth that oozes more gel.

As the gel falls out of its mouth and makes contact with the ground, a hissing sound can be heard as the acidic substance burns on contact.

Alex's first instinct is to turn and run, but as she takes the creature in, she makes note of its multiple legs, clearly built for speed and its dozen rapidly moving eyes. All of them directly focused on her. *I can't outrun this thing.*

The two beings stand in place, each rooted to the ground, complete stillness washing over their bodies. Alex watches as its eyes stare hungrily at her, waiting for her to move. Alex feels a lot like prey as the far superior predator stares her down, willing her to move so it can start the chase and hunt her like an animal.

Alex moves her hand ever so slightly, shifting the outstretched pistol to aim at the centre of the creature's body. Her fingers tremble on the weapon as she watches half of the creature's eyes follow the gun and the other half stay on her face.

With a rapid decision-making process that Alex's mind is not used to, she quickly fires three rounds into the beast's chest while beginning a backward run. She manages to make it ten steps before the creature regains its stability and starts the chase.

Using the distance Alex has created, she launches herself sideways down an adjoining hallway just as the creature jumps for her, soaring through the space where her body had been just seconds ago. Alex careens down the hallway and lands painfully on her face. Quickly turning, she scrambles to her feet and looks back to the opening she just jumped through. Blood trickles down from her forehead, split open from the contact with the ground. Blood now escapes from both the front and back of her head. Simultaneously she wipes the blood from her eyes and raises the weapon up to aim at the opening. Holding her breath, she waits for the creature to leap through after her. Instead, she is surprised to find the creature standing on the very edge of the threshold, eyeing her with an intense amount of rage.

Still holding her breath, Alex stares down the hallway, as she realizes what is happening, she lets out a deep sigh of relief, the air releasing out of her strained lungs. The creature is being held back by a thin force field, just as the worm was. It seems the creature can only stay where the lights are, which unfortunately, is the same place she needs to be if she is going to make it through this portion of the Cataloguing.

Steadying herself, she brings her weapon up again and fires at the creature, watching as the ball of energy passes through the forcefield and harmlessly dissolves into nothing. The creature looks down at the three wounds in its chest from the previous rounds and back up to her, rage boiling behind its eyes. Its mouth hangs open, and a large amount of acid drips out, singeing the floor in front of its many feet.

Taking a deep breath, Alex turns away from the creature and pulls out her phone, using the flashlight to illuminate the path before her. There is no way she is going to be able to get past that creature without stepping directly into its path. The only way is to move away from the creature and try to loop around. Alex steps forward and leaves the creature behind. Anticipating that more dangers may be waiting in the darkness, she tucks the pistol into her pants pocket (originally designed to hold a water bottle, but it also, to her surprise, fits an alien gun) and pulls out the bomb launcher. Using both hands, she pulls it up to her chest and points it ahead into the darkness.

If she remembers correctly, there were multiple ways to get to the same destination. *Maybe that is the point of this test? See if I can figure out how to avoid the creature and still get to the second table.* She begins moving her feet forward and does her best to recall the maze patterns and routes.

As she walks along in the darkness, guided only by the small light from her phone, she stumbles across her house key lying harmlessly on the ground. She lets out a small laugh and picks up the key, returning it to her pocket.

Finally, she comes to a crossing that is once again illuminated by the small lights in the floor. With hesitation, she steps into the pathway and turns both ways. The creature is nowhere in sight. With haste, she keeps the gun aimed ahead of her and moves along the designated travel path. To her relief, she moves with no resistance.

Feeling like she might pass this test, she opens into a quick run. Rounding what she feels must be the last of the corners, she skids to a halt and staggers back as she is put face to face with the same snarling, angry creature.

Quickly backstepping, she fires a round from the launcher. Missing the creature by inches, the bomb thuds into the wall directly behind it. She fires another round, this one landing on one of the creature's legs, the small clamps from the bomb dig painfully into the creature's leg. With a frustrated and disturbed howl, the beast lunges forward as Alex pulls the second trigger. Both bombs detonate simultaneously, the first bomb blows the creature closer to Alex, and the second explodes on its legs, sending the creature into a violent tailspin. The creature hurtles toward Alex, out of control from the blasts, and lands on her with a heavy thud.

The wind is knocked from her lungs as she and the creature tumble down in a mess of legs and gel. As the creature's mass settles on her, she feels the acidic gel that covers its body starts to burn into her skin. Quickly, she scrambles for her weapons but is left grasping at nothing as she realizes they have been knocked from her grip.

The creature flails around dramatically, its immense weight still pinning her down. It works fervently to turn toward her to get its mouth within reach of her face. The acid burns more vigorously into her skin, and Alex's mind panics, sending her into survival mode. Quickly and without thinking, she thrusts her arms upward into the back of the creature in an effort to remove the heavy, acidic thing that is crushing and burning her to death.

As she thrusts upward again, the blade attached to her forearm glints in the floor lights, catching Alex's eye. Quickly she thrusts again, this time willing the blades to thrust out as well. With a slicing sound, the blades push sharply in the centre of the creature's body. A final strangled moan comes from the creature as it goes limp.

Alex, still burning from the acid contact, moves quickly to dislodge herself from the weight. Finally, she is able to wriggle free, but her body is now covered in the acidic gel. She looks around with a panicked feeling.

"I thought you were supposed to protect me!" she screams to the edge of the chamber. "I thought you were supposed to keep me out of danger! Help me! Can't you see I'm burning to death!" A small sob escapes her lips as she stumbles forward and lands on a knee, the gravity pulling her down fast and hard. She looks at her hands and finds the first layers of skin are gone, leaving a deepening red layer along her skin. The acid continues to burn through her flesh.

Realizing that Stellie is not going to help her, she stumbles up to her feet, pushing up against an invisible weight, and continues to follow the lights, leaving the dead creature behind. Limping forward, her mind jumps back to the guns. Stumbling to a halt, she turns around to retrieve them, retracting her blades back into their holders at the same time.

With guns in hand, she moves through the final parts of the maze, pace slowing as the acid continues to burn through her skin, now eating into muscle and fat.

Weakly, she reaches the base of the stairs and collapses. With extreme effort, she crawls forward and upward. As she reaches the peak, she lifts her head to see a pool of blood. At first, she is confused. *Whose blood is this?* With a small hysterical laugh that is more like a bark, she realizes that it is her blood. Moving her eyes away from the growing pool, she looks around at her new surroundings. On top of the table is a small bucket of liquid, with a label that reads, "Αλβεραξ Αντιϖενομ."

"Of course, it's in an alien language," she mutters. With pain lancing through her body, she continues to crawl forward, her muscles protesting as they are eaten by acid. She leverages herself to a standing position. Her body is quickly deteriorating, and the pain is enough to leave her blind, nearly knocking her unconscious. She moves closer to the bucket and peers inside. The smell is fruity and pleasant, so on a leap of faith, she dips her finger in. Immediately, the pain in her finger subsides. She pulls it out with a surprised gasp and looks at her fully healed finger. With renewed hope, she quickly takes the bucket and douses it all over her body, feeling immediate relief. She lowers herself to the ground, and she watches in amazement as her body heals and she generates a new layer of skin. All but the wounds on her head are now healed.

Alex lies on the ground for several moments before she finally finds the will to stand. As she does, the familiar horn blares, and the lights flip on once more, and she is left blinded again.

CHAPTER

10

Struggling to regain her sight and feeling the strangeness of her baby smooth, new skin, Alex moves toward the table. Her muscles have renewed strength, still pulled down by the atmosphere but not exhausted from her battle with the creature. They no longer shake with exertion. *That stuff is magic!* She thinks to herself.

"Alexia, my dear Alexia," Stellie's voice rings through the chamber once again. "You continue to surprise us." She turns her body to the crowd and raises her arms up as if to say 'look at this'.

Behind Stellie, and around the room, Alex can see that all the aliens are staring at her with intense eyes, a new expression spreads across their collective faces. Some remain openly curious and anxious, while others are downright afraid. *Have I done something wrong? Was I not supposed to kill the creature? Am I failing this test?* Oh, how quickly her mind can turn on her, making her doubt her decisions, that only moments ago saved her life!

“What happened to keeping me safe Stellie?” Alex says to the tall purple alien. “I could have died down there. Why didn’t you help me?” The exasperation in her voice comes through clearly.

Stellie turns to face her head-on, dropping her arms to her sides once more, “Alexia, you did not die, therefore my promise withstands. The whole point is to see where your strengths and weaknesses lie, and that is exactly what we are doing. So, if we can move on, that would be lovely.” Turning back to the crowd, Stellie moves into the next portion of her speech. “Cataloguers and Council Members, we very well may be witnessing history being made. As promised the Cataloguing will continue.”

“❄♒♓⬧ ■♏♏♎⬧ ⧫□ ⬧⧫□❑!” a shout comes from the crowd. Alex turns to find the source of the outcry. Her eyes settle on an alien that closely resembles a human, except for the bright red skin and third eye in the top of its head.

“⌖♏ ♍♋■■□⧫ ♋●●□⬧ ♒♏❒ ⧫□ ♍□■⧫♓■⬥♏ ♒♏❒ 👍♋⧫♋●□♑⬥♓■♑📪 ✋⧫✌⬧ ♍●♏♋❒ ⧫□ ⬧♏♏ ⧫♒♋⧫ ⬧♒♏ ♓⬧ ⧫□□ ♎♋■♑♏❒□⬥⬧ ⧫□ ♌♏ ♋●●□⬧♏♎ ⧫□ ❒□♋❍ ❑❒♏♏●⍓ □■ □⬥❒ ◻●♋■♏⧫⬧📪”

While Alex is unable to understand the alien, the tone rings through clearly. It is very upset about something.

From all around the room, aliens nod in agreement. Alex’s mind drifts back to her family on Earth. She is scared for her own life but the worry that she may never see her husband and daughter again floats to the front of her thoughts. Her mind fills with images of her laughing daughter, her pensive husband. As Alex’s mind drifts to her loved ones far away, her eyes are drawn to something. She follows the pull and locks eyes with a brown alien that looked at her with such familiarity before. As she watches the alien, her vision begins to blur, and he becomes the only thing she can stare at, the only thing that remains in focus. Unlike all the aliens here, he is the only one who does not nod, he does not react to the outburst at all. His rounded body remains eerily still. Those humorous but intense eyes focus on her, while the crowd around him moves in an agitated motion.

Alex maintains eye contact with the being and is startled when she feels a connection to him, as if her mind is being linked with his.

"Finish the Cataloguing, don't let them suspend the testing." The voice, clearly not her own, rings through her mind. *"We need the results."*

As fast as the connection began, it is gone, and the brown alien goes back to blending into the crowd. Alex's vision returns to normal and the fog she felt in her mind lifts. Turning to Stellie, she speaks loudly, "What are they saying? Have I done something wrong? Something that would void the Cataloguing process? If not, I would like to request that the Cataloguing continue."

As the words tumble out of her mouth, her brain struggles to keep up. *Why on earth would I want this to continue? I nearly died in the last round. It makes no sense to listen to a creepy alien voice in my head. Snap out of it, Alex.* But despite her internal thoughts, her external words plead with the lead alien Cataloguer to allow the process to continue.

Stellie looks awkwardly from the angered crowd, back to Alex, and finally to Brookstone, who has moved forward to stand directly next to her. Stellie towers over Brookstone, yet as the small being stands next to her, his presence appears larger than hers. He stands there, not in a show of support but rather a display of dominance. His slight frame seems to overrun Stellie's nervous demeanour. Brookstone eyes Stellie harshly, disgust written across his face. He mouths something to Stellie, and Stellie raises her hand, urging the crowd to quiet down.

"My friends," She glances nervously at Brookstone once again. "I am the Cataloguer in charge of this session, and you are all here as my guests to the process. Please find order once more." With a supportive nod from Brookstone, the crowds' grumblings subside, and eventually, all the aliens seat themselves again. Stellie turns to the red alien and continues, "Sando, I understand your reasoning to stop the testing. You are correct, we have not seen results like this in any of our histories; however, this is what the Cataloguing process was designed for. With the support of our Council member," she tips her tall head slightly in Brookstone's direction, "the process shall continue, and the final score will determine the fate of our new Stone Set Holder, Alexia."

Turning around, Stellie rests her weary eyes back on Alex. "Alexia, the final phase of the Cataloguing is basic instinct. Please proceed."

This time Alex is braced for the shocking blackness that comes after Stellie finishes her last words, but still, the sudden absence of light leaves her disoriented. As the black filters in around her, Alex picks up on a repeat sensation. The ground beneath her feet begins to vibrate once more, and a dull light fills the chamber, leaving the crowd cloaked in blackness. As her eyes adjust to the dim light, she becomes aware that the maze around her is gone, leaving her standing in a large open space once more. At the far end of the chamber, the final table is illuminated with light, giving her a clear ending.

Alex checks her weapons, the bomb launcher is still heavily slung over her shoulder, and the pistol is firmly in her hand, both seemingly undamaged by the acid from the creature. The knives strapped to her arm also appear to be in working order. She thrusts her arm out and watches in continued amazement as the blades shoot out and then slide easily back in as she lowers her arm. Moving forward, she takes a step away from the table, and the light behind her flickers out. Taking another step, she grows increasingly aware of how easy this feels, much easier than the previous test. Even still, she grips the pistol tightly.

Another step forward, her mind racing, looking for danger in the dimly lit space. Moving forward, her other senses start to notice something. She stops where she is, planting her feet firmly, her body moving to a defensive position and the grip on her pistol tightens even further. She focuses on the smell now wafting toward her. With a deep inhale, Alex takes in a lungful of smoke. Coughing to clear her throat and nose, she hears the scared cry of a small child. Alex can't believe her ears; *How could a child be here, that doesn't make any sense.* Yet, she clearly hears the wail, the mother in her immediately recognizing it as a child in distress. Looking around frantically, she spots the start of a small fire at the other end of the room which is in the exact opposite direction of the final table. Smoke billows thicker than it should for a fire of that size. Every second she stares, the fire grows larger and larger. Directly in the middle of the inferno is what appears to be an alien child. The child looks at her with desperation in its large eyes and begins to wail louder.

The mother in Alex does not take a moment to think, does not need time to assess the situation. Immediately, her body is pushed forward, toward the child. If she moves quickly enough, she can grab the child before the flames engulf it. Alex moves as fast as possible, drawing nearer to the child with each breath. As she rushes towards the child, she notices the floor in front of her starting to change shape. Walls begin to lift around the child entrapping it and the flames, into a large circle.

With more strength than Alex thought she had, she sprints ahead, closing the distance to the child and raging inferno. With a tremendous amount of effort, she leaps over the wall and swoops down to pick up the screaming child while awkwardly holding both it and the pistol in her hands. The young one's skin radiates heat from the fire, and it screams with pain and fear as she picks it up.

With fear settling uncomfortably in Alex's stomach, she grips the child firmly and looks out over the fiery inferno, watching the walls lift higher and higher around her. With a scream of defiance that matches that of the child, she launches herself toward the flames and catapults her body over the wall. During the process, the small child grows quiet, and Alex fears she may have injured it with the movement.

With a soft landing that leads to a full-body collapse, Alex finds herself sitting on the other side of the wall, gasping for clean air, and holding the shaking child. Looking down, Alex peers closely at the child for the first time. It is quite small with rough, scaly skin. Its eyes are huge in comparison to its head, and its eyes peer off in different directions, looking for something. Small hands and feet cling to Alex's torso, digging into her skin with thick nails. Luckily, it seems to be uninjured, just dazed. *What kind of monsters bring a child into these tests? Who exactly am I dealing with?*

Unsure of her next move, Alex looks up once more and notices a small woman standing at the far edge of the chamber, closer to where the table is illuminated. Only the woman's body is visible in the darkness, and Alex is unable to see the details of her face. Shakily, she moves to a standing position and hauls the child up with her. The claw-like hands and feet loosen their grip on her body until she is supporting all its weight limply in her arms. Moving toward the woman, Alex feels the child start to wiggle. Alex peers down and finds both the child's eyes are trained on the woman, its tiny arms extend out to her with anticipation, "Momma," the child gurgles, its large alien mouth moving awkwardly.

Piecing it together, Alex starts to move toward the woman with the intent of returning the child, but as she draws nearer, the woman begins to back away. Alex begins to walk faster, not understanding why the woman would back away from her child, but as she closes the final steps, the woman becomes more visible, Alex can see the fear that is stricken across her face.

Confused, Alex draws to a halt and looks down at the child once more. A terrified look crosses her face, and a small scream escapes her lips as she looks at the thing she is holding. The child has morphed into a giant lizard creature and is clawing out at the woman. The hands that once clung to Alex now arc into long pointed talons, with nails over an inch long. The awkward mouth that cried for its momma is now shaped like a lizard's mouth. A forked tongue slithers out, tasting the air around it. Its independently moving eyes stare at the woman with a look of hunger.

Alex quickly drops the creature and backs away. As she does, the lizard lands on the ground, its clawed feet splaying out underneath it. Moving quickly, its legs skitter across the ground with a scratching sound, heading straight toward the woman. The woman screams in terror, unable to move as the creature jumps onto her leg, digging its claws into her skin. Alex stares in horror as bright red blood trails down the woman's leg and the creature takes a massive bite out of her leg. With more speed than Alex thought possible, the creature continues to climb up the woman's leg, and comes to rest on her chest.

Suddenly remembering herself, Alex pulls the pistol up in front of her and aims it at the creature. If she shoots, she will likely hit the woman as well, but if she doesn't, the creature will eat her alive. Having to make a quick decision, Alex pulls the trigger and watches in amazement as the bolt of energy springs forward from the gun, hitting the creature directly in the back. The creature drops off the woman and lands at her feet, spasming as it slowly dies.

Alex takes a few shaky breaths and moves toward the woman. As she advances, the woman's full body shudders, and both she and the dying creature vanish, leaving Alex rooted in place and very confused.

Turning back to the illuminated table once more, she is pleased to find she has covered more than half the distance to the table. She steps forward and starts to close the remainder of the distance. Moving with caution, she begins to feel herself sliding backward, despite her clear steps forward, as if the ground is pulling her back. Quickly, her brain recognizes the feeling of a treadmill. She increases her steps to match that of the moving ground and continues to advance toward the table. The ground beneath adjusts once more and continues to pull her backward, increasing in speed. Alex tucks the pistol into her pants pocket once more and uses her arms to propel herself forward until she is at a full sprint. As her breathing begins to max out and her lungs start to burn, Alex is thrown off balance by a small shudder radiating from the ground. Her arms flail out to the side, and she struggles to maintain her balance, barely keeping her feet under her. The ground around her starts to move once again. This time, walls begin to rapidly rise next to her, reaching a full height of roughly twelve feet in mere seconds.

Glancing around nervously and trying to maintain her sprint, Alex stares in terror as the walls begin to move in toward her, threatening to crush her. They move at a slow and steady pace but sooner than she would like, Alex is able to touch both walls with her outstretched arms. Suddenly, the moving ground beneath her comes to a stop, and Alex is pitched forward as her feet move from a sprint to a standstill.

Crashing into the ground ahead of her, Alex finds herself sprawled face down, feeling every part of her body protest from the impact. Blood springs from the wound in her forehead, split open again when her head bounced unceremoniously off the ground. With a low moan, she pushes herself to an all-fours position, watching as the blood drips down to the ground. Lifting her head, she rocks back on her heels and reaches out to feel for the walls. Unfortunately, while the treadmill stopped moving, the walls did not. They continue to move steadily toward her. Standing up with great difficulty, Alex glances up toward the table. From this distance, she will not make it to the table in time, not without being crushed by the walls.

Taking a deep breath, she pivots and plants her feet on the wall to her right and presses her back against the opposite wall. Using all her remaining strength, she begins to walk herself up the twelve-foot wall. The higher she rises, the harder it gets for her to move with her legs being pushed toward her chest and her leverage points lessening.

With one final push upward, she pops out the top of the walls and clambers to one side, lying face down, her entire body shaking from exertion and blood stinging her eyes. After several moments, the walls stop moving as they make final contact with each other. Alex is left resting atop the two walls, her chest flat down as her body heaves to catch its breath and slow her heart down. Moving like she is in a nightmare that she will not wake from, she pushes herself up to a crouched position and shuffles her way to the edge of the wall, closest to the table. With unsteady hands and a shaky body, she lowers herself down to the ground, dropping nearly four feet and landing with a soft thud. The moment her feet make contact, the walls begin to lower themselves back into the floor.

Alex turns, her entire body trembling from adrenaline, exhaustion, and pain. She takes the final few steps toward the table. Her tired eyes rest on a button in the centre of the table. The button is inscribed with an alien language, "✿□◆ ♎⚨♎ ⚨◆!"

"Next time I do this process," Alex grumbles under her breath, "I'm going to demand they translate everything to English."

With wary fingers, she reaches out and presses the button. Immediately, the lights around her flare back to life, and she is bathed in brightness once more.

CHAPTER

11

yes squinting against the sudden onslaught of light, Alex works to steady herself, bracing her exhausted body against the third and final table.

At first, there is nothing but light to fill the room. Eventually, noise begins to rise in the chamber as the crowd murmurs sounds of discontent. Alex looks around in confusion. To one side, she can see Stellie and Brookstone talking in hushed and rapid tones, their lips moving in their foreign language. Stellie bends awkwardly at the hips, leaning down to hear what Brookstone is saying, while he makes no effort to reach up to her.

All around her, aliens move around and look at her with harsh glances. Something doesn't feel right. Her instincts are detecting a new danger that she hasn't felt before, the danger of an angry mob. She scans the crowd once more, in search of some signs of respite. Her eyes find Androx, who looks at her with a new fear on his face. He gives her a small, sad shake of his head and backs further away from her, as if the massive distance isn't enough to keep him safe from her. Alex feels a pit in her stomach. Something she did during her Cataloguing has caused the masses to turn against her.

Finally, Stellie moves to speak, addressing the crowd first, "Cataloguers and Council Members, quiet, please. The final scores have been calculated, and Council Member Brookstone and I are reviewing the results. Your patience is appreciated. In the meantime, Alexia, please approach the podium."

Alex moves forward on tired feet and comes to stand before Stellie and Brookstone. The two aliens turn to her, and it is Brookstone who addresses her first.

"Alexia, your results have given us much to consider." Brookstone's voice is a low baritone that rumbles through Alex's chest. It leaves her with a heavy feeling and tips her instincts into something being unsaid. *This alien is not your friend Alex, be careful with what you say and do around him.* "As you are aware, the Cataloguing process is designed to test your strengths and weaknesses. The tests will morph into what they believe will best measure your abilities. As a Cataloguing team, Stellie and I do not have any input to the test parameters. With that being said, the tests you were put through, were…interesting in nature. This team has not seen results like these in many decades, nor has anyone in this room. Given the nature of your results and the parameters of the tests, you will be placed into immediate custody and transferred to Barter for filing."

Alex stumbles away from Brookstone in fear, unable to speak.

Stellie turns to address the crowd, satisfied with Brookstone's response. "Esteemed members of the Council and Cataloguers, Alexia Harmon's results indicate that she is unfit to be a Stone Set Holder." The crowd roars with approval. "She will be immediately removed and transferred to Barter. Steps will be taken to erase the Stone Set from her possession, and she will be imprisoned on Barter for the remainder of her human life."

Guards move from the corners of the chamber, originally hidden by shadows. They approach Alex with sophisticated-looking handcuffs and surround her from all sides. They encircle her, and she is forcibly driven down to her knees. The long-forgotten weapons are pulled from her body, and the dual blade system is detached from her forearm.

A guard forces her arms behind her back and places the cuffs over her hands. Alex can feel the cold metal of the cuffs start to extend beyond her wrists and encompass her entire hands, leaving her unable to move her wrists or fingers. Another guard pats her down and removes the cell phone and key from her pocket, tossing them to the side. Alex stares in horror as the last part of Earth is stripped from her possession. Finally, the guards place a helmet over her head that leaves her cut off from all sight and sound.

Fear boils up in her throat, and she screams in terror as she is hoisted to her feet and dragged out of the chamber.

CHAPTER

Alex can feel herself being pulled from the chamber and dragged back down the hallway to the elevator. The helmet blocks out all her valuable senses, and she is left with nothing to gauge where she is or where they are taking her.

After a lot of jostling and moving, Alex feels herself being thrust into a small cage. With her arms still secured behind her back, she hits the ground with a thump. Pain radiates up to her shoulder and into her back. Awkwardly, she manages to work into a seated position and moves to rest her back on the wall of the cage, cold bars pressing against her sweaty back.

As she rests, she can feel the air around her change and the ground under her begins to rumble. If she is not mistaken, she is in a shuttle of some sort, being moved to a new location. After roughly twenty minutes of travel, she feels the shuttle set down once more, and she is hoisted out of the cage.

Two guards push her forward until she is pinned against a wall, the front of her helmet pressing painfully into her face. At first, nothing happens, but as she waits, she feels the guards' grip on her tighten. The metal peels back away from one of her hands, and a button is pressed against her finger. She feels a familiar pinching sensation all over her body. *This was the same feeling I had when I transported to the city of Valyrn. I must be teleporting to Barter.*

The pinching sensation subsides, and she feels the metal of the handcuffs slide back over her exposed hand. Alex is once again pushed forward by the guards. She is startled to find that the wall that was in front of her only moments ago has disappeared, confirming her suspicions of teleportation.

The guards lead her along a route that makes her feel like she is in another maze. They pause periodically, in what Alex assumes are moments used to open doors.

Finally, they stop, and Alex feels the guards begin to unhook her helmet. With a jerky motion that catches her nose and makes her eyes water, the helmet is lifted off. Glancing around, she takes in the dark room. She looks to the guards who avoid eye contact, treating her as something that does not deserve their respect but also wary of her at the same time. They work to remove her hand restraints.

With all the restraints removed, the guards quickly back out of the room and slam the heavy metal door shut, leaving Alex alone in the cold, dark room.

The room is devoid of any life or light. There are no windows, only a small opening in the door that allows light to seep in. She looks around with a shaky breath and reaches her hands out to the walls. The room is no bigger than her outstretched arms and is only a few inches taller than her head. Crouching down, she edges her fingers along the surface, feeling the cracked indents of the old and dirty floor. In one corner of the small room is a hole in the floor that she assumes is for beings to do their business in. Alex jerks her hand back in disgusted horror as her fingers brush against the edge of the hole.

So, this must be Barter. What a lovely place! Alex gives a strangled laugh. The noise from her throat echoes off the walls and bounces back to her.

Still crouched down, she seats herself on the ground, as far from the hole and door as she can, and presses her back against the wall. She pulls her knees up into her chest and lets her mind turn inward to her racing thoughts.

How did I end up here, in this hell? Is this my ending? What about my family? My daughter? A sob comes from her lips as tears roll down her cheeks. She so desperately wants to go home.

Alex sits in silence for a long time before finally falling asleep. Her mind unable to carry on, she is thrown into a dream land filled with vicious aliens and creatures of all shapes and sizes.

CHAPTER

13

A bruptly, Alex is woken from her sleeping nightmares, only to be launched back into her living nightmare. A loud noise has caught her attention; she turns her head toward the door just as it swings open.

Framed by light from the exterior hallway stands Brookstone. "Hello, Alexia. Horrible place to be wouldn't you say?" He pauses for dramatic effect and takes in his surroundings with a distasteful grimace. "Oh, you pitiful thing. Get up out of the dirt and let me look at you."

Alex moves to stand while careful to maintain a safe distance between Brookstone and herself. *I'd rather stand in the poo hole than be next to this creature.* In this small space, Brookstone's deep voice echoes off the walls and vibrates in her chest, as if it is amplified like Stellie's was. She looks around awkwardly and tries to dust her jogging clothes off, but her hands come away even dirtier than before. *What I wouldn't give to have a shower right now,* she thinks to herself, *and some food.* Her stomach growls at the thought.

"That's better." Brookstone rumbles. He looks her up and down with a low hum. "Now, now, you certainly don't look that threatening. But the Cataloguing doesn't lie. Oh yes, there is something dark in you, isn't there, Alexia? Something just below the surface that threatens us all. We made the right decision to send you for filing." With a startlingly quick movement, Brookstone is directly in front of her. He is roughly the same height as her but lifts his chin in a way that makes her feel as if he is staring down on her, as if she is just a peasant in the presence of royalty. His robes still cover the majority of his body shape, but Alex can make out two arms and two legs moving below the billowing outfit. His frame closely matches that of her own.

"I'm going to explain to you how this works, Alexia, and I'll do my best to dumb it down for someone of your inferior species. Keeping it simple for you to understand. You are a threat to us, whether you know it yet or not. You cannot be allowed to exist as a Stone Set Holder and travel freely amongst our galaxies. You certainly cannot return to Earth and inform them of what you have discovered, even if there is only a slim chance they will believe you. No, you will be filed here with the other degenerates and our society, my society, will carry on existing as it always has."

Alex feels herself starting to shake under the intense glare of Brookstone. His voice has drawn down to a whisper and his words take on a razor-sharp tone.

"But before you can be filed, we must remove your Stone markings." Alex steals a quick glance down at her hands.

"Yes, those. You don't deserve to possess those." Brookstone passively strokes his own hands, and Alex catches a glimpse of similar markings on the insides of his palms. "The process for removal is quite violent." An evil grin spreads across his face.

Alex's face goes slack as she recognizes the look of joy on this maniac's face. This is something he is looking forward to.

"The procedure is one that I invented a few hundred years ago. You see, I will start by inserting a large needle into your eye and into the soft squishy part of your brain." He takes a pudgy finger and lifts it up to hover just in front of Alex's eyes, making her go cross-eyed. "And for that we need you awake and coherent. I will do my best not to do any long-lasting damage, but accidents do happen. From there, I will extract the memories that the Stones have left behind."

"What memories? I don't have any memories that aren't my own." Alex manages to stutter.

"No, and that is the point. We need to remove the memories before they work their way into your conscious mind, and you become even more dangerous. After that step is complete, we will move to your hands. Now I know some of my colleagues would prefer to remove your hands entirely, but I don't want to do that. No, you see I am a scientist. I want to explore you. I haven't legally had a human on my table in nearly two hundred years." The way he says 'legally' leaves Alex with the impression that he has certainly had humans here illegally before.

Brookstone continues, "I'm going to need time to research, experiment if you will. So, I will be taking my time with you, and once the markings are removed, I may just spend more time exploring the rest of you. Such a rare creature you are! How could I pass up this opportunity to learn about your secrets? Who knows what valuable information you could reveal?"

"After all that is done, assuming you survive, you will be sent for filing. This step is much more boring, no exploration at all, just a simple liquefaction and jarring preservation process."

Brookstone looks at Alex again and sees a look of terror staring back at him.

"Oh, nothing to worry about, we just extract your conscious mind from your physical self, liquify your body, leaving your consciousness intact, place you in a jar, and send you down to the filing room in the depths of Barter to live out your sentence. I believe you would refer to it as 'Hell'." With a quick laugh, he turns to leave. "I'll be back for you in a few days, Alexia. Sleep well."

The door slams shut behind him, and Alex is left to cower at his lingering words.

These creatures are monsters! This is their high-functioning society? How could Earth have possibly been rejected for being unable to adapt to the ways of their society? They are barbarians compared to us. This is it, I'm going to die here, or liquify here, which actually sounds way worse than dying. Either way, I'm about to meet my end. Alex's mind moves a thousand miles a minute, leaving her to shake and cry on the floor as the doom of her situation settles in.

Another few hours pass by as Alex moves in and out of exhausted consciousness. Again, she is startled out of her stupor by another noise from outside her cell.

With wary eyes lingering on the door, Alex stands and pushes herself against the back wall, fearing that Brookstone has come back to scare the living daylights out of her once more, or worse, collect her for his experiments. Suddenly, a large bang shakes the door as something heavy strikes it.

With a sliding sound, something is dragged out of the way of the door, and it swings open. There in the doorway is the brown alien from her Cataloguing. His humorous eyes settle on her, and he gives her a startlingly bright smile.

"Hello, Alexia, I am Rickert. Sorry about this mix-up; if you would please follow me, I have come to save your life."

CHAPTER

14

Something deep inside Alex's heart and mind tells her to trust this alien, although she can't put a finger on why. It's as if that little voice is speaking to her again, the voice that isn't hers. With one last look around her cell, she steps out toward Rickert and out into the hallway. On the ground next to the door is the guard that was stationed to watch over her, now lying unconscious in a heap. Alex glances up to Rickert, and he continues to smile broadly at her, clearly very pleased with himself.

"I know you must be a little confused, but I assure you, I am on your side. You need to trust me, Alexia, do you think that's something you can do?" She gives him a small nod. "Perfect! We are going to need to move quickly, but there is no way you will be getting out of here looking like that, much too human. Here," pulling a small bag off his shoulder, he pulls out a new set of clothes that closely resemble those that the guard is wearing, "put these on."

Giving a sheepish look to Rickert, Alex strips down to her underwear and sports bra, throwing her foul-smelling jogging clothes back into the cell. Quickly, she pulls on the guard uniform and does up the series of snaps and clasps. Standing up straight, she looks back at Rickert who gives her a smile.

"OK, that's better, but your face and skin colour are still a dead giveaway, not to mention the blood running down your face." Alex grimaces as she imagines what she must look like. Reaching back into the bag, he pulls out a bracelet and hands it to her. Taking it cautiously, she slips the thing onto her wrist. At first, nothing happens, but then she feels a sharp pinching as metal pins shoot out of the bracelet and puncture her skin. Immediately, her skin starts to shimmer and take on a green hue. She looks in shock as her entire body is transformed into something that resembles one of the aliens she has seen wandering in this galaxy. She can feel a dull throb on her forehead as something else shifts in her appearance. She lifts her hands to touch her head and gasps when she feels a small horn protruding from her skull. The wounds on her head are still there, her fingers sticking painfully into the one on her forehead as she pokes around her horn. Pulling her fingers away from the open wound, Rickert hands her a hat and a damp rag, seemingly having thought of everything. She quickly wipes off her face and then pulls the hat over her head. Her knees wobble as the gashes sting under the pressure of the hat, but otherwise it fits quite comfortably. The hat even has a built-in space for her horn. As she adjusts the hat, she notices that even her hair has changed colour and is now a vibrant purple.

Rickert begins to chuckle at the horrified look on her face, "No worries, Alexia, it's all temporary. Once the bracelet is removed, your appearance will go back to what it was. Can't have you looking too much like the rest of us now, can we? Not when you are who I think you are." Alex looks at him curiously. Oddly, she doesn't feel threatened by what he says, but she does feel worried. *Who exactly do you think I am?* Her thoughts start to drift away from Rickert and her surroundings, her anxiety creeping back into the centre of her chest. As if Rickert can sense the drift in her thoughts, he reaches out and gently touches her shoulder, a soothing calm comes over her.

She starts to breathe again, and her focus is pulled back to Rickert.

"That's much better," he says. "Now follow me. This feels too obvious to even have to say, but don't talk to anyone, just keep your eyes forward. It is normal for me to be seen down here, and it's not uncommon for me to have a guard accompanying me, but we don't want to push our luck."

With that, Rickert stuffs the unconscious guard's body into her old cell and closes the door. Turning quickly on his heel, he walks away from the cell with Alex hot on his trail. Together they work their way out of the complex jail system. Just like when Alex was brought down here, they pause periodically to open doors which she can now see this time around. Rickert waves his palm in front of a screen each time to release the locks. After the third time, Rickert catches her curious gaze. "Oh these," he holds up his palm for her to see, it features similar markings as her hands, "these handy little Stone markings will get you into a lot of places. One of the conveniences of being a PPC member, no one expects us to do anything naughty." He gives her a mischievous little smile.

Continuing their trip up and out of the jail, they encounter only a few guards. Each one stationed outside of various cells, guarding their occupants. Every guard gives Rickert a small nod but otherwise ignores them.

After a long walk and a lot of stairs, they reach one final door, this one heavier than the last dozen, implying that it is the final barrier keeping the prisoners in place. With a wave of his palm, the door swings open and Rickert steps out into a brightly lit room.

Whitewashed walls cover the sides of the room, brightly reflecting the light around, leaving Alex feeling like she is once again stepping into a different galaxy. This room is so clean and organized compared to the jail below. A row of aliens sits along the far wall, silently working on their computers or watching holograms in front of them.

She steps through the door, and it swings silently shut behind her. Starting to feel like they are going to make it out unnoticed, Alex begins to ease her breathing, still following closely to Rickert.

As they approach the far end of the room, a deep call rumbles through the room "Rickert…" a familiar voice rings out, leaving Alex paralyzed. Rickert turns smoothly and smiles broadly, giving no sign that he is in the middle of a prison break. Alex turns slowly, fear climbing up her throat as her eyes land on Brookstone.

"Brookstone, my oldest friend, using the long-lost English language I see, I like your style. What can I do for you?" Rickert steps toward Brookstone, while also subtly stepping in front of Alex, partially blocking her from view.

"I see you have also brushed up on the language, such a wicked and awkward thing, isn't it? Yet I'm drawn to using it for some reason. I may use it more often as I do enjoy watching the idiots around me stare in confusion." He glances humorously at Alex, thinking he just insulted her deeply, and then looks back to Rickert. "I'm surprised to see you here, Rickert. I thought you were heading to Solax. As you know the Council is gathering to try and decipher why a Stone Set would choose a human. I thought you would be interested in that conversation?"

"Ah yes, that is where I am heading right now. I just needed to make a quick stop at my favourite place to refill my lungs with its glorious smells and let my eyes rest on its beautiful sights." Brookstone's nose crinkles up in revolt at Rickert. "I jest, my good man. I simply needed to drop off some paperwork. I have a few more items to attend to before I head back to Solax. It may be a few weeks before I can make it there, but I trust the Council to do its job."

"Safe travels then, I'll be on this disgusting planet for a few days while I work through the removal process of our newest guest." At the mention of Alex, her spine stiffens, and her green skin goes pale. Brookstone senses the change in her demeanor and glances at her once more. He eyes her with suspicion, wondering if it's possible she is understanding them, after all, they are speaking a language that she should not know. With a sneer at her, he turns back to Rickert. "I would love to join the Council as well. As you know, I have observed Earth for many years, but I simply cannot take myself away from this more pressing matter."

Rickert nods in understanding and the two beings stare at each other with what appears to be a mutual suspicion. *Their friendship is clearly fake.* Alex thinks to herself. *Obviously, these two do not like or trust each other.*

With one final distasteful look to Rickert and Alex, Brookstone turns on his heel and marches in the other direction, exiting through a small side door.

Rickert turns back to Alex and motions for her to follow once more. They exit out the main doors and find themselves outside on a desolate-looking planet. Stepping away from the doors, Alex turns to see the building she just exited is actually relatively small, no larger than the main white room. *The jail cells must be underground. That makes escaping on your own even harder.*

The planet around her is a deep red, reminding her of Mars. The ground beneath her feet crunches as she walks, small pieces of bright red shale cracking under her weight. She feels light on this planet, as if her mass is less than it was on Earth. *The gravity must be lighter here.* Compared to the intense weight of her body on Valyrn, she feels like she bounces along.

She is surprised to find that she once again has no problem breathing on this foreign planet. Above the building is the same air conditioning type unit that she saw stationed above the city on Valyrn, only much smaller. *Strange to think I'm on an entirely different planet now, and yet I can still breathe.* She marvels at her simplicity. *Something to wonder about another time, Alex, let's focus on escaping right now.*

Unlike Valyrn, this area of the planet seems to be boxed in with a large forcefield covering the small building and what appears to be a parking lot for spaceships. Alex stares up in awe, craning her neck to see the full length of the forcefield.

"It keeps the life support system contained," Rickert says as they walk away from the building. His tone is hushed, despite there being no one around them. "The system on Barter is small, only meant for this little space and the prison grounds below. Keeps everyone here alive, but you die instantly if you step outside the forcefield. Another security measure to make sure no one ever escapes from Barter." He smiles sadly, like the brutality of it wounds him.

Quickly, Rickert leads her away from the building and toward a row of spaceships. He takes her to the fifth ship in line. A large double-decker beast that looks more like a yacht than a spaceship looms before her. Alex marvels at the sheer size of it, her mind instantly flashing to how expensive it must have been. She chuckles at herself; *I wonder what they use for money around here?* Rickert walks underneath the tall black ship and approaches a long flat section of the wall. He waves his hand in front of a small control panel and the belly of the ship opens to reveal a small ramp. The duo climbs up into the ship and the ramp lifts behind them, sealing them inside.

Isolated from the world of Barter's prying eyes or ears, Alex lets out a shaky breath, feeling as if she has been holding it since the white room. The space in the lower part of the ship is barren, full of metal components, uncomfortable-looking benches, and a pilots' chair. The pilots' chair is seated in front of a simplistic-looking control panel. Lights flash sporadically and knobs and switches sit in various positions. A large gel pad is at the centre of it all, a faint outline of a handprint can be seen pressed into the sticky-looking substance. Rickert slides into the chair and adjusts the seat so that his hand is lined up with the gel pad.

"Easy, Alexia, the hard part is over."

"Alex."

"What's that?"

"Please call me Alex."

With a bewildered look, a smile creeps across Rickert's face. "Alex," he says, testing out the word "OK, Alex it is. Well, in that case, you can call me Rick! What fun!" He gives a hearty laugh and turns toward the front of the ship and seats himself in the main seat. Alex finds herself a small side seat and sits down behind him. Still laughing to himself, Rick puts his hand on a control panel and the ship comes to life. Small wires jump out from the panel and wrap themselves around his hand. With what appears to be nothing more than a thought, the ship's engines fire, and they lift into the air. As they rise steadily, the ship jars suddenly to the right and then angles sharply left, causing Alex to shift uncomfortably in her seat. She looks around for a seat belt or harness. Finding one behind her, she fastens it over her shoulders and hips.

"This is a rudimentary way of travel for me so bear with me while I work the controls of this finicky machine. Now, where is the button for the cloaking device?" Coming across a large purple button, he gives it a poke and a shimmer falls over the windows of the ship. "There we go, I paid a lot of money for that feature. Now no one will be able to see or detect us." Eventually, the ship steadies out, and Rick uses his opposite hand to enter something into the ship's control panel.

As Alex sits there, the ship pushes up toward the forcefield. Alex feels her body tense as the nose of the ship approaches the fine blue mesh that marks the barrier. They glide through without so much as a bump. The red planet disappears from the view of the windows as they shoot up toward the sky. The ship jumps forward, and they are launched into outer space. Soon, Alex can see nothing but blackness and stars in front of them. After several long moments, she starts to think of her family again.

"Rick?"

He chuckles at the shortened version of his name, "Yes, Alex?"

"Where are we going? I need to go home. Are you taking me back to Earth?" As she asks the question, the feeling of dread builds in her stomach as she anticipates the alien's response.

Rick looks back to her, a flicker of sadness crosses his face, "No, my dear, I can't take you back to Earth. For that you would need a Stone Set of your own, and from what I understand, you do not have your Stones with you, which means we would need to find them. At the moment, it is simply too dangerous for you to be out in the galaxy. After all, you are an escaped fugitive. Besides, we have a few things to take care of before we can send you on your way back home. For now, we are heading to my favourite place, but it's my little secret, so you'll have to forgive me, but I cannot tell you quite yet."

And with that, Rick turns back to face out the giant window, leaving Alex to cry quietly behind him.

CHAPTER

15

A lex quickly comes to learn that space travel via ship is a long and tedious process. During the first few hours, she sits quietly behind Rick, staring out the window as stars fly past. After that, her mind begins to wander and her body wilts from exhaustion. Catching the tired look on her face, Rick steps away from his control console, having set the ship to autopilot long ago.

"Come this way, Alex. Let me show you to your room." With a heavy feeling in her bones, this time from exertion rather than gravity, she stands up and follows him to a narrow ladder. Letting him lead her to the upper cabin of the ship, Alex steps up and out after him and is surprised by the amount of open space. The main part of the ship houses a small kitchen and dual-purpose seating and dining area. Beyond the kitchen is a bathroom that Alex looks longingly towards. Across from the dining area are three doors. Rick takes her across the space to open the middle door.

She walks through the door and looks at the small but comfortable space. "Here is where you will be sleeping.

Our journey will take about two months." Alex looks at him in horror.

"I can't be here for two months; I need to get home!"

"Oh yes, I suppose I should explain some things to you. Why don't you wash up and meet me in the dining area? There is much to discuss." He turns away from her and climbs back down the ladder.

Alex looks around the room; inside is a small bed, a desk, and a closet. The walls are empty, and a single light hangs overhead. She moves across the room to the closet and peers inside. Here she finds a set of freshly laundered clothes that are miraculously her size, although she is getting the impression that nothing is coincidental with Rick. She grabs them from the shelf and exits the room, and shuffles tiredly across the ship.

Entering the bathroom, she closes the door behind her and secures the lock in place. She turns to face the mirror and jumps backward in shock and fear. Staring back at her is a green alien with a horn on her head. *Oh right, the bracelet.* After taking a moment to examine her temporary hair, skin, and horn, she works to remove the bracelet.

Looking for a way to release the vicious pins from her skin, she locates a small button. With a light push, the pins slide back into the bracelet, and her skin fades back to its normal color, and she feels the horn disappear. Setting the bracelet to the side, she turns back to the mirror and takes in her own image. It's still quite a shocking sight to see herself in an alien's uniform, covered in dirt and grime. *This is undoubtedly the dirtiest I have ever been.*

After a quick scan of her wounds, she finds them minor in nature, with the worst of them being the cut on her forehead. She hops in the shower and spends the next thirty minutes moving between vigorously scrubbing her skin and sobbing quietly under the water as it falls on her.

Finally, she feels clean enough to exit the shower and pulls on the fresh clothes. The beige neutral set hangs loosely from her body. Using her fingers to comb out her hair, she steps in front of the mirror one final time. A clean and sad version of herself looks back at her. So much has happened in such a brief time. The person looking at her is hardly the person that she was when she was pulled from her home on Earth. Her brain moves rapidly inside her head, and thoughts flow to the surface about her family and her life back on Earth.

I miss my daughter. I miss the feeling of her small hands in mine, the feeling of her tiny body pushed up against my leg in one of the mighty hugs that she likes to give me. I miss my husband and his corny dad jokes. I miss his cooking and the sound of his voice ringing through the house. For crying out loud, I even miss the ridiculous way he dresses. Pain fills Alex's chest as she is overcome with feelings of grief and loss. *They aren't dead, Alex; they just aren't here.*

As she finishes in the bathroom, she throws her old clothes into a laundry basket and tucks the bracelet into her pants pocket. Opening the door, she steps out to find Rick back in the seating area. "Feeling better?" he asks her as he takes in her clean body and puffy red eyes. "Well, you look cleaner at least. Come, sit, let's talk about some of those things that are making you so distraught."

She moves to take the seat across from him and eyes a bowl of something in the centre of the table. "Help yourself," he says, pushing the bowl across to her. "It's a delicacy in our galaxy. I'm not quite sure how the name translates to English, but here we call it ●⋇○◆□ɱ.ɱ." He gives her an apologetic shrug and watches as she hesitantly picks up the green squishy food. Taking a small bite, her lips curve into a smile as the sweet taste spreads across her taste buds and the liquid rolls down her throat.

"This is delicious."

"Hence the reason it is a delicacy. Help yourself to as many as you would like. There is also more food in the fridge. Unfortunately, everything is labeled in my language so you may find yourself in for a wild ride while you work through it." He gives her a little wink and then grows serious. "So, let's start with what is troubling you, your family back on Earth, correct?"

Surprised that he guessed so accurately, she stares at him "Yes, how did you know?"

"Oh, it wasn't a guess. You see, I am very in tune with the thoughts and emotions of other beings. Speaking of, sorry for the rude intrusion into your mind during the Cataloguing. Usually, I like to have a pre-established bond with the recipient of my telepathic communications before I thrust myself into their mind, but as you know, there wasn't time for that. When I jumped into your mind to tell you to continue testing, you were thinking about your family. When I opened the pathway, it opened a two-way communication path, but don't worry, with a little training, you'll be able to control what I see and what you hold back from me."

"Anyway, back to your family. They are safely back on Earth, in fact, they haven't even noticed your absence, so rest your weary mind." Alex stares at him in disbelief.

"What do you mean they haven't noticed that I'm gone? It must have been more than twenty-four hours since this whole nightmare started. Surely, they would have noticed that I am gone by now."

"Time is a funny thing, Alex, especially when it comes to Stone Holders like you and me." Seeing her confused look, he continues. "You see, the Stones are the conduit that allows the PPC's members to travel through time and space. But even more complex, they also control the space-time continuum for every galaxy in the universe."

"The orb, traditionally called the Pillar, controls space travel, taking you to any destination you want. The rectangle, traditionally called the Perma, controls time travel." A familiar smile shows across his face. "Pillar and Perma? PP? Get it? We are the Pillar and Perma Council! PPC! A little wordplay if you will." Seeing that she is not nearly as amused as he is, he awkwardly clears his throat and continues.

"When you took hold of the Stones, they imprinted into your DNA, leaving those marks behind, but we will get further into that later. In addition to that, they also gave you the ability to control the space-time continuum. This is where it gets messy; when the Stones pulled you from your galaxy into ours, the timeline stopped progressing on Earth. You see, we PPC members have been keeping a dirty little secret from the common folk."

"Only galaxies that house a Stone Set, both a Pillar and a Perma, can exist with a linear timeline. When you took the Set out of Earth's galaxy, you took the last remaining Set, so everything on Earth is frozen, neither moving forward nor backward. And until the set is returned, that galaxy will stay that way." He gives a little chuckle. "So, you see, you have nothing to worry about Your family is fine, they are just stuck in a never-ending time freeze."

Working to grasp his words, thoughts bounce around in her head, threatening to strangle her. As her mind races and her anxiety takes grip, Rick seems to pull away from her with a pained look on his face. Her mind eventually lands on a question. "But I thought you all assumed there were no sets on Earth? That's what Androx and Stellie told me." Alex stumbles over her words as her brain tries to keep up with the onslaught of information that Rick is giving her. This isn't the most crucial thing she wants to ask, but she can't seem to get her brain to ask the right questions, the questions her heart wants to know most. *What the hell do you mean my family is stuck in a never-ending time freeze*? No, that's a question she will have to process on her own for a bit.

"Those nimrods?" Rick responds with a chuckle. "They are nothing but bureaucratic worker bees. The inner workings of the PPC and the Stones are largely kept secret from the general population."

"How do you know they are frozen? How do you know the Stone Set that chose me was the last on Earth?"

A guilty look crosses over Rick's face. "Well, we have been working to remove the Stone Sets from Earth. For centuries we have been tracking them and pulling them away from the Milky Way galaxy, hoping to put it into a state of permanent pause."

"What? Why?" She is disgusted to hear this.

"There are other galaxies we wish to inhabit, and we need the Stones to set them into motion. Simply put, Earth ranked low on our food chain, especially because you didn't even have a member representing you on the PPC. But you being here, the Stones choosing you, that changes things. The Council surely won't ignore Earth anymore, and they definitely won't pause the galaxy. Even we won't override the will of the Stones that way, we hold too much respect for their wishes."

"Then why look to remove them from Earth in the first place?" Alex can't believe what she is hearing.

"Honestly, we thought the Stones were trapped there, and we couldn't understand why they would willingly choose to stay in such an inferior location."

"We are not inferior, we are not stupid, and we are not simplistic!" Alex's anger floods over with all the snide comments about the human species bubbling to the surface and spilling out onto poor Rick. He shrinks back from her, pinching his forehead as her emotions and words overtake him. Regaining his composure, he continues.

"I understand, I have always understood. In fact, I believe you may just be the strongest one in our galaxy, the one capable of the most exciting things."

"What do you mean?"

"The Stones, they chose you. That means you are strong, there is no doubt of that. But compared to the rest of the Council you may be the strongest of us all, and we are supposedly the elite of the species. The things we deal with and the crises we work through would melt the minds of even the most sophisticated species. But if the

Stones chose you, then they must feel you are needed and that your strengths are required for something. Hence, the reason I asked you to complete the Cataloguing. That process shows us who is truly capable of handling the Stones and the responsibilities that come with them. It tells us what your strengths are, and you Alex, you had many surprising strengths."

"But I failed, and I understand, there is no way I can handle all this," Alex motions to the air around her, as if she can summarize the last few days with the wave of a hand.

"Oh no, you misunderstand! You didn't fail because you couldn't handle it. You failed because you scared us. You failed because we cannot handle someone of your abilities. Alex, you failed because you are too powerful."

CHAPTER

16

"**Y**ou're wrong," Alex shakes her head profusely. "I'm sorry but you're wrong, you have the wrong person, the tests were wrong, it's just all WRONG!" The last word comes out as a shout as Rick stares back at her with patience on his round brown face.

She pushes away from the table and staggers to a standing position, a slimy green fruit still in her hand. She backs away from the table and tries to put as much space between her and Rick as she can manage, given the restricted space of the ship.

This can't be happening. It's not happening, this is a dream. She clenches her eyes shut and crouches down in the far corner, placing her head between her knees. Her breath comes in rapidly and unevenly as her body shakes with adrenaline and fear. Once again, her anxiety overtakes her, and she is sent into a panic attack.

Unable to hear anything around her as the blood pounds in her ears, Alex is pulled deep into her own sorrows. For a few long minutes, the world around her ceases to exist as her mind and body fight against each other. With a very gentle touch, Rick places his four-fingered hand on her shoulder and again, a feeling of calm spreads through her body.

"Breathe, Alex, breathe," he soothes.

With the telepathic help of Rick and her efforts to slow her breathing, the panic attack passes, and Alex is left curled up on the floor, shaking from the physical response her body has.

Eventually, Alex moves to a more comfortable position, leaning against the wall and facing out toward Rick, who sits cross-legged in front of her. She keeps her knees tucked tight to her chest with her arms wrapped around them, taking on a defensive stance.

"I'm sorry that was so overwhelming for you, Alex. We will go slow, I promise, but I need you to trust me. You are so much stronger than you know. You are a thing of prophecies." His gentle blue eyes rest on her as she stares down at the ground. Unable to hear anymore or learn anything new, she stands up slowly and moves to her new bedroom. Heavily, she collapses onto the bed and quickly falls into a dreamless sleep.

* * *

The next several days are spent in a haze, moving only from her bed to go to the bathroom or to find food. Rick watches her carefully as she moves about the cabin but does not say anything to her. Alex is grateful for the little alien; his presence and silence are a comfort to her.

Occasionally she senses that he feels torn between her and something else.

"Alex, I need to leave the ship for a bit." She stares at him, a mixture of emotions running through her mind. "Don't worry, the ship is set to autopilot. There will be no problems, and I will only be gone for a little while. I need to continue with my duties as a PPC member. I can't allow my fellow Council members to notice an interruption in my service. I must go back and start attending Council meetings to find out what is happening in the galaxies. Find out what their plans are to find you and try to put in as much misdirection as I can to protect you." Alex can't comprehend what he is saying, her mind is working too frantically. She turns away from him and stumbles back to her room, but her ears pick up on a faint whooshing sound, and just like that, she is left alone on the alien ship.

* * *

Roughly five days after boarding the ship Alex emerges from her bedroom in search of food once more. But this time, instead of taking her strange meal back to her room, she sits down with Rick at the small table.

He gives her a small smile, and together they eat in silence.

This tradition carries on for several days as Alex slowly recovers from her traumas. Rick continues to depart the ship occasionally but is careful to always be there for shared mealtimes, wanting to give her the support she needs. Eventually, she breaks the silence that has drawn out between them. "You said something about a prophecy, that I was the thing of prophecies. What did you mean by that?"

Happy to have something to discuss, Rick starts talking. "Thousands of years ago, when the Stone Sets were first found, they were found in a place of magic and prosperity. The two sisters who made the discovery, named Pillar and Perma, found themselves with the power to control the space-time continuum. Back then, the society we know today didn't exist, and most species and cultures were living in the dark ages. In fact, most galaxies remained unexplored and barely connected in the sense that the Stones had distributed themselves amongst the galaxies that they felt worthy of life. It was Pillar and Perma who brought the galaxies together and formed the society. But at a terrible cost."

"As you can imagine, building a high functioning society consisting of several galaxies takes time and work. Pillar and Perma began to play with their own timelines, travelling back in time to new galaxies and leveraging their knowledge to push the civilizations forward much faster than they were ready for. Eventually, the sisters figured out a way to avoid aging altogether. They were able to jump through time in a way that kept them from growing any older but continued to maintain the steady progress of the societies. Sadly, the toll on their minds was significant."

"Perma was the first to break. After a jump within her galaxy and to a far-off future she came back speaking only in riddles and permanently afraid. She told Pillar of an unknown future, where the lands were razed with fire and destruction. Haunted by creatures from the depths of hell."

"Pillar tried to get her sister to tell her where or when this future was, but Perma quickly moved beyond verbal communication as her mind deteriorated. Just before her death, Perma wrote a prophecy."

Rick clears his throat and recites the prophecy:

"The future holds a dark age.
The lights will dim and leave the
civilizations in darkness.
This dark age will bring death and destruction to
the galaxies, unlike any that time has seen before.
At the head of this destruction stands one being, a
being that cannot be stopped by their peers, cannot be
sated by power, and will not be controlled by morals.
Only one being can end the destruction, only
one being is powerful enough to kill that
which is created and end the tyranny.
They alone, this unseen warrior,
are the Defender of man."

Alex stares at him as he recites the prophecy. "And why exactly do you think this prophecy is about me? Nothing in there tells me that I fit that bill."

"That's very true," Rick replies. "But after the death of Perma, Pillar did as much exploration as possible. She worked to uncover additional Stone Sets, pulling them from galaxies and handing them to worthy individuals. It was the first time anyone outside of the sisters had been in control of time and space travel; she created the

Planetary Peace Council. Grateful for their new role, they devoted themselves to Pillar's cause to help her discover more details about this doomed future that her sister spoke of. Through their travels, the group uncovered more prophecies and more data that helped them build the bigger picture. But again, the more they discovered, the more they were prone to madness. Over the ages, thousands of Stone Holders have succumbed to mania. A sickness that comes when they start to distort their own timeline. And if the mania didn't get them, most of them just simply disappeared, assuming to have died somewhere lost in the time stream."

"Roughly three hundred years ago, a ruling was passed by the PPC, aimed at protecting the minds of the Holders. It was declared that no member of the Council was to use the Perma Stone for time jumps. The restriction limited Stone Set Holders to only using the Time Stone to ensure their space jumps remained linear. No being was to exist outside of their own timeline or in their own futures or pasts. Anyone caught breaking this rule would find themselves with their Stone Set being confiscated, and they would be incarcerated on Barter."

"The Council also formally declared that the prophecy was nothing more than hearsay. A fantasy based on the manic minds of our time-addled ancestors as simply a consequence of their unbridled time travel. Since this declaration, the Council members have stopped exploring the prophecy, leaving the information unchecked and the truth of it unknown. All that is, except for the two of us."

Alex looks at Rickert with wary eyes "Let me guess, you and Brookstone?"

"Again, that is correct. I have been a Council member for nearly two hundred years, and in that time, I have managed to piece together the known facts of the prophecies and have painted myself a picture."

"As I see it, based on all that I have gathered, the prophecy speaks of a Defender from outside of our control. They will hail at our time of greatest need and bring with them strengths beyond what this civilization has seen in over a thousand years. This being will be one of supreme mental power that can be harnessed into a formidable weapon."

Alex stares at him with her lips pressed into a hard, thin line. "OK, that's all fine and dandy, but none of that describes me. I'm not mentally strong, for crying out loud I've had ten thousand panic attacks since arriving here!"

"Give yourself a little credit, my friend. I have seen inside your mind; I know the power that lies there. Can you imagine what you would be capable of if you started to believe in yourself? I choose to believe in you, Alex. I choose to believe that you are the Defender we need." Rick looks at her hopefully. "Can I show you something?"

"Sure, why not," Alex replies with an exasperated tone.

Rick reaches across the table and grips her hand. Suddenly, the inside of the spaceship is gone, and Alex is left standing on a new planet. With a shock, she wrenches her hand out of Rick's grip and is left gasping.

"Sorry, sorry! I forgot you were new to the powers of telepathy." Rick looks at her guiltily. "Everything you see is just a figment of your mind. Nothing is real, you cannot be hurt by what you see. You cannot interact with what you see, nor can anything interact with you." He pauses, "Can I try again?"

Still reeling from the experience, Alex gives him a small nod and puts her hand back out in front of her. With her hand once again in his firm, four-fingered grip, Alex is thrown back onto the planet.

This time she takes a moment to gain her bearings and looks around her. The planet is a husk of a civilization. All around her, buildings burn, and beings run and scream in terror. Alex takes a step forward and watches in horror as the giant light bulb she saw illuminating the sky of Valyrn falls to the ground, destroying everything in its path, leaving nothing but mayhem.

Her eyes drift back up to the place where the light hung only moments ago. Flying in the sky is a being that leaves Alex feeling cold, despite the heat of the burning city. The being flies around in tight circles, swooping down occasionally to pick up aliens, tossing them high in the air, and watching them fall to the ground with a wet splat.

Alex stares in terror as the being comes to land just ten feet in front of her. True to Rick's word, the being cannot see her and takes no notice of her presence. Up close, Alex can see that the being resembles a giant insect. Huge pincers jut from its body and slash through the air at aliens that run by, slicing them cleanly in half. With a whooping sound, the creature tosses its head into the air and laughs maniacally. Turning on two legs, the alien creature moves closer to Alex. Its eyes dart around, taking in the chaos around it, searching for more ways to spread destruction and death. Alex stares at its face. She is shocked to find the eyes are strikingly human, sending alarm through her body. *How can I find a resemblance to anything human in this monster?* But the rest of its face is vastly different from a human. Its nose is like that of a small elephant. Their mouth opens horizontally and reveals thousands of small teeth. The wings curl around the back like an angel of death, rippling as the creature walks and twitching with excitement.

The creature moves to stand over a dying alien. Opening its mouth wide, it leans over the being and brings its head down, hovering inches above its head—

Alex pulls her hand from Rick's grip once more. "What the hell was that?!"

"That is our future, Alex; every prophecy, every time jump, every piece of data always ends there. That is our destruction."

CHAPTER

It takes Alex a long time to recover from what she saw. Several more days pass before she can speak, fear having constricted her throat, leaving her verbally paralyzed. It doesn't help that her dreams are growing eerily strange. She is seeing things that her mind can't understand. Each morning she wakes up in a cold sweat, her mind feeling as if it had been working in overdrive all night, leaving her feeling mentally exhausted. Yet, when she tries to recall the dreams, she cannot focus on them long enough to pick out any details.

Once again, Rick gives her the space she needs. While not offering any words of support or comfort, but always being nearby, just in case she needs to talk. By nature, he is a very calming presence for her. She feels herself relax when they share a space, her trust in him growing, despite the terrifying things he keeps showing and telling her.

On the fourth day of silence, Alex approaches Rick and stares at him closely, a thousand questions bubbling below the surface. "I think I'm ready to know more."

Rick closes the book he was reading and glances up at her, with a heavy sigh he shakes his head. "I wish that were true Alex, but your mind is in a fragile state."

"Stay out of my mind, Rick."

"I wish I could believe me, but you are throwing your emotions around like they are candy at a parade. Being in such close proximity with you for the past weeks has been quite mentally taxing for me as well."

Alex gives him an apologetic look. "I'm sorry, I had no idea."

"If you truly want some mental privacy and to give me some peace and quiet, I suggest we start training you. What do you think?"

"First, tell me one more thing about the prophecy..." Alex presses him for more information. "When exactly does this prophecy take place? How do we know it is in our lifetime?"

"Good questions, I first discovered the foul ending about twenty years ago. I was jumping illegally through my own timeline and landed among the scene that I showed you. I barely made it out with my life. Since stumbling across it, I have been afraid to go back, but when I try to jump past that time, I'm always met with the same scene. It's as if there is no future beyond that, not one that the Stones can show me anyways."

Considering his answer, Alex asks another question. "Last prophecy question...for now... Has anyone else come across this future?"

"It's highly unlikely, seeing as it's illegal and all the current Stone Holders are serious rule followers." He pauses, and his face grows sour, "Except Brookstone, of course. He has also seen the future, and he has definitely linked it to the prophecy, just as I did. I'm sure he is actively exploring it, just as I am. But his methods are unconventional, I don't know what exactly he would do with that information, or how he would interpret it."

Satisfied with his answer and seeing that Rick is uncomfortable talking about his old friend, she moves the conversation back to training. "What does 'training' mean exactly? How are you going to train me?" Mostly she wanted to know if it was going to hurt.

"It's actually quite easy. Follow me." Rick leads her to the third door in the small space next to her bedroom. "I'm surprised your curiosity hasn't brought you to look in here yet, or even ask about it."

Well, I've been a little busy trying to not mentally overload and die, Rick. Alex thinks haughtily to herself, but she just shrugs at him.

Rick opens the door and steps inside, Alex following behind him. "Welcome to the Knowledge Computer." Inside the small room is a series of high-tech computers. Alex looks around, clearly impressed with the setup. As she explores the room, Rick asks something that catches her off guard, "Tell me, have the dreams started yet?"

Surprised once again by his intuition, she nods to him while still exploring the room, touching the wires and knobs, which run into the sophisticated computer. Despite all her tech-savvy abilities, this is not a computer she can figure out just by looking at it.

"Hmm, I suspected as much, I could feel your discontent while you slept. Those dreams are the Stones communicating with you. The communications can be extremely overwhelming to someone who is not mentally trained to handle the onslaught of information they hold. This training will help you immensely with that."

"The Stones can communicate?" Alex asks.

"Oh yes. I'm sure you know by now that the Stones are sentient beings. They can make decisions and act on them in the same way as you and I. While we aren't completely sure of their motivations or their true purpose, we do know that they choose to communicate to their Holders when it best suits them. Not all Holders will experience the communication path, this likely has something to do with the bond between the Stone Set and the Holder. If the dreams have started, then you have an established communication path." Alex looks at him curiously, trying to find a way to ask about other communication methods. Rick notices her shift in stance and prods further. "Have you heard anything else from your Stones?"

Alex looks at him and gives a small nod. "I think so. I have been hearing a small voice in my head, almost like my conscious, but different and stronger. Could that be the Stones?"

Rick looks at her incredulously. "It's quite possible, but I haven't come across a communication path that strong in all my years on the Council. It would be quite unique." He looks excited, like Alex has just checked another box in his prophecy checklist. "If that is the case, then we definitely need to start training you, work on your mental agility, and increase your knowledge. That way, you will not only be able to block me out but also communicate more effectively with your Stone Set."

Alex gives him a grateful look, "OK, where do we start?"

With a happy smile, Rick turns to the computer and pulls out a chair, motioning for her to have a seat. Alex sits down, and Rick pushes her in toward the computers. These computers aren't like the ones back home; there are no monitors—only wires and restraint-looking devices.

Warily, Alex eyes the devices as Rick picks one up. "There is no pain with this process, Alex, although it may leave you feeling disoriented after the first few sessions. Your mind will need time to adapt to this new way of knowledge absorption."

Rick slips a headset over her head. Alex is grateful that the wounds suffered during her Cataloguing are fully healed. He adjusts the wires, sticking a few to her temples and the soft part at the base of her skull.

"The computer hooks directly into your mind, allowing for the flow of information to go directly into your memory banks for processing," Rick explains. "There are millions of files on this computer. You simply think of what you want to know, the information is located, and then uploaded into your brain. It's highly sophisticated technology, and it is only available to those that are on the Council. I suggest you start with language. That will give you the ability to understand our dialects, I think you'll like that, and it's a pretty easy place to start."

Looking nervously at the computer, Alex thinks of the word language. With a small hum, the computer springs to life. Alex can feel a strange tingling sensation in her head as the knowledge is dumped, unfiltered, into her mind. As the information rushes in, she has to close her eyes against the rapidly forming headache, but in seconds, she can feel an entire language forming in her mind. Just as quickly as it started, the flow ceases, and she is left with nothing but a small dull ache in her head.

Rolling away from the computer, she pulls the headset off and looks to Rick, who smiles down at her. "So how was that?"

"Just fine, I suppose, but how do I know if it worked? I don't feel like I know any new languages."

Rick gives her a laugh, "Well, a good indication is that I asked you that question in my natural dialect, and you understood it and were able to respond back to me in my language." Alex looks at him in disbelief. Rick laughs harder at her. "Oh, I have forgotten what it's like to receive your first knowledge dump. Don't believe me? Why don't you go to the fridge and take a look, see if you can read the labels on the food."

Alex stands up and quickly walks out of the room and into the kitchen, pulling open the fridge door. Sure enough, everything in the fridge is now labeled with something that she can read. She pulls out the slimy green fruit that she first tried, "Limtree." She reads the label aloud. She puts the fruit back and closes the door, and turns back to find Rick standing in the door frame, still smiling broadly at her.

"Holy crap! Let's do that again!"

CHAPTER

Despite Rick's warnings, Alex spends the next three days plugged into the Knowledge Computer. Her mind is a busy whir as she learns as much about the foreign galaxies as she can. At first, she starts out with simple keywords like Earth, Valyrn, or Planetary Peace Council. Over time, as her knowledge expands, she starts to grow broader in her searches. She now pulls massive amounts of data into her mind with words like history, Stones, and species.

After the third consecutive data dump, Alex disconnects from the machine and takes note of her weary body. Standing slowly, she exits the room and makes a mad dash for the bathroom. As Alex is violently ill, she tries to remember the last time she ate or drank anything and cannot come up with an answer.

After several intense minutes of sickness spewing from both ends, Alex limps out of the bathroom to find Rick chuckling, "I told you so."

With an aggravated look, Alex snaps at him, "Why didn't you come get me? Force me to eat, to take breaks?"

"What? Am I, your mother?" Rick laughs at the funny phrase and then continues. "In all reality, Alex, it is extremely dangerous to interrupt someone while they are hooked into the computer. To interrupt someone during a data flow could mean serious brain damage. Besides, I was travelling on PPC duties. I didn't realize you were plugged in for so long. Now, may I suggest, once again, that you go slow. Your mind will do everything you tell it to. It will make sacrifices to accommodate. For example, it will stop running your body, it may even forget to tell you to breathe or to tell your heart to pump blood. Ultimately, you could quite easily die."

"Well, that would have been good to know three days ago," Alex grumbles. "OK, fine, I'll take it easy. Besides, I can't imagine hooking up to that thing again any time soon. I feel awful."

Again, Rick laughs at her expense, earning him a baleful glare from her. "Go rest. When you wake, we can spend some time in the real world.

***

Alex sleeps for two days straight while her mind works to catch up on all the information it has absorbed, and her body heals from the trauma she put it through.

Waking up, she feels her stomach growl and rolls out of bed. Stumbling bleary-eyed to the kitchen, she moves to the fridge and pulls out something called "Makerjot." *It's almost more confusing and concerning being able to read the labels.*

She heats her food up in the rapid warming device next to the fridge and pulls out the steaming pile of gray-and-green food. Taking a quick sniff, she is assaulted with an acidic and tangy smell. She sputters a little bit but decides to try it anyway. So far, her food adventures have been exciting. The foods in this galaxy are much more complex than those on Earth. Her basic palate struggles to keep up with the onslaught of new flavours and textures. Rick assures her that there are even more tastes that she is unable to sense, but her human tongue isn't sophisticated enough to detect them.

She makes her way to the table and wonders where Rick is—usually she finds him here, reading a book.

She glances around and sits down to eat her food. After twenty minutes, her stomach is full, and she feels energy ringing through her body once again. Still wondering where Rick is, she heads to the ladder and drops down into the spaceship's cockpit. Here, she finds Rick fiddling with the controls. Clearly he is not sure what he's doing.

Startled by her sudden appearance, he jumps a few inches in the air, and his hands snap away from the control panel. "Oh, you startled me," he says, grasping at his chest. "I feel like a schoolchild being caught doing something naughty."

"Are you doing something naughty?" she questions.

"Well, that depends on whom you ask," he replies with a devious smile. "Technically no. Travel by spaceship is definitely allowed, and actually a very popular way for the common folk to travel. But you need to have a license, and in a manner of speaking, I do not. I have actually only driven a ship once before; on my way to rescue you from Barter. The Knowledge Computer was able to give me what I needed to figure out the basics. Sadly, there wasn't much on the subject. It's not a form of travel any member of the Council really needs to know about, seeing as we have the Stones and all."

"Speaking of, why don't we just travel via Stone? Or teleport using one of those fancy button things?"

"Travelling by Stone can only be done by one user at a time. While I could travel by Stone Set, you would be left behind. So, until we get your Set safely back in your hands, we have to stick to the rudimentary travel ways." He motions to the ship around him. "As for the teleportation stations, there are a few reasons."

"Reason one: those are closely monitored. To use the teleportation stations, the user has to press the button for themselves. That way the station can take a scan of your DNA and transport you safely to your destination. Another user cannot press the button for a teleporter. It has to be the intended traveller. Then, every travel route taken using a teleportation station is logged with the Embassy of Valyrn. When you entered the Cataloguing process, we took a scan of your DNA, creating you a file. Now, every time you travel through a port, it will ring through to the Embassy. Considering you are supposed to be locked up in Barter, that would be very strange. Although they probably know by now that you have escaped."

"Reason number two: where we are going doesn't have a teleportation station. Not all of our planets are accessible by teleportation. For example, you cannot teleport to Solax, the planetary home of the PPC. That can only be reached via spaceship or Stone Set. My secret little hideout is not an inhabited planet, it is not a space that the PPC has taken under its control, so you definitely won't find it housing a teleportation station."

"I see, so you're still not going to tell me where we are going. Just when I thought we were starting to trust each other." Alex lays a thick layer of guilt over her words.

With a heavy sigh, Rick gives in. "Fine, while my main home is on Solax, my secondary, and secret home, is on Muskoux. It's here that I have continued my research into the prophecy. It's here that all my research is housed. I keep it a secret because there are certain powerful beings that I don't want stumbling across what I know."

"Would that powerful being be Brookstone?" Alex asks.

Rick gives her a nod. "Him, for sure, and possibly others. The Council banned research into the prophecy, so no need to wave it in their faces."

"You mentioned before that Brookstone has also been looking into the prophecy. How do you know that?"

"Because we started exploring them together," explains Rick as a sad look comes over his face. "Brookstone and I are the oldest members of the PPC, him being a member only slightly longer than I have been. When I first met Brookstone, I wasn't even a PPC member yet; my father was the current member, and my brother was next in line, but that's a story for another time."

"Brookstone was a vibrant young man, brimming with life and curiosities. We immediately became friends, and over time, he started to share some of his research with me. I found it fascinating; we spent weeks poring over what he had discovered. When my father surprisingly handed his Stone Set down to me, Brookstone and I started traveling to far away galaxies in search of new information. It was he who introduced me to the darker, illegal side of time travel. It was he who first convinced me to time jump and start exploring spaces outside of my linear timeline. Even at the time I knew it was wrong. The Council had banned it for a reason, but Brookstone was a part of the decision to ban it, so I figured he knew what he was doing."

"We made the illegal time jumps together a handful of times before I started to feel the pull on my mind. It felt as if I was holding too many memories that overlapped with each other. My mind struggled to pull them apart. It was like having multiple personalities in my head. I told Brookstone that I didn't want to time jump anymore. He called me weak, said I wasn't worthy of exploring the prophecy with him, that he regretted involving me at all."

Rick's face grows even sadder as he relives the moments his most meaningful friendship perished. "I tried to convince him that there were other ways to continue exploring, that we had enough information, we didn't need to keep time jumping. He wouldn't hear it; he was convinced the answer lay just beyond his grasp. I could see he was becoming obsessed. I could also see the pull it was having on his mind. The gentle and easy-going Brookstone I once knew was dying and, in his place, a mad man was taking over."

"It was roughly fifty years ago that we went our separate ways. He was playing with his own timeline so much, that like Pillar and Perma, he stopped aging. Even now he doesn't look a day over seventy-five. I was always surprised the Council didn't investigate this absence of aging, but I think his seniority left them feeling cowardly, not wanting to question him. But I knew what was happening. Since then I have distanced myself from him. I am sure he has continued his research. Using any method necessary to gain more information. I think he originally started out trying to stop the prophecy from being fulfilled, but now I'm not so sure."

"What do you mean?" Alex asks. "If he isn't trying to prevent it, then what is the purpose of trying to figure it all out?"

Rick gives her a sad look. "Well, I think in his madness, he may be trying to become the Defender, so that he can save us all from damnation."

CHAPTER

19

A lex, with the help of Rickert, spends the next two weeks working on her mental and emotional control. He puts her through a variety of tests to manage her emotions, teaching her how to filter them before they take hold of her mind. For hours at a time, she sits at her desk and works through coping mechanisms, using them to focus her mental energy on controlling the emotions rather than letting them control her.

In a funny way, it reminds her of the therapy sessions she went through back on Earth. Rick has taken on the new role of her therapist, except his methods are a bit out of her world, literally.

The coping mechanisms she uses are similar to those she would find on Earth; light a candle, do ten push-ups, draw a picture, snap a rubber band on her wrist, etc. But unlike her practices on Earth, Rick steps into her mind and shows her how to truly turn inward. To really process the thoughts or emotions and control what power they hold over her.

A common technique they use is putting something in the box. It's a process that Alex learned on Earth. When something bothered or upset her, she would mentally picture herself putting something inside a box. She would mentally walk down a set of stairs and descend onto a beach, then she would walk over to a lone palm tree and use her imaginary hands to uncover the box of her own design. Her box acts as a one-way mirror. She puts the thoughts or feelings into the box, and while she can no longer see or feel them, they can continue looking out. The theory is that they may change over time or adapt to her new way of thinking. So, if she ever wanted to revisit the feelings, they may not be so painful.

Rick enjoyed this method very much as he was able to step into her mind and guide her through the process, making it more effective for her.

As the weeks draw on, she feels her mental capacity growing, and with each step forward, she can feel the mental draw on Rick ease as well. He has less frequent headaches and seems to wake more rested.

While she gains control of her waking thoughts, she also gains control of her dreams, or rather the images the Stones put into her mind.

While she was in the jail cell on Barter, Brookstone told her the Stones imprinted their memories into her mind. Until now, they have been coming through in fragments. Something she couldn't quite fully understand, but as time goes on, the memories become more straight forward in her mind.

During mealtimes, Alex has taken to the routine of telling Rick about the Stones' memories, or at least what she can remember from her dreams. Parts of it are still fragmented and broken. Rickert cautions her that she should only reveal what the Stones want her to openly communicate.

"The memories a Stone Set gives you are very sacred things between the Holder and the Stones," he tells her. "When you search the memories, you will feel which ones are acceptable to share, and which ones are not. Especially if you have such a strong bond with the Stones."

After a while, the dreams stop coming and Alex is left with the full memory set. Hidden away in her mind is the entire living history of her Stone Set. She can see as far back as their creation; when Pillar and Perma pulled them from a foreign planet, now called Solax, and gave them to their first owner, a stout little alien named Jaceer.

She can see all the Holders that came after Jaceer, including how the Stones came to be on Earth. As she tells Rick about the Stones landing on Earth, he is genuinely surprised to discover that this Set has been there for nearly three thousand years, and that it was one of many. "I thought that Earth was virtually untouched by our kind. We have been led to believe that Earth was not worthy of our technologies and leadership. Are you sure?"

"Yes, my Stone Set was one of nine on Earth, but as the years drew on, the Holders and their Sets vanished entirely, leaving only my Set behind."

"Do you know who the Holders of the other Sets were? Were any of them members of the PPC?"

Alex shakes her head, "I can't see that. It's like the Holder of my Set at the time lost touch with the other

Holders. Like he was abandoned on Earth. I can feel his despair as if it was yesterday, but this was hundreds of years ago."

"What else can you see about the Holders of your past?"

"I can't say much, partly because some of it is secret, but also because it still doesn't quite fit together in my head. I can tell you that the last alien holder was over fifteen hundred years ago, and then she handed the Set down to the first human, and from there, the Set has been handed down in that family line for thousands of years. The last member of that family line died, and the Stones found me. From what I can tell, the Stones were never used by their human Holders. They didn't have the knowledge to work them, and the Stones never truly connected to them, not the way they did to me anyway." Alex glances down at her hands. The red markings still prominently etched into her palms.

"Well, if that's true, that makes a lot of sense as to why we were left in the dark. We knew there was obviously a Set left somewhere on Earth. Otherwise, its time continuum would have stopped when the last Holder left, but we could never track them down. That's why the PPC kept going back, kept checking in on Earth. However, I think the Stones had a greater plan."

Alex looks up at him and makes eye contact, doing her best to control her emotions, to not let Rick feel what she is feeling.

"I'm right, aren't I?" Rick takes in her change of body language and makes an educated guess. "The Stones had a plan on Earth all along. They were waiting for you!"

CHAPTER

20

"**C**an you tell me more about the knowledge transfers?" Alex asks across the dinner table one evening. The prospect of evening is all relative. In space there is no such thing as day or night, just a long stretch of blackness that compresses them from all sides. Thankfully, the ship does have a feature that automatically adjusts the lights in communal areas at certain times, signifying to them that the evening approaches, or that daytime begins. It helps to keep their circadian rhythms in check.

Rick looks up from his bowl of green porridge-like dish and looks questioningly at her. "What do you mean?"

"Well, I understand that knowledge is being transferred into my head, that I can feel and see. There has to be more to it. It's like there are all these new pieces of information in my head, but when I try to put them together, try to form the picture, it comes out all fuzzy. Like I can't understand or see it."

"Oh yes, that. You're partially right. There is more to it. Your brain is like a large computer. It will take in as much information as you throw at it and store it in various parts. It's your subconscious mind that has to filter through all the new information and put it into something that makes sense. As we continue our training of your telepathic power, this will get easier. Speaking of, how are the dreams for you? Getting easier to understand?"

"Yes. I can clearly see the Stones' history now; it's all starting to fit into chronological order." Alex gives a chuckle. "I always made fun of the alien nuts. Thought they were crazy, but no, they truly were seeing aliens. Ha! If only they knew what I know. Why exactly was Earth kept at arm's length from the rest of the galaxies? While we are not as advanced as you, we aren't the barbarians we once were."

"That's true," Rick replies, giving her a thoughtful glance. "To be honest, Earth is not something I have watched too closely, having been consumed with my hunt for the prophecy and all. Which is ironic because the Defender apparently hails from Earth." Alex rolls her eyes. She is not nearly as convinced as Rick is that the prophecy is about her.

"The big push to leave Earth untouched actually came from Brookstone. He is the current PPC member who has been charged with assessing its readiness to join the PPC. There were others of course who would visit periodically as we tried to track down the last Stone Set, but Brookstone gave the final report. Each time he would return from Earth, he would give the Council a recap of what he had seen, and each time, we would vote to leave them as is."

"How did Brookstone assess Earth? You think people would notice an alien wandering around them."

"Oh, they did! All those nuts you spoke about, they were likely seeing our Council Members. While we tried to be discreet, some of us even donned the shapeshifting gear that I had you wear coming out of the prison, it didn't always work. Although, I can assure you we don't abduct people…OK, well, maybe Brookstone has been…." A sad look comes over Rick's face and he mutters under his breath, "Oh, my friend, what has happened to you?"

* * *

Rick was right; the more she trains her mind, the easier the knowledge becomes to understand. Soon, Alex could feel herself becoming a walking encyclopedia. Her mind is full of details and facts that she never even thought to question before.

She is becoming sharp. No longer plagued by panic attacks, she starts to think objectively and strategically. She spends hours scouring over all the information in her mind, focusing on the few details of the prophecy, the information known about Brookstone, and the inevitable doom of their society.

"The Knowledge Computers have limitations," Rick warns her. "They only know what the PPC members have inputted into them. There are secrets we have all withheld; for example, I have not entered any of my newfound knowledge about the prophecy, as I'm sure Brookstone hasn't either. Members also don't like information about them being entered, each of them preferring to remain private. So, take everything you see with a grain of salt. It may be missing key pieces of information or be slightly altered, only showing you what the original author wants you to see. I guess what I'm saying is, don't stake your life on the information from the Computers. You may not have the whole picture."

"OK, so when or how will I get the whole picture? If I am the Defender, don't you think I should have a good idea of what the big picture is?"

"Actually, no, from what I can tell, the being that fulfills the prophecy is an outsider, someone who is unfamiliar with our ways. So far you fit that description well, but I fear the more you know, the less adequately you fit the bill. Unfortunately, even my knowledge has limitations. How I interpreted the data about the prophecies may be skewed. Who's to say? Prophecies are fickle things."

"All that being said, I do want to share with you all the information I have. I believe you need to choose what your role in the prophecy will be. I know it seems that this responsibility is being thrust upon you, but in reality, a true Defender must choose their future. Obviously, this being cannot make the choice until they are satisfied with all the information. That is why we are destined for Muskoux. My secrets are there, and my secrets will become yours to protect and learn from. Speaking of which, we are only a few days away from my hideout. I suggest you spend them gathering your thoughts and readying yourself. It's time to put all that mental agility that you have gained to the test."

CHAPTER

21

Rick was right; the planet is something that would have sent the old Alex's mind into a tailspin.

As they disembark the ship, a flurry of sounds hit her eardrums. Birds chirp in a cacophony, water surges in a nearby waterfall, trees sway in the rushing breeze, almost making a grinding noise as they move past each other. Compared to the intense quiet of outer space, the noise is deafening.

Alex focuses on her new skills, turning inward, not out of fear, but with power. She focuses her mind and controls it, feeling her body respond. Confidently, she walks down the ramp and onto the soft soil beneath the ship. Rick watches her with a newfound appreciation and respect. "Well done, Alex, I can see your hard work is paying off."

Alex gives him a small smile and turns back to her surroundings. While her mind may be in control, she still finds herself able to admire the intense beauty that surrounds her. They landed on the top of a tall hill, and all around her, beautiful yellow and red trees shoot toward the sky and tower over her, leaving her in a cool shade. Above the trees, a ball of fire floats in the sky, much like her own sun on Earth, but the light it casts is a vibrant red. The planet around her, bathed in red light, shimmers in glory. The ground is covered in purple and red moss, making her feel as if there would be no pain accompanied with a fall— only the soft envelopment of pillows around her.

She smiles as she takes in the sounds. The chirping sound that she heard earlier were not birds, rather the moving of the wind. Something about the wind here makes a soft sound as it hits the trees and moves through the branches. The air has a fragrant smell. *Flowers?* she thinks to herself. Looking for the source of the smell, her eyes settle back on the trees. The branches are covered in delicate yellow petals as flowers burst forth and track the sun, moving their flamboyant heads to soak in the red rays.

Alex steps further out into the world around her as Rick exits the ship behind her. "Gorgeous, isn't it? All our planets used to be full of nature like this. Sadly, as our civilizations popped up, natural beauty was replaced by buildings and structures. Albeit, still beautiful in construction, but not the same." He stares around in appreciation. "And you'll notice how your lungs fill with oxygen? This planet has a unique ecosystem designed to provide all living life with the resources they need to survive. A lot of our civilizations were given manufactured ecosystems that mirror ones like this, like the one you saw on Barter. But it's not the same as the real thing. No, the air here is crisper than that in the cities. On the flip side, it does make for some interesting wildlife. When anything can survive, the beings that walk the surface tend to thrive a little too well, causing what you would refer to as overpopulation. So, tread lightly. The ship's landing pad and the path we are about to travel on are protected by forcefields. Step beyond them, and you will be at the mercy of the planet."

Rick heads down a narrow path and away from the ship, leaving Alex to follow along behind him. Slowly, they wind their way down the hill, Alex being cautious to stay on the trail. True to Rick's word, Alex can see creatures skittering in the trees behind the forcefield, seemingly watching her as she travels. At one point, a series of eyes pop out from behind a stump, followed by a furry little face and body. The creature closely resembles a chipmunk. Alex bends down to look closer, and a smile shows across her face, "Well, aren't you sweet?"

At the sound of her voice, two other arms pop out from the creature's rib cage, and its mouth flies open in a gaping hole as wide as her hand. It launches itself at her throat. Alex stumbles back as the thing contacts the forcefield and slams roughly into the invisible wall. It slides down the side and runs away unharmed.

Behind her, Rick laughs, having watched the exchange. "Dreckers! Nasty little creatures. Cute, but with a big bite."

Turning back to him, Alex gives him an embarrassed look and works to stand back on her feet, dusting the dirt from her clothes. Following Rick closely, she is careful not to stop and interact with any of the creatures she sees outside the forcefield. Finally, they reach a small cabin. "The forcefield extends beyond the cabin on all sides by about ten feet. You will find marker posts on the ground, stay inside them, and you will be fine," Rick warns her.

They approach the door of the cabin and are about to enter when Rick turns abruptly, "Oh yes," he turns to her, suddenly remembering something. "I should mention that I have a pet. He is extremely friendly, so please don't be alarmed if he runs toward you and tries to jump on you." Satisfied with his warning, Rick turns back to the door and waves his palm in front of the lock. With a soft click, the door opens, and Rick enters. Alex hangs back, wary of his warning; *What exactly is Rick keeping in there?*

"Kody, my boy! Oh, I have missed you! You look well, I can see the planet has provided for you in my absence." Rick's joyful voice rings out of the cabin and dances in Alex's ears. She has never heard his voice so happy; it makes her heart smile.

Slowly, she enters the cabin and is bombarded by a small black creature. It rushes toward her on four short legs and leaps up at her. Its front two feet land on her hips as it eagerly tries to lick at her face. Jumping down, the creature does a spin and launches up at her once more.

Its ears bounce enthusiastically as it spins in all directions. Its short and stubby body is covered in thick black fur. Kody bounces around the room, his short tail wagging vigorously as it runs between Alex and Rick.

"Rick!" Alex exclaims, "This is a dog!" She laughs heartily as the furry little black dog runs happily around her feet, leaping up to do fancy spins in the air. She crouches down and scratches him behind the ears. He happily sits down between her bent legs and wags his small tail.

"A dog?" Rick looks at Kody with fondness and laughs along with her. "He is a wonderfully loyal companion, although here he is called a Floofin."

Alex spends the next few minutes petting Kody, thankful for the friendly reminder of her life back on Earth. Eventually, her love bucket is refilled to a suitable level, and she stands up, looking around the cabin for the first time.

The inside is quite beautiful. The walls are constructed of the same stunning red and yellow trees that make up the forest outside, reminding Alex fondly of red and yellow Lego pieces. There are bright open windows that allow the soft red light to filter in and cast small shadows around the room.

A quaint kitchen takes up one-third of the footprint. Across from it is the main bedroom, a guest room, and a bathroom. The opposite wall is quite a remarkable sight. Alex approaches it with awe. Pictures and literature litter the walls, with twine connecting them in what appears to be an uncoordinated fashion.

The more Alex stares, the more she is overwhelmed by the amount of information that Rick has collected, all of it related to the prophecy. Rick comes to stand next to her and smiles, "Well, here you have it, all the information that I have." He looks proudly at his wall, as if it is an extension of himself. Alex eyes him with a fondness that has developed over the past few months. *I sure hope he's not crazy*, she thinks to herself.

Looking back to the wall, she gives an appreciative whistle, "How am I going to absorb all this?" she asks, looking around for a Knowledge Computer.

Rick laughs at her. "The old-fashioned way, by reading and talking!"

CHAPTER

Months pass by in what feels both like a century and a blink of an eye. Rick and Alex spend hours poring over the information he has collected, working together to confirm old theories and conclusions or to build entirely new ones. They take breaks periodically so that Rick can go about his daily life. "Have to keep up appearances!" He tells her as he pulls out his Stone Set to travel back to Solax.

The information they scour comes from all over the galaxies. Rick has collected information in a variety of forms; pictures, words, and artifacts brought from other times and locations.

Alex scans the information for what feels like the thousandth time. It all seems to contradict each other. Except when it comes to the destruction and the Defender; that is always the same. Doom will come, that cannot be avoided, but the destruction will end at the hand of a Defender.

The original prophecy from Pillar, the first one to mention the certain doom, foretold of a lone Defender, an unseen warrior.

Yet, in one of the hand-drawn pictures hanging on the wall a shadow of the Defender stands in front of an army. In Alex's mind, the Defender appears to be urging the army on, challenging them to rise and fight.

"Rick, what is with this drawing? It doesn't connect to anything…." she points to the photo, which hangs off to the side, separate from the rest of the mess on the wall.

Rick comes up beside her and peers over her shoulder, a concerned look coming across his face. "I collected that from a prophet in the far reaches of the galaxies. I don't remember the exact details. He had some story about a Defender held up on the backs of the outliers, or at least that was his interpretation. He drew the picture while in a mad haze from eating too much of a hallucinogenic plant. Either way, I wasn't able to link it to any other prophecy pieces. Nowhere else is there any mention of an army supporting the Defender." He continues to stare at the picture with dislike spread across his face like a memory flashing behind his eyes. Alex tries to register his body posture and decipher what he is feeling, but all she can register is discontent.

As they continue to draw parallels and work through the puzzle together, Alex is constantly drawn to the picture. It alone contradicts the lone Defender aspect. To Alex, this picture means that the Defender may have an army. Alex looks at the photo and tries to imagine herself as the shadowy figure leading the masses. *Can that really be me? Do I have the ability to lead an army?* Part of her is terrified by the idea, but the more controlled and disciplined she becomes, the more she believes in herself, believes in her abilities. Another small part of her, the part that genuinely believes she is the Defender, is grateful that she doesn't have to defend the galaxies alone.

* * *

Rick tosses and turns in his sleep, his dreams full of prophecies and villains.

"We need to jump; we can't be here!" His voice comes out in a panic, shaking with fear and adrenaline. He tosses fitfully, calling out into the air.

"Not yet, we haven't gotten what we need." The return shout is clipped, agitated. Brookstone is tense.

Rickert looks around, hearing the long-lost sounds of rustling in the trees that surround him in his dreams. They are out there, he can sense it, even as he sleeps, he knows they are there. They watch from the shadows. Not much is known about this planet or this time. What is known is that the native species are cannibals. Anyone entering their territory is at the mercy of their appetites. He shivers at the memory as he lies in his bed, his body shaking.

"Please, we don't need this, we have enough information. We can make do without it." He pleads with his friend.

"No! You don't understand, we need this! It's the key to the prophecy. So shut up and follow me." The words come from the lips of a rattled mind; someone who is on the verge of madness. Rickert knows this and yet still he follows, still supports, still encourages.

They seem to float through the jungle, the dream fading in and out as the mundane parts are glossed over.

The ground sinks under their feet, threatening to swallow them whole. *Why does everything on this planet want to eat me?* The thought is a weak and desperate attempt to distract himself, but his dream self chuckles nonetheless.

He follows behind Brookstone while his eyes dart around the forest surrounding them. The rustling above them is growing louder. His eyes pull upward and find the canvas of leaves thick, blocking out all the light that should be radiating through. The edges of his dream grow dark as they move farther into the depths of the jungle.

Finally, they find the mouth of the cave and step inside. A sticky wall of air greets them, moving into their lungs like a hot, moist blanket. He struggles for breath, gasping at the clean air of his room, but in his dream, he sucks in the pungent atmosphere.

Moving forward, they trade trees for dirt and stone. Their feet crunch and crackle as they move deeper into the cave. The last of their light dims as they travel into the heart of the planet, forced to travel in darkness while using their hands as guides.

His dream is black, there is nothing around him, but still terror races through his sleeping body. Then a faint light greets him from the depths of the cave. The memory grows brighter once more.

"He must be sleeping. It's perfect, like the prophecy wants us here, I told you!" Brookstone's hushed voice reaches out to him, his friend lost somewhere in the darkness.

"Let's just do this. We need to get out of here." Rickert speaks aloud once more, the words escaping his sleeping lips, echoing into the dark space of his room.

Slowly the duo creeps forward, stepping into the light of the open space. The cavern extends out and up into a large chamber. In the centre is a small being sleeping soundly. Scattered all around are drawings and sculptures. He stares at them, taking in the madness that comes with every artist.

The being snores lightly as the two men shuffle through his belongings, searching for some hint of the prophecy. A source led them here to this artist, and he is supposed to hold invaluable information about the Defender.

"Aha!" Brookstone's exclamation echoes around the room, but the sleeping being only rolls over and continues to snore.

"Shhh!" Rickert hisses across to his friend, praying he stays quiet, but looking at him, he can see that Brookstone is too far into madness, and there is no controlling him. "You got what you need. Can we go now?"

His friend stares at the canvas in his hands, a crazed smile spreading across his face. "No, I need to know more." With more speed than expected, he crosses the space to the artist and delivers a hard and fast kick to the being's stomach.

With a huge grunt and a lot of coughing, the being is pulled from his peaceful slumber and dragged into the world of the conscious. "What?! What is happening?" The artist skitters backward, away from the two intruders looming over him.

"What is this? Tell me what you drew?" Madness drips from his Brookstones' voice, scaring both Rickert and the artist. He shoves the drawing into the artist's face, forcing his eyes to cross.

"I don't know, I swear it." The artist recoils as a fist crashes across his face, sending him reeling. "Please, I don't know, I was high, I had eaten Drockleberries." The crying artist points to a large pail of sickly green berries.

Suddenly the pail is in Rickert's hand, seemingly having transported there, a trick of the dream. Rickert smells the contents and turns to Brookstone, "These are highly hallucinogenic. If he consumed these, then he won't remember a thing."

As the words leave his lips, a sound drifts through the cave. All three beings turn to the cave tunnel and stare in terror as a lone creature stands in the entryway. Staring at them with hungry eyes, the predator clicks its teeth in anticipation of a meal.

"We need to leave, now!" Rickert looks desperately to his friend, searching for some sign that there is sanity left in him. But only madness stares back.

Brookstone squares his shoulders and pulls out a concealed weapon. With a loud blast, the cannibal is thrown backward, with its chest torn open from the impact. As it falls to the floor, another being steps into the light, and then another, until their escape is blocked by a wall of cannibals.

With one last desperate look to Brookstone, Rickert lunges across the room and rips the drawing from his grasp. "I'm sorry." He whispers it, knowing that this will be the end of their friendship. With one final look back at the advancing cannibals, he grasps his Stone Set and whooshes away, leaving his friend and the artist at the mercy of the native beings.

Rickert lurches upright, sweat dripping down his forehead and neck. His hands grip the bedsheets, and he works to figure out where he is. The feeling of grief weighs heavily on him as he relives his last encounter with Brookstone.

He brushes the sweat from his brow and lays back down, tears flowing freely from his eyes.

* * *

"When are we going to find my Stone Set?" Alex questions Rick, as they stare at the prophetic information once again.

Rick looks tired, like he didn't sleep well. "It's not as simple as finding them. In all honesty, I know exactly where they are."

"What?!"

"Easy. While I know where they are, it's not up to me to take you to them. They brought you here for a reason, but they also left you for a reason. I believe the Stones will reach out to you when they are ready to be found."

"Why did they disappear?" Alex asks, having been wondering this question for months. "Is that normal?"

"Oh yes, when the Stones are not handed down to their next recipients, when they are left to find their new Holder on their own, they often test the waters with the chosen person. When your Set found you, they must have been confident that you were what they were looking for. Otherwise, they wouldn't have left you those marks." He points to her hands. "Despite their connection with you, they still clearly felt something was missing that would make you truly ready to be a Holder. It could be something as easy as knowledge and training, which is what we have been covering for the past six months. Although, it could also be something else such as the right time, or for you to be physically ready to take on the burden of them."

Alex takes in what he has said and mulls the information over. "How will we know when I am ready?"

"I'm not exactly sure. It has been so long since a Stone Set has found their own recipient that we have extraordinarily little knowledge of the process. From what I do know, when you are ready, it will be obvious."

* * *

As time goes on, Rick is careful not to expose her to the news coming in from the outside world, not wanting to overwhelm her with information or skew her view on her role in the prophecy. However, Alex can hear the holograms through the thin wall separating their bedrooms. News of her escape from the Barter prison spread far and wide only a few hours after her rescue. She can hear the news reporters giving frequent updates on the galaxy-wide hunt for her. The PPC directed all civilians to be on the lookout for her and to report any suspicious activities. Alex knows that Rick is in a difficult spot, considering his active role in the PPC and his desire to protect her.

Rick often travels to alternate galaxies, conducting PPC business, and while he is away, Alex is left on her own for long stretches of time. She never ventures far, only walking the short trail to the ship for exercise. Her body aches from the lack of use, and she misses the long-lost feeling of going for a run. Occasionally, she boards the ship to use the Knowledge Computer, accessing information about the species Rick tells her about, trying to learn how to acclimatize to her temporary home.

"I feel so out of place here," she tells Rick one afternoon as they take a break from their reading. "I can't leave the safety of the barrier, and I know so little of this planet. There is nothing registered in the Knowledge Computer about it."

"Hence, the reason it is my secret," Rick reminds her.

"Right, but still. I feel weak and ill-prepared for what lies ahead." Alex is starting to come to terms with the fact that she may very well be the being in the prophecy. As her mental powers grow, so does her confidence. She is no longer the scared and overwhelmed woman she was back on Earth. Here, in this environment, and with the constant help of Rick, she has moved past her basic mental capacity into something more.

"Well, that is partially true," Rick nods at her. "Mentally, your powers are growing, and we can do more even in that department. Physically, you are still human which, by nature is far inferior to most other species you will find here in Gatlin. Fortunately, there are steps we can take for that if you are willing?"

"What do you mean?"

"Well, there are procedures that one can undertake to enhance their physical and mental abilities. I caution you though, they aren't to be taken lightly, and there is no guarantee they will be successful given your human genealogy. There are significant risks, not only to yourself but also to the likelihood of you fulfilling the prophecy. You know my opinion on that particular topic."

"I know, the further I move from being human, the harder it may be for me to fulfill the prophecy. But we don't know that for sure. The bits you have collected all seem to be scattered. We think the Defender is an outlier to start with, but we don't know that they are always that way." Alex rolls her eyes and takes several minutes to consider what he says, slowly working her way through the strange soup Rick has cooked for them. "Is there someone whom I can talk to about these procedures? Or something in the Knowledge Computer? How do we know that this isn't exactly what my Stone Set thinks I need to be worthy?"

Rick looks at her thoughtfully, "Yes, there is someone more experienced that you can speak with. I have a good friend who performs the procedures, and I trust her enough with the secret of your existence. As for the last comment about being worthy; that's harder to say. The Stones haven't made themselves known yet, which means we are missing something. It may not just be knowledge they are looking for you to have. I'd say based on the way you have worked through the Knowledge Computers database, you have just as much knowledge as any of the PPC members. Our next step is to try something physical. So yes, if you are up for it, we will travel to Aya, and I will introduce you to the best surgeon in this galaxy."

CHAPTER

23

T hey board the spaceship together once more and depart from Muskoux. The distance is roughly half of what it was from Barter and Rick assures her it will be nearly a quarter of the time. "We don't have to travel as slowly now. The news of your escape has blown over, so no one is searching for you as actively. We can travel without our cloaking device in place, and we don't have to worry as much about check stops."

As they travel, Rick tells her about the origins of the planet they are travelling to. "This particular galaxy houses two main medical moons, Aya and Meera, both of which orbit Valyrn. We are going to Aya. This is where my friend works. She has agreed to meet us covertly to discuss the procedures with you, and if you wish to proceed, she is willing to perform them as well." Alex gives him a nod.

"Aya was a desolate moon until the PPC came along and brought civilization to it. Because Aya and Meera orbit around Valyrn, there is always one medical moon close to the inhabited planets, making travel by spaceship more ideal. Of course, there are also teleportation stations, but ship access is always required in the event there is a teleportation outage."

"Now the planet is covered with a variety of treatment centres, thousands of hospitals, recovery facilities, and therapy buildings scatter their surfaces. It's not pretty," Rick says as he wrinkles his nose. "Very medical feeling, but it is efficient. Species of all kinds come to either of the medical moons for treatment of physical, mental, and supernatural ailments."

"Supernatural?"

"Yes, sometimes, beings such as myself can lose control of our powers, either becoming overtaken by them or losing them entirely. When things like that happen, we seek medical treatment, just as you would for a physical ailment."

Alex thinks this over and is impressed by the dedication to health in this galaxy. "Can anyone access these medical treatments?"

"Well, not exactly. There are Factions that live outside the main society, Factions that aren't registered by the Valyrn government or included in the PPC agreements. These groups are not able to receive our medical treatment. However, from what I know of them, their civilizations do not require our external aid."

Alex has heard of these Factions before having learned about them from the Knowledge Computer. Turning inward, she focuses on the information in her mind and forms the story about the Factions. Suddenly, she becomes aware of a large gap in her knowledge. "All the information in the computers says these Factions live outside the bounds and control of the PPC; in fact, you don't even know where these Factions are…" Alex pauses to consider her next words. "Do you think the Factions could be the army of the Defender? The ones from the picture?"

Rick looks at her thoughtfully. "I hadn't considered that. To be honest, I haven't put as much weight into that picture as you have. When I first saw you at the Cataloguing I assumed that if you truly did have an army standing behind you, then it would be members of the human race that supported you." He pauses a moment. "It does make a lot of sense that it would be the Factions. That could be why there is no information about them in the prophecy. They live so far outside of our sights that we cannot predict their futures nor see their role in ours." He smiles at her, "Alex, you may have just made your first move as our Defender."

* * *

Just as Rick says, rather than a month of space travel, it only takes them ten days to reach Aya. When they arrive, they enter through a small medical bay that is isolated from the main portion of the planet. Before disembarking, Rick reminds Alex to don her appearance-changing bracelet. Popping it onto her wrist, she gives a little gasp as the pins poke into her skin, changing her into the green horned alien once more.

"We are meeting my friend Veela. She is a kind soul at heart but can come off as quite…abrasive. Bear with her, she has a lot of practice in surgical rooms working on unconscious souls, but not much experience speaking with the conscious ones."

As the ramp of the ship lowers, Rick and Alex descend side by side. Waiting at the end of the ramp is a tall orange alien. Her skin looks soft and smooth, and her vibrant orange hair flows down the side of her head and down her back. Her lab coat sits open, revealing a modest beige shirt and pants combo. She looks at Rick, and immediately, the sour look on her face turns to a smile, her long full lips curving up toward her ears. Her three eyes dance with delight at Rick, and her four arms reach out to embrace him. She is quite a bit taller than him, but she bends down and pulls him into a firm embrace. Oddly enough, she seems well practiced at this display of affection.

"Rickert! It has been too long," Veela speaks in their native tongue, which translates smoothly in Alex's enhanced mind. "While these are very strange circumstances, I am still so glad they are happening. Anything that brings us back together again."

Still holding onto Rick's shoulder with her bottom two arms, she pulls her body away and looks at him lovingly. Her top arms tuck her fallen hair behind her long oval ears in an obviously nervous display. Alex gets the distinct feeling that these two aliens were once much more than friends.

Finally, stepping all the way back, Veela lets go of Rick and turns awkwardly to Alex. All the tender emotion drains from her stance. "Hello, Alexia, my name is Veela. Rickert has told me all about you." She gives her a curt nod, taking note of her little horn and rolling her three eyes at Rick. Remembering that unfamiliar beings do not touch here, Alex returns the greeting with a small smile.

"Well, come this way. I understand you have questions about my services."

Veela leads them away from the ship and down a long dim hallway. They pass several closed doors and climb a set of stairs. Here, there seems to be more life and activity. Careful to avoid the busiest rooms, Veela leads them to her office. The trio enters the large room, and Rick closes the door behind them.

"Thank you for meeting with us, Veela. As I told you over the hologram last week, Alexia is the newest Stone Holder. She is also, as you know, an escaped prisoner of Barter."

Veela lays a harsh look on Rick. "Yes, Rickert, I am well aware of how she mysteriously broke out of prison, and now she has been declared legally deceased. What I was not aware of, nor does anyone know, is that you helped her escape and have been harbouring her ever since. What were you thinking?"

Rick looks at her with a guilty expression on his face, as if being scolded by a lover. "It's not an easy thing to explain, but one that I would gladly bring you into if you would hear me out."

Veela's face softens, "I am always willing to listen to you."

The duo shares a tender moment that leaves Alex feeling like the third wheel, an outsider once more, looking in on something private.

Remembering themselves and their surroundings, Veela clears her throat. "I assume we won't be doing that here and now. No, we have business to attend to.

Alexia, Rickert tells me you wish to know more about the procedures I can perform."

Alex nods to her, relieved that the topic has shifted back to something more comfortable.

"There are three main types of things I can do to someone of your genealogy. First, I can alter your mind; this is called cerebral advancement. Second, I can alter your physical being; this is called corporeal advancement. Lastly, I can enhance your supernatural possessions; this is called paranormal advancement. The first two are relatively easy with someone of your make-up; it's the last one that is going to be a challenge."

While Veela explains the procedures, Alex begins to feel a strange sensation. At the mention of the physical and supernatural enhancements, she feels a strange tingling sensation start in her hands and forearms. Trying to focus on it, she looks down at her relaxed hands. With her attention pulled inward, the sensation subsides, and Alex is left with only her thoughts. *That was strange.* Alex thinks to herself, turning her attention back to Veela, who has continued to speak.

"Your kind is not naturally made with supernatural powers; in most cases, the basic building blocks do not lie in your DNA. That being said, there are some rare cases in the human history of someone being born with something extra, a sixth sense as you may call it."

Alex nods at her once more, familiar with the term but also surprised to hear that it is real.

Veela continues, "This is something that, if you possess it, we can enhance it. We can run a series of tests to determine where you are on the supernatural scale and then perform a procedure to enhance that power. So, Alexia, what do you think? Is this something you would like us to pursue?"

As Veela explains the last part and poses the question to Alex, the strange sensation washes over her once more. Starting again from her hands and moving strongly and quickly up her arms, into her chest, and settling into her heart, like a tidal wave rolling over her body. Alex stares down at her hands. Nothing physical appears to be happening, but for the first time, she can feel the Stones calling out to her and connecting with her. She turns inward and listens to the feelings rising inside her. Closing her eyes, she blocks out her surroundings. A faint hum comes to her ears as she feels the Stones connect through the markings in her hands. Images of approval dance in her head. *I feel you.* She calls out to them with her mind. *I feel you! Please tell me what I need to do? What will make me ready?* The Stones continue to send her images of approval, urging her to move forward with the enhancements. Alex smiles, feeling the relief of knowing that she is finally on the right track.

"Alex, are you OK?" Rick's concerned voice drifts through her ears, and the images slowly fade, leaving Alex alone with only her own thoughts. Opening her eyes, she nods slowly to Rick.

Turning to Veela, she speaks for the first time in a while. "Yes, we should move forward with the enhancements."

"Excellent," Veela smiles. The doctor in her is clearly excited by the upcoming challenge. "Which enhancements?"

Alex looks from her to Rick, "All of them."

CHAPTER

24

Veela leads Alex down the hall and onto a landing pad similar to the one they left behind an hour ago. This one houses her own small ship that she will use to carry them to her lab.

As they approach the ship, Rick pulls Alex to the side and allows Veela time to prepare her ship for travel.

"Are you OK? Something seemed to shift in your telepathic presence, almost as if there were two beings dancing around in your mind." He looks at her with a mixture of concern and curiosity.

She pauses for a moment, unsure of how much she should tell him. *Rick has never given me a reason to doubt him. He has been my constant ally throughout this whole experience.* Yet, something in the back of her mind is telling her to proceed with caution. "I was just weighing the options and needed a moment to collect my thoughts. You probably just felt the weight of my split decision. Nothing to worry about. I'm fine." And just like that, Alex lies to Rick for the first time.

Rick looks at her as if he doesn't truly believe her but is willing to accept her answer. With a pensive look on his face, he nods to her and turns back to the ship. Alex feels a pain in her heart, a pain that one feels when lying to a loved one.

Together, the trio flies to Veela's lab on the opposite side of Aya. They disembark into a warm and welcoming area that catches Alex off guard. This space is clearly not only Veela's lab but also her home. The interior is bright and cheery, filled with pictures of friends and family along with all the niceties of a place called home for many years.

Veela leads them through her home. "First, we will start with the tests to ensure compatibility. If we are able to proceed with the procedures, we will do them here." She gestures to her surroundings. "You cannot be entered officially as a patient into any of the hospitals. But don't worry, I am fully set up to conduct what is medically required. I have all the state-of-the-art equipment; it was part of the deal when I created it for them." She smiles, pride showing on her alien face.

"Veela is a genius; she has been around for a long time and has changed the medical world. She has invented most of the new equipment that is used today, and she is responsible for the supernatural treatments being performed. Without her, those of us with supernatural powers would still be suffering in silence." Rick speaks of Veela with love and admiration, making her blush a deep orange.

"Anyways," Veela says, giving Rick a small smile, "Alexia, you may be spending a lot of time here with me. The tests and procedures are not quick. The surgical work itself can take several weeks, possibly even months to complete. They have to be done in phases, with periods of healing in between, and then you must fully recover afterward. This also includes time to learn how to control your new powers. With that being said, my home will become your new home for the next few months. If you are willing and comfortable, of course?"

Alex can feel her heart split in two. More months spent on an alien planet means more months spent away from her family. With every day that passes, Alex can feel herself being pulled farther and farther away from her life on Earth. *How am I supposed to return to my normal life after all this? Thanks to the Knowledge Computer, my mind is already full of information that wasn't there when I left Earth. Now, on top of that, I'm considering physical and mental enhancements? Will my family even recognize me? Every step I take here moves me further from them.*

Sadness encompasses Alex's enhanced mind, but it does not cripple her as it once would have. Instead, Alex processes the emotion with a newfound coldness; something foreign to her. It leaves her feeling robotic and inhuman. She simply takes the emotion, processes the logical feelings, and pushes the sadness away. Without a further thought given to her grief, she turns back to Veela.

"Yes, if you will have me as your guest, I will gladly stay here."

Veela nods with excitement, but it is Rick who looks at her with concern. Already guessing his hesitations, she addresses him directly, "I'll be fine, Rick, trust me, this is what I'm supposed to be doing."

He gives her a concerned smile. "If you are sure, Alex. Then this is where I take my leave, ladies. I will check back in periodically to see how you are progressing. Alex, may I speak with you privately?" He looks apologetically at Veela and leads Alex to a corner of the house.

"Rick, I'll be fine," she assures him again.

"It's not so much you that I am worried about, I trust that you have a plan. It's more the galaxy that I am concerned about. What if we cannot wait for these enhancements? Veela said it could be months until you're fully recovered..."

"Rick, if I am the Defender of this galaxy, if I am truly the Defender of man, then the doom and gloom will wait for me," Alex responds, more confidence in her voice than in her heart. "Besides, there are no indications that anything has even started, we have the time."

"If you're sure..." Rick looks at her uncertainly. "I think I need to start bringing more beings into our cause. With your permission, I would like to bring Veela in; she is smart and well connected. More importantly, I trust her with my life and now yours."

Glancing over at the tall orange woman, Alex assesses her from a logical standpoint. Taking out the emotional aspect that Rick clearly holds for her. She knows little about this alien, but Rick seems to trust her. She didn't report Alex's arrival to the authorities, and considering that Alex is a wanted fugitive, that is a testament to her trustworthiness.

Alex turns back to Rick and nods. "Yes, bring her in, but be cautious. We know that most of the PPC do not believe in the prophecy. If they find out you have been researching it, even after you were told not to, you could land yourself in Barter." Rick nods rapidly, excited at the possibility of sharing his secret with Veela.

"Rick, one more thing; while I am undergoing the procedures, I need you to look into something for me. I need you to find out where the Factions are. I think I need them. Call it a Defender's intuition or whatever, but I believe I need them to win the war."

* * *

With Alex settled into her new temporary home, her host leads her to the medical portion of the property. A small building set off the back of the main house stands two stories high and is wide enough to hold all the medical supplies required for her testing and upgrades. On the first floor is Veela's lab. Here, they will conduct the tests required to determine if Alex is capable of withstanding the upgrades. The second floor holds the operating and recovery rooms.

"This is where the real magic happens," Veela tells Alex excitedly. Veela is an odd creature. She is often very awkward around Alex, often unable to hold a basic conversation. She rarely partakes in small talk, but when it comes to her work, she is a bushel of life and energy. Alex has found the woman can talk for hours if it is about her research or work.

"Now, Alex, I must warn you that nothing we are going to do will be easy. Even the tests are complicated and painful. You will find the next few months to be physically and mentally exhausting. I will be your main caretaker, and I will do my best to keep you sedated. Periodically, there will be times when I need to wake you up to check your mental responsiveness. These moments will be...unpleasant. I'm sorry in advance." Veela pauses. "Are you sure you want to proceed?"

Alex looks at the tall lady. Mustering as much courage as she can, she replies, "Yes, I'm ready."

CHAPTER

25

onths have gone by since the human escaped. It's like she was pulled from the face of the galaxy. The PPC and officials of Valyrn spent months looking for her, searching all the inhabited planets and even some of the uninhabited ones. Eventually, the search was called off, and the human was declared officially deceased by the PPC. Brookstone knows better; he knows she is still out there, threatening to spoil his plans.

He could see it in her as soon as she started her Cataloguing. He could see the potential she had, and he knew that if he could see it, then so could Rickert, who sat in the crowd. He noticed when Rickert opened his telepathic bond with her, something that they used to share, something that is so personal.

"Oh, Rickert, if I find you played a part in her disappearance, then I will take action." Brookstone's voice rings out around his small office. He has spent countless months scouring the galaxy, plotting areas out on maps, and then travelling to them using his Stone Set. All in hopes of finding and killing the human.

"She is a stain on my legacy!" He exclaims aloud to no one. "She could ruin everything!" He slams his hands down onto the desk and lets out a low growl that fades into a sigh.

He is tired. He has been alive for hundreds of years, roughly three times longer than should be possible, but science has come a long way. The advanced technology mixed with the power of Stones means he is in charge of his own timeline. He has lived most of his life dutifully, but the prophecy still haunts him, keeps him going, always pushing him. He knows it to be true. He can feel that in his bones. He is the Defender, of that he is sure, and there is no way he is going to let some unsung hero swoop in and take it from him. Not after everything he has done to get here.

Brookstone has given the last two hundred and fifty years of his life to the PPC and protecting the galaxies. Each time a new threat came up against them, he was the one at the front of the Council. Guiding them to a solution, helping them choose the correct path, and every time he has come out victorious. The Council is made up of a bunch of newbies and burnouts. The Stones have been handed down so many times to unfit and unworthy family members. The pool of genuinely worthy beings is diluted and opaque.

Brookstone was the last true recipient of the Stones. While no one on the Council knows this, he was chosen by his Stone Set just as the human was. He was chosen as the worthiest; the Stones picked him. Nothing was handed to him, and he had to earn everything he has in this life.

Brookstone moves out from behind his desk and walks over to the opposite wall. Here, he has created a map of the prophecy. Everything he has discovered in his two hundred and fifty years. Everything that he could learn, steal or kill for. *But it was all for a worthy cause, all for the big picture.* He thinks to himself, reassuring himself for the millionth time. *I am the Defender; I do not need to justify my actions.* Still, the guilt weighs on him. When he committed his first murder nearly one hundred and seventy-five years ago, he was a desolate shell of a being for months, unable to eat or sleep. When the second time came around, it was a little bit easier. Brookstone was constantly reassuring himself that he was the Defender, that this was his destiny, and he had to do whatever it took to fulfill the prophecy.

Now, each murder is a just spot on his subconscious. While he still wears the guilt like a blanket wrapped around his shoulders; it does not paralyze him, and it does not weigh him down. Instead, it keeps him company. But Brookstone is tired; he is also lonely in his cause. *Being a Defender means going at it alone, moving in the shadows, hidden from the prying eyes around him.* He knows the prophecy;

They alone, this unseen warrior, are the Defender of man.

He still misses his friends. He was once the life of the party, at the centre of it all. Rickert was the first being that he really bonded with, even before he was a PPC member. Having him join the PPC only a few years after Brookstone was an orchestrated beauty on Brookstone's part. Brookstone saw him as a true kindred spirit and someone he could share all of himself with. So, he made sure there was a space for him on the Council. He wanted their relationship to be so much more than just friendship. He wanted love. He wanted a life with Rickert. But Rickert felt differently, his bonds tied to an up-and-coming doctor on Aya. Brookstone settled for friendship with him while vowing to always be there for him, as long as Rickert stood by him.

As time went on, things changed, and they drifted apart. Eventually, Rickert distanced himself entirely from Brookstone; cooling their friendship until the flames in Brookstone's heart went out completely. The loss of their connection turning his heart to ice. With no one to share his theories, ideas, or life with, Brookstone became the being he thought the prophecy needed him to be, alone.

Brookstone stares at his prophecy wall, his eyes scanning it, looking for some unseen connection, some clue he hasn't seen before. He knows he won't find one, and more importantly, he knows he doesn't need anything more. The prophecy is so close to being upon them, even if he did have to force it along after being tired of waiting for the damn thing to show up. After all, he has played with his own timeline so much that who knows what the long-term impacts to the overall timeline may be.

This office space is his secret hideout on Zeya. Here, he can work for days on end without being interrupted. No one expects someone of a scientific nature to take up space on the planet that is solely used to manage the transportation of the Gatlin Galaxy. Here, he works to fulfill the prophecy, working to put it into action.

The room is small but large enough to hold everything he needs. It is located underground and attached to a small shipping office on the surface of Zeya. On the surface, it appears quite small, but in reality, the entire property is massive, spreading several layers deep and many miles wide. The main space he uses as an office is dark. The only source of light is a small fixture on the ceiling, a desk lamp, and a spotlight that points at the prophecy map. The sparse furniture consisting only of a large desk, an office chair, and a bookcase.

A dull thump echoes through the room, forcing Brookstone to bring his attention away from the map and turn his eyes to a door to his right. With a heavy sigh, he calls out, "Patience, my friends, I'm coming."

The banging continues and grows more intense. Brookstone hauls himself away from the wall and opens the door. He flicks on the lights and walks down a set of stairs to a well-lit room. This has been his lab for the past twenty years; this is where he does his experiments.

Along one wall is a workbench filled with vials, testing equipment, and surgical devices. In the centre of the room is an operating table fixed with heavy-duty restraints and sedation equipment. On the far wall are the pinnacle of his creations, his friends, as he calls them.

Twenty-five years ago, he completed a time jump to an unknown future era and was put face to face with the creatures of their doom; the creatures that would rain terror on the world. Brookstone remembers the day as if it were yesterday, the way the creatures looked at him, the way they knelt at his feet, looking up at him with subservient eyes. That's when he knew he was the Defender. Only he had the power to make the creatures bow, to control them. He could stop the devastation that would befall his galaxy.

When he jumped back to his time, twenty-five years in the past, he began his search for the creatures, hoping to wipe out their existence before they could become the thing that destroyed the galaxy. Frustratingly, each time he came across something similar and destroyed it, he would jump ahead in the timeline and still be put face to face with the same future. It never changed; he was constantly faced with the submissive creatures. No matter where he went in the galaxy, the creatures existed, raining their destruction upon the innocent. Still spreading death and mayhem while bowing only to him.

After five years of searching and destroying entire species, Brookstone determined that these creatures do not yet exist, that they must be a creation that has yet to be made. That's when he began to look at the prophecy differently; what if both figures in the prophecy are one and the same? What if the Destroyer is also the Defender?

CHAPTER

26

Veela was right; the process is excruciating. The doctor undersold the pain that Alex would feel. They start out with testing to determine what exactly they can do for her. They have two main goals—increase her physically with the goal of enhancing her strength and basic capabilities. Then they will move on to expand her supernatural powers beyond the basic range of a human. Veela has admitted that she doesn't know precisely what the outcome of the supernatural powers will be. She has done a lot of research into the capabilities and limitations of humans, but still, her findings are inconclusive.

They start with the physical upgrades. Veela feels that if Alex can survive the physical, the mental will be more manageable.

Veela starts Alex out with a series of tests to determine her baseline. She is weak even by her human standards. All the muscle definition she once had back on Earth is gone, and her runner's body has become soft from inactivity.

She lifts, pulls, drags, and pushes heavy weights across the lab floor while Veela stands over her with a holographic scroll, taking notes on her performance.

She puts Alex through a variety of tests, including bone density, oxygen capacity, blood cycling, and dozens of other tests that Alex doesn't understand. Normally, Alex would do some research into the tests that Veela was attempting. However, there is no access to a Knowledge Computer here as Veela is not a member of the PPC. If she's honest, Alex isn't sure she even wants to know what she is up against.

Once the baselines are created, Veela creates the surgery plan. They will start by carving out Alex's muscle structure then inserting new veins to allow her body to carry oxygen and blood cells more efficiently. Then Veela will insert additional muscle mass throughout Alex's body. This will enhance Alex's overall strength, allowing her to gain and maintain muscle at a more rapid rate. For this, she will also need to be capable of processing the oxygen required to feed her muscles, hence the enhanced vein structure.

To ensure that her muscle mass doesn't outgrow her bone structure, they will install thin strands of alien metal along her bones to increase their density, making her even more robust.

Next, they will increase the size of her heart and lungs. "Your circulatory and respiratory systems need to be able to support your increased body demands. If we enhance your basic systems, you will be able to take more punishment," Veela explains. Alex looks at her warily, she knows she is going to war, but the idea of actually being in combat scares her.

Lastly, they will increase her senses. Once the procedures are complete, Alex will be able to see in the dark and detect heat signatures. She will be able to smell things from distances far greater than that of her current nose. Her touch will become more sensitive, being able to pick up subtle heat changes and textures. Her hearing will become more in her control, allowing her to increase beyond her current human capabilities or decrease sensitivity to a tiny amount. Taste is the only sense that will remain the same, "I don't need to be more overwhelmed in that department," Alex tells the eager doctor.

Veela gives her the night off from testing and shuts herself in her lab, leaving Alex to wander the house by herself. She takes in the sights around her, marveling at the alien artwork that lines the walls. *I didn't take Veela for an art enthusiast. I didn't think the scientific mind appreciated art like this.*

As she explores further into the house, she comes across a picture of a young Veela and Rick, smiling happily while at some sort of intergalactic fair. The love in their eyes makes her wonder what drove them apart. It also makes her nostalgic for her own husband, missing the love he gives her, the way he makes her smile, the way he holds her hand. Alex feels the familiar creep of loss moving into her chest. Sadness threatens to overtake her. It has been almost six months since she has been in his warm embrace. As quickly as the feelings rise, Alex works to push them down, assessing the emotion and deciding that there is no room for it in her head right now.

Alex goes to sleep feeling numb and robotic. She makes note that she may be closing herself off too much from her emotions. She will have to check in with those suppressed feelings eventually, but for now, she has to focus on surviving what Veela has planned for her.

CHAPTER

27

rookstone began creating his own army roughly fifteen years ago. He manufactured brand new species. He searched the Knowledge Computers and used his Stone Set to travel to far-off galaxies, collecting the most dangerous species, then dissecting them, only to piece them back together again. He used the knowledge he had from his trips to the future and the images of the creature as a blueprint for creating the new species.

It took many attempts, with a lot of trial and error. Many creatures died on his table, some that he abducted solely for the intent of experimentation and others as the result of his own creations. After many failed trials, Brookstone had done it. He had created the thing from the future. No longer just an idea, but now a living, breathing thing—the creatures are fondly called Shreikers because of the power their shrieks can have.

Brookstone walks through the room to the opposite wall, which is lined with cages. Inside the cages sit the Shreikers, one per cage to prevent them from dissecting each other. As he approaches, the creatures move from their seated positions to stand on two legs, lifting their pincers into the air and make a clapping sound, hailing his arrival. He smiles at them and moves to grab their feed buckets. The large insects whoop loudly when his hand grabs the bucket, and he begins to scoop sludge into them.

Bringing out a remote, he walks up to the door of the first cage. Inside is his leading beauty, Dru. She is the latest of his creations, the baby of his army. She stands nearly twelve feet tall, taller than any species in the galaxy, and she is a host to many unique abilities. With a whooping sound, Dru backs away from the door before he has to press the button on the remote. The button sends a neuroshock to her brain, one that would leave her temporarily crippled and writhing in pain on the ground.

When Brookstone created the creatures, he gave them no abilities to think and act independently of him, except Dru. She is the only one that can make decisions. Despite their lack of free thinking, he also built in an insurance policy, the neuroshocks. Each creature has a small chip implanted in its spine. It's a way for him to control them and even override Dru's commands, although he rarely needs that level of control. If a creature disobeys him or shows aggression toward him, Brookstone is quick to dispose of it. "There is no room in my army for such disobedience," he tells the creature just before he murders it. Brookstone is careful to make sure the other creatures can hear and see the slaughter as a warning to them all that he is their master.

As Dru steps back, Brookstone opens the cage and steps inside. Dru eyes him and the bucket with her human-like eyes. When the bucket is placed on the ground, she eyes it hungrily but waits for Brookstone to exit before pouncing on it. Using her two powerful legs to close the distance, she dips over the bucket and devours the contents. It is an impressive display to watch her using her flexible jaw and thousands of teeth to break through the cartilage and bone. Her long nose winds down in front of her to help scoop the food into her mouth. She makes snuffling sounds as she tears through her meal.

Smiling at her, he turns away and repeats the process with the remaining three creatures in the lab. Each of the creatures is slightly different as a result of him tweaking his process each time to produce a smarter, more dangerous creature. Here, in the main lab, sit his main points of pride, the leaders of his army. These four creatures will take his army and spread the destruction that the prophecy depicts must happen. Dru will lead them all though; she is everything, the pinnacle of all his work. When Brookstone sets the prophecy into play, he determined that Dru will be the one to lead the charge, the creature that controls the masses. While they will all bow to him, they will be controlled by both of them. She is his commanding officer.

With one final look at his three commanders and Dru, he turns to another door and waves his palm in front of it. A series of locks releases, and the heavy door swings open. He descends another set of stairs that opens into a vast space. This room is the size of ten football stadiums put together, all buried underground, much like Barter.

Careful to put on a sophisticated set of hearing protectors, Brookstone flicks the room's lights on. As the lights come to life, rows upon rows of creatures are illuminated. Thousands of cages stretch out before Brookstone, all the individual creations of his sophisticated mind.

He smiles as they begin their chorus of whooping sounds, a sound that would destroy the mind of unprotected ears. This is his glory. This is what he was made for— to be the master of the species that will doom them all.

CHAPTER

28

The weeks pass in a painful blur, with Alex being heavily sedated most of the time. Occasionally, she drifts into consciousness, especially toward the end of the surgeries when her enhanced body starts to move through the anesthesia faster than she once would have. New blood pulses painfully through her veins, feeding new muscles. All her joints and limbs are bruised and swollen from the harsh alien metals being fused onto her bones.

She breathes shallowly as her lungs adapt to their new capacity. Her heart beats in a weak and uneven pattern, surging the painful blood around her body.

In her sedated state, Alex feels the Stones calling to her, urging her to stay alive. She listens to their soothing calls in her mind, focusing on them and pulling her mind away from the pain of her body. She does not dream; she does not think, she only listens to the Stones while feeling her connection with them deepen.

CHAPTER

29

I t all made sense. Once he shifted his thinking to include the Defender and destroyer as the same being, it fit perfectly in Brookstone's mind. He had the knowledge and the power to create the new species, and with them being subservient to him, he would have the power to end the destruction. That was something he and Rickert uncovered together, the destruction must happen, and the civilizations must fall. Every future held the same ending. There was no avoiding this.

What took a long time for Brookstone to understand was why; why was this future their inevitability? As his time as a Stone Holder continued, and he watched other Stones Sets being passed down from generation to generation, he saw the dilution and weakness. The current civilization is flawed, and its leadership corrupt. The flaws extend well beyond just the leadership now as each planet is at its bursting limit. The PPC is so passive that it does nothing but avoid conflict by sidestepping anything that might threaten them. That, combined with each species thriving beyond what they should because of the all supporting ecosystems installed by the PPC, overpopulation is becoming a major problem across the galaxy. It's unsustainable with the current state of affairs. Eventually, the species will turn on each other, and civil wars will erupt throughout Gatlin. Resources will be diminished and eventually the galaxy will succumb to the disaster that the PPC has put before it. This is an ending that they will not recover from. That is why Brookstone must manufacture an ending he can control— a way to level the civilizations, bring them to their knees, and then build them back up.

The leader in Brookstone also wants to be rid of the PPC, tear them down. *They are obsolete, ineffective, and just simply a disgrace,* he thinks to himself. When Perma created the PPC, she allowed the Stones to choose their Holders; this meant the worthiest were chosen, and the PPC was formed on the backs of the best the galaxies had to offer. This included species of all types.

But now, the members of the PPC primarily hail from Gatlin. Because the current Holders have all been cherry-picked by their elders, there is no strength anymore. Authentic leadership is being ignored or excluded because the ignorant and selfish want their children to be the Holders.

In the two hundred and fifty years that Brookstone has been exploring the timelines and the galaxies, he has come to realize the flaw of time travel. When Pillar and Perma opened the gateways and started to build up new civilizations, they broke the timelines that were supposed to occur naturally. Each species in the new worlds were supposed to begin at a different time, thus allowing the dominant species to start a new rule. There would have been an ever-shifting role of power on a planet or even in the galaxy. The most elite species would have been the natural ruler. Instead, they aren't given their rightful place, a seat at the head of the table, simply because they missed the right conditions in which to rule.

The more he thinks about it, the more he is sure that forcing the fall of the PPC and the civilizations is the right thing to do. To be the Defender of civilization, he must first destroy it and force a hard reset of the galaxy. Creating the chance to start anew, a chance to start on a level playing field. If nature is allowed to start once again, without the manipulation of the Stones, then the best of the civilizations will rise to the top place of power.

The picture of the Defender standing in front of the army is the key; he is drawn to it. When he and Rickert found it many years ago, it landed in Brookstone's mind as the missing piece, but Rickert disagreed. Brookstone still believes this is why Rickert left him, but he could not simply ignore the picture. Despite Rickert's urging to leave the picture be, insisting that it was an outlier, something that didn't matter. Brookstone continued to time jump in search of the army, his army.

As he searched, and as Rickert distanced himself, Brookstone began to lose hope. The future he saw, the one with him at the head of an army, he couldn't find it. This problem, coupled with the lack of an enemy that he was supposed to save them from left Brookstone in an awkward place, a place that his scientific mind did not like.

On one of the long nights alone in his office, Brookstone made a realization. If he can be both the Defender and the destroyer, why can't his army be the same?

CHAPTER

30

When Alex awakens, she is terrified to find herself blind and bound. Scared that the doctor is indeed up to something sinister, she cries out, seeking help from anyone who may hear her. At the sound of her voice, Alex is overcome with pain as her overly sensitive ears magnify the sound beyond what she can handle.

She tries to throw her hands up over her ears, but they are held back by the restraints. In the attempt to move, she is once again overtaken by otherworldly pain. Her body has not been used in several weeks, and her muscles have atrophied and hardened. It's not only the procedures that were painful but also the laying stagnant for so long.

In the corner of the room, Alex becomes aware of a shuffling sound and then a soft hushing. "Easy, Alexia, try not to move. I have restrained you only so you don't wake up and damage yourself. If you promise not to try and get up, I will remove the restraints," Veela's soft voice comes from beside her bed.

Nodding slowly and carefully, Alex feels the restraints being removed. Slowly, she flexes her arms and legs slightly out to the sides, aware of every ache and pain. While the pain is steady, it is not overwhelming. "You were unconscious for most of the healing, and the pain you are feeling now is from a lack of using your body," Veela explains. "I tried to move your limbs around as best I could, but there was only so much I could do."

"Why can't I see?" Alex asks, careful to keep her voice a whisper.

"Your eyes are not quite recovered from the procedures; the exposure to light may blind you. I figured it was better safe than sorry."

Agreeing with her wholeheartedly, Alex uses her mind and does a mental scan of her body, individually checking in with each part of herself. She feels her muscles work and slide under her skin as she stretches and feels the increased weight of her bones in the bed. She inhales deeply and is surprised to find it takes twice as long to fill her lungs. As she inhales, she experiences her heightened sense of smell. She can now smell everything in the room, including the meal on Veela's breath. She wrinkles her nose, growing nauseous from all the odours. Her fingertips grip the sheets, and she feels the small threads that make up the material, each one giving her a new sensation. The heat from her body radiates into her hands, and she can almost measure her exact temperature. If she is correct, she is running a slight fever.

Over the next few days, Veela allows Alex to begin moving around the small medical room. First, starting with sitting up, then walking, then light exercise. Her body responds amazingly, and Alex has to be careful of her newfound strength. She nearly crushed the tall orange alien while leaning on her for support when she first tried to stand.

"It's best if you fully recover from the physical portion before we move to the supernatural," Veela tells her one afternoon as Alex works out in the home gym that Veela has set up for her. Her muscles take on definition faster than her human ones did, and soon she is built like a rock. All the fat has disappeared from her body, leaving only trimmed muscle in its place.

Her favourite part about the transformation is her ability to run. On the makeshift treadmill, Alex can run at nearly forty miles per hour for roughly two hours.

Before the procedure took place, Alex made it clear to Veela that she wanted to look the same when it was all said and done. Nothing was to change in her height or looks. Looking at herself now in the bathroom mirror, she can see the differences even if Veela didn't intend them. Her eyes sparkle more, and her shoulders are broader. Her legs and arms are thicker, both from muscle and bone density. *My family won't recognize me. I look like a monster,* Alex thinks to herself, with sadness and guilt. *I am choosing to distance myself from them, choosing to grow the gap before I return to them. Even if I do make it back, even if I do survive this war, what is to say they will accept me? That anyone could love this version of me?* And for the first time in months, Alex cries. She feels the emotions she has pushed down. Rather than pushing them further down, she allows them to bubble up.

She sobs deeply at the reflection in the mirror. As she cries, she hears a light knock on the door. Trying to hide her puffy, red eyes, she opens it to find Veela standing outside the bathroom, looking at her awkwardly. "I'm not overly good with conscious beings, but I think you could use a hug. Am I right?"

* * *

Once Alex has reached her peak physical condition, Veela declares that it is time to move on to her supernatural powers. This is the part Veela is most looking forward to, and she nearly vibrates with excitement.

"I have done as much research as I can, and I have everything lined up," she tells Alex in a cheerful voice. "Once again, you will be heavily sedated in the beginning, but there is a lot of work to do, so I will be moving you in and out of consciousness. This process will not be as physically painful as the last, but it will be more mentally taxing. The goal is to go slow enough that your brain is not overwhelmed. We don't want to force it to give up on your body. Just in case, I have physical life support on standby." She points to the large machines to her right, next to the medical bed.

"We will go slow, starting with the easiest powers of emotion-sensing, then mind-reading. Lastly, if we are lucky, we will enhance your telepathic control. The last one is the hardest. It's an exceedingly rare power that few beings possess. In between each one, I will wake you up, and we will test the power. There is no need to get to a place of full control before we continue to the next one, but we do want to ensure we aren't doing any damage and that the powers are fusing fully to your mind. Are you ready?"

Alex lies on the table and, with one very deep breath, nods to her, "Let's do this."

CHAPTER

31

Brookstone paces his office, back and forth for nearly an hour, glancing anxiously at the map spread out on the table. The voices in his head grow assertive, pulling him, making him paranoid. "QUIET!" he yells out into the silent air around him.

His voice carries down the staircase and is met with the familiar whooping sound of his army below. He smiles fondly as his friends cry out to him, reacting to his voice.

Brookstone turns to where Dru is tucked safely in her cage and places a hand on her bars.

"Where could she have gone, Dru? A human cannot simply escape, not from Barter, not when she has no galactic experience. She must have had help. But who, and why?"

He lets out a frustrated growl.

"It has to be Rickert, he saw her potential, and he was in Barter the day she escaped. How could I have missed it? I used to know him so well. I could read him like a book." He looks desperately at Dru, who clicks back at him in response.

"Well put, Dru, time does change everything. He is different now; I've been watching him. He seems erratic, and he spends less and less time on Solax. Yet, I can't seem to track where he goes." He chuckles to himself. "I guess he guards his secrets as well as I guard mine." He gestures to the lab around him.

It had occurred to him to go back in time and simply kill the human. Eliminate her while she still sat exposed in the jail cell on Barter, but even Brookstone knows better than to change the past. Throughout all of his time jumps, he has never once changed the past. He knows the price to pay for that. It can alter the entire future; everything he knows, everything he has in his timeline, could be different, or worse, gone. Going back and killing her is not an option.

"Well, my girl, maybe I should watch his friends instead. I wonder if that silly doctor of his knows something." Deciding to pay the doctor a visit, he pulls out his map and Stone Set. Placing the Stones in his hands, he focuses his mind on her hospital on Aya. With a small whooshing sound in his ears, he feels himself pulled through time and space and finds himself standing in front of the doctor's office. He gives his robe a light dusting and then knocks on the doctor's door. No answer.

Looking up and down the hallway, he quickly opens the door and slips inside. The office is indeed empty, and it appears that the doctor has not been there in several weeks.

Brookstone rounds the corner of her desk and starts to sift through her papers. There is a lot of information regarding telepathic power enhancement, physical upgrades, etc. All the basic things of a doctor with her specialties.

As he turns to leave, something catches his eye on the far corner of her desk. Drawing closer, he pulls out a partially hidden sketch. On it is a roughly drawn image of the human anatomy. "Now, my dear Veela, why would you have this?" Brookstone chuckles, "Gotcha."

CHAPTER

32

A lexia sleeps comfortably on the medical bed while Veela watches over her. She has performed one of the three mental enhancement procedures in Alexia's mind. Now she is waiting for the pain of surgery to subside before waking her to test the power.

Rickert stops in periodically, each time looking more tired and worn down. He has taken to spending the nights with Veela; it brings her memory back to the old days.

Even after they went their separate ways, her heart was always called back to him. For years she buried herself in her work, numbing the pain. It helped with shutting out the world for a time, but she is growing older, and soon, the medical world will outpace her. She has already set it thousands of years ahead of what it should be. The medical communities think of her as a medical marvel.

What they don't know is that Rickert helped her substantially. Somehow, he always knew of some innovative technologies or theories. He would give her ideas on what to create or hint at what problem could be solved. He would always give her motivation, always make her feel the problems ahead of her were the ones that could be solved. So, she took his words and sometimes even his written schematics, things that he would never admit where he got, and she would design the next best thing in medical science.

She didn't do it for recognition or fame; no, that's not who she is. Veela did it to help the species she saw suffering around her. The PPC treats the galaxy well, helping its civilizations thrive. However, it doesn't understand the medical world, and it doesn't understand the toll they have. Veela has a theory that each time a member of the PPC jumps, they create a ripple effect. An effect that alters the mind of the Holder and of those around them, or at least that is what Veela has surmised. It doesn't matter if they follow the PPC rules for time jumping; any sort of jump causes long-lasting brain damage.

She watched Rickert jump for years, and slowly, she watched his mind change. It was subtle at first, but in time he started acting very differently. When she confronted him, he grew very defensive, accusing her of spying on him. *Another symptom of his deteriorating mind*, Veela thought to herself as he berated her.

That was the moment he started to pull away, but she wasn't the only one he pushed away. As he shoved her aside, he also left Brookstone behind. Veela never particularly liked Brookstone, and she always felt he was a bad influence on Rickert. She didn't dare tell Rickert that, after all, Brookstone was his oldest friend.

But she knew the two of them were up to something. For days at a time, Rickert would disappear with

Brookstone. She assumed they were travelling to some far-off place. Despite his unexplained absences, the worst part of it always emerged when he returned. His mind would be savage, and he would have emotional outbursts. It was too much for Veela; it was too much for their relationship.

So, they parted ways. In his wake, Veela was left with a new research pathway to follow. The impacts of Stone travel on the psyche of Holders and bystanders. It wasn't new in the sense that the PPC and the medical community didn't know the basic impacts, even Pillar and Perma knew of the consequences of time travel. That is why the Council banned it nearly three hundred years ago. What they don't know is how space travel can impact the minds of the Holder and those around them.

It never made sense to Veela why Rickert always came back so different. She knew there was no way he was jumping through time, after all, that was illegal. No, her Rickert would never do that. So, it had to be something else, some unexplored impact on the brain.

It gave Veela a new purpose. She began studying the PPC members. Taking in volunteers from the Council and running them through tests. She also studied the family members of the test subjects and found that those closest to the Stone Set Holders also suffered from brain alterations as a result of the jumps. It fascinated Veela; *if the jumps have this level of impact, then what does the future of our society hold?*

Veela's mind never stops. As she watches over the sleeping Alexia, she goes through the thousands of possibilities of her recovery. She thinks of what will happen to her poor human brain once she finds her Stone Set, once she starts jumping through space. How can this small woman possibly be their Defender?

Veela did not know about the prophecy until Rickert enlightened her only a few weeks ago when he first brought Alexia to her. At first, she was enraged that this is what Rickert had been working on his whole life. This is how he chose to spend his time when he should have been with her and working on their relationship!

Her scientific mind could not grasp that a man as intelligent as Rickert would place so much weight on such a silly thing like a prophecy. Although, the more he told her, the more it started to line up and click in her brain. There were undeniable facts that came along with the information he handed her. Things from their past that could not be dismissed as hearsay. And then, he showed her their future. This terrified her more than anything for more than one reason.

First, it confirmed that Rickert was indeed jumping through time, moving around, and creating major unknown ripple effects. Second, the future itself was terrifying. The creatures he showed her, the state of the civilizations, it was all too much. But it was effective; it made her a believer, it made her commit to Alexia, made her fully commit to what she could be. She had to be the Defender, and if she wasn't, they would make her into one.

That is the main difference between Rickert and Veela. Rickert believes this is all destined to happen, that time will simply run its course, and the future will thrust itself upon them.

Veela knows better because she knows that the future doesn't work that way. She knows that the decisions they make here today will determine their future. They need a Defender, so Veela is going to make them one.

Lost in her own thoughts, Veela nearly misses the sound of someone at the front door of her home. Leaving the unconscious Alexia in her medical room, she exits the lab building and enters her home, heading for the front door.

As she reaches for the door handle and pulls the door open, someone pushes on it from the other side and thrusts the door inward. She stumbles back as the doorframe is taken up with the looming image of an angry Brookstone.

"Hello, Veela, where is she?"

CHAPTER

33

Veela regains her composure and positions herself back in the entrance, blocking Brookstone from entering her home.

"Brookstone, who are you talking about?"

"You know whom I'm talking about," he responds with agitation.

Veela makes note of his shaky voice and twitchy body motions. *His mental state is deteriorating. I need to tread lightly,* Veela thinks to herself.

Steadying herself further, she reaches to the table beside her and discreetly presses a button.

"I assure you I do not, and you have no right to come to my home like this. This is my private space. If you need something, I would be happy to meet with you at my office during more appropriate hours."

Brookstone laughs at her. "Oh, I have been to your office, and you'll never guess what I found." He holds up her drawing of the human anatomy, something she sketched out during her research of Alexia's physiology. Her face goes pale.

"You went through my things? You had no right," her voice begins to shake as she silently begs for the signal from the button to find its recipient. "Brookstone, you need to leave."

"I don't think so. You know, for all the years you were fooling around with Rickert, I have never been to your home." He looks around and wrinkles his nose, clearly unimpressed. "So rude of you not to invite me over for dinner, wouldn't you say? Maybe you should invite me in now, give me the grand tour. After all, we were practically family." His tone is menacing, and it leaves Veela feeling cold. While she is taller than him, he has more muscle mass than her. If he tried to push his way into her home, she would not be able to stop him.

Brookstone takes a step toward her, moving in a way that makes Veela feel violated. She steps back, just as a whooshing sound emits from behind him. Stopping his motions, Brookstone turns and finds Rickert staring at him. Rickert's body is rigid with anger and apprehension. His face painted clearly with rage for Brookstone.

Veela lets out a sigh of relief and is forever thankful that Rickert installed the panic button that would reach him anywhere in the galaxy.

Rickert comes to stand in front of Veela, stopping just inches before Brookstone, their eyes level with each other. Veela stares at the two beings as they subconsciously mimic each other's body positioning, each of them puffing up their chests, squaring their shoulders, clenching their fists. It catches Veela off guard just how much Rickert and Brookstone look alike. *Did they always look so similar?*

It has been so many years since she has seen the beings together like this.

Rickert eyes him angrily. "Brookstone, as I am sure Veela has told you, you have no right to be here. Why did you come?"

"You know why I am here, Rickert, you and this degenerate doctor are hiding the human. As for what purposes, I do not know." His voice is stiff, but as he looks at the face of his old friend, it softens, and his chest deflates slightly. "What are you doing, Rickert? Release the human; she is not the Defender from the prophecy. Please, hand her over, don't do this."

Rickert sighs, and some of the anger leaves his body as well, but he remains on edge. "Brookstone, you need to leave. You're being paranoid. We have no human here; I stopped working on the prophecy years ago. I hoped you had as well, but I see that's not the case." Rickert raises his hands, as if he is going to place them on Brookstone's shoulders, but then he thinks better of it and lets them drop back to his sides. "Please, move on, my friend. It's not healthy to dwell on things beyond our control."

"Beyond our control, ha!" Brookstone steps backward in a motion of defiance. "Nothing is beyond my control. I highly doubt you have stopped working on the prophecy. Otherwise, I wouldn't be standing outside *her* door." He spits the word 'her' out as if Veela is some sort of disgusting germ. The moment of vulnerability between Rickert and Brookstone is gone, leaving only wariness, distrust, and hurt feelings.

"Brookstone, you know the law; you cannot raise a hand against me, nor Veela. We have done nothing wrong. You need to petition the PPC and follow our rules." Rickert grasps at straws, trying to buy them more time. He knows full well that if Brookstone enters the property, then Alexia's life is over.

"You are forcing my hand, Rickert. I will jump through your hoops, but I will return for the human. When I do, her time here will end, of that, you can be certain."

With a whoosh, Brookstone vanishes, leaving Veela's doorstep empty. Rickert and Veela stand facing each other.

Veela lets out a small sob, fear bubbling out of her chest. Rickert rushes to her and embraces her. "I'm sorry, Veela, I'm so sorry." He continues to hold her for a few moments longer, only pulling away to look into her eyes. He holds the stare. This is Veela's favourite part about him, his ability to calm her, to make her feel safe. He lightly strokes her hair, cradling the side of her face. "I had no idea he would look for Alex here."

She takes a long shaky breath, closing her eyes, trying to push the fear aside. "What now?" she asks, her voice still a trembling mess.

Rickert slides his hand down her shoulder and finds the hand of her top arm. "You must hurry Alexia along as I have no doubt that he will be back. I am certain he will try to kill her and us if we stand in his way."

CHAPTER

34

Veela works quickly to finish the remainder of Alex's enhancements by speeding along her recovery time using synthetic drugs to enhance her mental capabilities. She implants medical chips and alters the functionality of Alex's mind to allow room for the new powers. Usually this process would take months, but they don't have that kind of time. Veela now walks along the thin line separating finishing the enhancements quickly and trying not to kill Alex.

Veela does not have time to wait for Alexia to recover from the first surgery, so she pushes a small dose of amphetamines into the life support system. Gradually, the woman's eyes flutter open, and her brow furrows in pain.

Words whisper out, rasping past her dry lips. "I don't think I can survive this," she says to Veela through gritted teeth. "It's too much." Veela watches as Alex squeezes her eyes shut, trying to block out the pain. *She must be in agony. Please survive.* Veela wills the small woman to live.

"Just focus on the sound of my voice, Alexia. This first power is all about emotions. Search for my calm, can you feel it? Does your mind tell you that I am calm?"

"No, it tells me that you are terrified."

Veela laughs weakly, "Perfect, it's working." Alex grits her teeth harder and inhales deeply, visibly trying not to pass out from what must be the overwhelming sensation of feeling someone else's emotions. "OK, OK, time to go back to sleep, Alexia." Veela pushes another dose, this time feeding her a powerful sedative. Veela watches as the pain subsides, and Alex drifts off once more.

"Will she come out the other side the same person as she was before?" Rickert asks, stepping out from the shadows. He didn't want Alex to know he was there. He blocked himself both physically and telepathically from her view.

"I hope so, but honestly, these procedures have never been performed on a human. Nor do we have any history of doing all this to any one being, much less in this little amount of time. If she is going to survive, she has to want it for herself."

***

The following two stages are similar to the first, but now Veela must complete them as fast as possible. After testing the results of the first surgery, Veela hurriedly performed the second procedure. This one will allow Alex to read the minds of lesser beings. It won't give her the ability to read all minds. Those that are trained in the art of telepathy will be able to block her, but those beings are few and far between.

Veela works through the night and completes the surgery. She awakens Alexia momentarily to test the power and then quickly puts her back to sleep. The woman is groggy and nearly unresponsive. Her body struggling greatly to keep her alive as she deals with the mental and physical traumas that Veela is putting her through. Miraculously, she survives. Alex is able to pick up on Veela's fear and see the thoughts that surface through Veela's mind; picking out the bits that Veela wants her to see.

Veela was once trained in telepathy; having lived with Rickert made that a necessity, but her skills are rusty now. She does her best to block the threat of the looming Brookstone and show her only images of a successful surgery. Strangely enough, the human doesn't find comfort in seeing the images of her own surgery. Veela continues to struggle to understand how to connect with her.

After putting Alexia back to sleep, Veela moves into the third surgery. She would have preferred to catch a few hours of sleep and allow Alexia to heal, but Rickert insisted there wasn't time. Veela argued with him, telling him that time will make them more successful while limiting the chances of a negative consequence. She told him in her medical opinion that the plan was to take several weeks and that they needed to give Alex a break in between each procedure. She urged him not to compress it down to two days, but he wouldn't have it. He pushed her, telling her that it was for the safety of them all. So, a groggy and vexed Veela moves to hover over Alexia for the final time.

Rickert moves in and out of Veela's lab, but for the most part he stays nearby. Veela can tell that he is growing increasingly worried that Brookstone will be back. To be honest, Veela isn't sure what has kept him away this long. There is no way he will obey the PPC rules. Something else must be occupying his time.

Bending over Alexia, Veela slices into the woman's forehead, peeling back the skin roughly two inches. Next, she uses a sophisticated saw to remove parts of the skull, and then she starts playing in the malleable part that makes up the human brain. Veela's long fingers move rapidly around in Alexia's brain, tweaking synapses, adding neurons, increasing the somas, and finally increasing the quantity and size of the neurotransmitters.

Veela loves brain surgery, and the human brain is particularly interesting. There are few beings in Gatlin that can suffer from the types of mental disorders that humans do. Alexia suffers from depression; this is clearly written in her brain. The disorder takes on a clearly physical state in her mind. Her brain lacks the required neurotransmitters to prevent this condition. Veela pokes through her brain, studying her like she would one of her cadavers, but with a quick realization, she looks down at the woman on the table and tries to relate to her. Veela takes a moment and centres herself around the despair that Alexia must feel on a regular basis with her brain not giving her what she needs to truly find happiness. Veela is saddened by the thought. Wishing there was time to correct her levels, but knowing there is not, she finishes her enhancements and begins to close the surgical site.

Using a bone grafting tool, she heals the removed piece of skull and replaces the torn-away skin. She runs a skin graft machine over the wound, and in seconds, Alexia is put back together. Veela smiles to herself and sits down in her nearby lab chair with an exhausted thump. Her work here is done; now the rest is up to Alexia.

* * *

Alex awakens and feels excruciating pain in her head, leaving her feeling disoriented and distraught. She struggles to open her eyes. She looks around the room through heavy eyelids and sees Veela hovering anxiously by her bedside. The orange alien has her eyes fixed on a heavy book on her lap.

"Hi," Alex croaks the words out, making Veela jump and slam the book shut, her top two arms flying up in the air as she grips the book tightly with the other two.

"Oh my!" She clutches at her chest and looks down at Alex. "You startled me. How are you feeling?"

Alex shrugs at her, unable to talk through her thick, dry mouth. Rick shuffles out from the corner of the room and comes to stand next to Veela. His face is etched with worry, but his mind is closed off to her. Veela's mind, on the other hand, is like an open book. Alex struggles to shut her out, not capable of handling the frazzled and exhausted woman's thoughts. Veela hands her a glass of thick green liquid. Alex eyes it warily, but Veela is insistent. Alex takes a long drink and feels the moisture rush back into her body. She immediately feels physically rejuvenated and refreshed, but the pain in her head is still intense.

"How long was I out this time?" she asks weakly while making note of their anxious faces.

"Three days...." Veela replies.

"Three days? I thought you said it would take at least three weeks. What happened? Is that why I feel like I have been hit by a truck?"

The two beings look at her with concern, Veela also looking confused by the word truck.

"Brookstone showed up," Rick finally answers. Alex looks around in panic, afraid she might find him standing in some dark corner of the room. Rick lays a hand on her shoulder to ease her mind. "He didn't find you, per se, but he is quite sure you are here. We had to speed along your procedures...so, yes, that is why you may be feeling a bit more discomfort than normal."

As Alex continues to look around the room, she notices that Veela's lab is primarily packed up; equipment has been put away in boxes, her notes taken off the walls in a hasty manner. The doctor looks exhausted, as if she has not slept in several days, and Rick looks agitated and worried. *They have been through a lot while I was asleep. Best to go easy on them.* She cringes as the simple thought moves through her mind, pain lancing behind her eyes. Her brain works to process her own thoughts and manage the new powers that Veela has shoved into her head. "Are we going somewhere?" she asks aloud, trying not to visibly wince with pain.

"Yes," Rick speaks softly. "We needed to wake you up to ensure you were fit for transport, but we need to leave today. We cannot be guaranteed that Brookstone isn't planning something nasty against us. So, gather your strength, Alex. We need to get you on that ship and take you away from here."

"Where are we going?"

"Well, that is a bit undecided at the moment. Veela and I can't come to an agreement on the subject. We were hoping you could break the tie. First things first though, we need to get off Aya. Once we are on the ship, we can figure out our next move."

CHAPTER

35

I t's time. After finding the human and going toe to toe with his oldest flame, Brookstone can no longer sit by idly while he wonders what Rickert is up to with that human. He cannot let his plans be spoiled. Brookstone and Rickert both know that the PPC will never allow action to be taken against him or Veela; they have too high a ranking in society. So, he will go about it another way by forcing the prophecy into action. *The time of our destruction, and ultimately our saving, is nearly upon us.*

Brookstone has spent two days in complete isolation working with Dru to finalize her training and hone her control over the army. The three commanders are working well under her direction, following her lead, and communicating flawlessly. He has designed them to communicate telepathically; modelling the powers that Rickert held. *You're always on my mind Rickert, always in my heart. It's a shame that you, too, must die.* Brookstone thinks sadly to himself.

He has switched the diet of his army to something that more closely resembles the alien species that they will find outside in hopes of enhancing their desire to hunt. He has brainwashed them into destroying all that stands; everything that isn't natural.

Brookstone isn't insane; he doesn't want to destroy the worlds. However, he knows the prophecy, and he knows that there must be destruction. By creating his own army, he controls what they destroy and what remains intact. He has no intention of destroying the things nature has made. As the Defender, he will need nature to help the civilizations rebuild. He has it all mapped out and has gone through every variability to put plans in place. This will go smoothly. He will save the galaxies.

After determining that Rickert was up to something, Brookstone came straight back to his lab and set his plans in motion. Now he needs to test out his creations to see how they respond in the real world. He has done extensive testing in the lab to find their strengths and weaknesses. Now he needs to see how the civilizations will respond. How will the PPC try to rid themselves of one creature? How will they react to ten? That is one of the few variabilities that remain in his plans. How will the Council members react? While he does have considerable influence over their strategies, he does not have ultimate control, not like he does of his army.

He will need to conduct experiments to ensure the PPC reacts the way he expects. He needs to be at the head and encourage them to declare war throughout the Galaxy of Gatlin. They will implement a General, and Brookstone is the best candidate to be that General.

Brookstone knows how that sounds; *It's the ravings of a madman, a child throwing a tantrum,* he says to himself.

But it's the role a Defender must take. Their Defender must be in command. Their Defender must be known. What the PPC doesn't know is that the army can be brought to heel at the click of a button, that they will obey Brookstone on command. *They don't need to know that.*

Overall, the PPC is remarkably unprepared for war. They have no armies or strategies since there hasn't been a war for thousands of years. The PPC has always solved their problems using the Stone Sets, but they won't be able to this time. Brookstone has something dark and devious up his sleeve that makes his army unlike any enemy before.

He has done extensive research into his own Stone Set and put in hundreds of years of work. He has finally discovered what exactly makes the Stones function: light and heat. The Stones have always interacted strangely with light. Even when there was only darkness around them, they seemed to emit some light as if they were sucking it from the darkness itself. Brookstone studied that behaviour for years, trying to manipulate the darkness, find the true absence of light, but still, the stones continued to function. It was on an accidental jump to a frozen, desolate planet that Brookstone uncovered the true need of the Stones. Yes, they need UV rays, but they also need warmth from light.

When Brookstone landed on the frozen planet, the heat was immediately sucked from his hands, and the space around him had no light. There were no bouncing rays or twinkling stars, nothing. He was left with no way to jump for several days. It wasn't until the planet orbited around a nearby star, and the light rays touched the Stones, refilling them with light and heat, was able to jump back. Those were not his favourite few days. However, it was the moment he made his breakthrough with the mysterious Stones.

Using this knowledge, he built his creatures with light eliminating technology and heat-reducing bodies. When faced with a Stone Set Holder, they will activate a forcefield around the Holder and themselves. This field will throw them into complete blackness, then the creature's body will remove all heat from the space. From there, the ill-equipped PPC member will be left defenseless, and the creature will kill them.

It is the thing that brings Brookstone the most pride and sadness. He does not want to watch his comrades fall, but he knows the sacrifices that must be made to purge them of the weakness. So, he built his army with the tools they would need to slaughter the PPC. Once they have all fallen, Brookstone will reign the creatures back in and limit their destruction. In the end, he will be the Defender, the one to end it all and the one to rebuild them.

Brookstone paces his lab again, turning toward Dru. "Are you ready, Dru? I think it's time we send some of our minions out for testing."

CHAPTER

36

One day after leaving Aya, Rick, Alex, and Veela sit around the small table of Rick's ship. The ship, which has been set to autopilot, is taking them in a controlled orbit around Valyrn. The trio needs to decide where they are to go next, and Alex needs time to heal and train.

Her headaches are subsiding, but her powers are proving to be a lot for her human mind to handle.

Rick and Veela scour the Knowledge Computer, something that Veela was outraged to find even existed. "You kept this from me? Do you know what this could do for science? How far this could have moved us forward without having to use those silly Stones?"

"I'm sorry," Rick answers sheepishly. "The Council determined that some things are too dangerous in the hands of the basic population." Veela's anger flares higher at being called 'basic.' Rick backs away quickly, muttering something about 'dangerous topics of conversation' and turning on his heel. He leaves Alex alone with the fuming scientist.

Still mumbling under her breath, Veela hooks up to the computer. Within a matter of an hour, she has developed a full training plan and schedule for Alex.

Later, at the dinner table, Veela fills Rick and Alex in. "We will need about four weeks to train her physically and mentally, to a point where she *may* be 'battle ready'. Although, that is hard to say for sure because we don't truly understand what 'battle ready' means. I recommend we travel to Alars and start researching war and strategies. The Knowledge Computer is sorely lacking information on this topic since the PPC members deemed it was unnecessary to document such things. I believe we will have more luck on Alars." She looks at the duo, searching for their support.

Veela is not a leader, Alex thinks to herself. She can feel the woman's discomfort at taking on a decision-making role while she can see the images of uncertainty flash in Veela's mind. *She is brilliant, but she should not be put in a spot of making wartime decisions.* Alex makes the mental note.

Alex closes her eyes and puts her head in her hands, braced against the table, trying to force her powers into submission. Having the two other beings around her is a lot. While Rick is trained to block her telepathic abilities, Veela is not. Her mind and emotions are like an open book, but instead of letting Alex passively read what is written, the words are shouted from the pages, screaming at Alex to listen.

"I think that's a promising idea," she replies with her eyes still closed. "How long will it take to get there?"

"Ten days," Rick replies.

"OK, in that time we will start training. I need to at least be able to shut out the minds of others." Alex looks painfully at Veela, who blushes a deep orange in response, realizing that Alex is unintentionally picking through her mind. Suddenly her mind flashes to very naked images of Rick. Alex blushes as Veela hastily leaves the room.

* * *

Alex spends the next ten days working to increase her control over her new mental powers. She uses Rick as the teacher, Veela as a tutor, and both of them as test subjects. At first, Alex is clunky and easily overwhelmed. But just like the work she put in to control her own emotions and anxiety, she eventually comes to be in control of the telepathic aspect of her brain. The ship has been retrofitted with things to train both her physical and mental strengths. The small room containing the Knowledge Computer now also houses a small gym. When Alex is not training her mental powers, she is putting her body through the paces and working on getting it to its peak physical condition.

Alex finds she has little need for sleep anymore, only sleeping for eight hours every three days. Veela tells her that is a side effect of her increased physical and mental attributes. Either way, it gives Alex a lot of hours to train. Veela is pleased with Alex's dedication to training. The lack of required sleep means that the time required for training is down to nearly half of what was predicted.

Currently, Alex is sitting still in the centre of the small living and kitchen area while Veela walks around and reads a book quietly to herself. This has become part of Alex's mental training. "Can you sense what I feel when I read this passage? Can you tell me what I have just read? Can you communicate to me mentally that you would like me to close the book?" Veela is a very practical teacher; rather than forcing Alex to study, she makes her test. Repeatedly, the two ladies work through scenarios while Rick points out different ways to listen or control. Alex is surprised by how effective the methods are.

As Alex focuses, her attention is pulled to a muted sound coming from the ship's cockpit. Deliberately, she brings her attention away from Veela and turns to Rick. He moves to the ladder and descends into the ship's command station. After a moment, he calls up to Alex and Veela, "We are here. Alars is about thirty minutes out. Time to ready ourselves."

He climbs back up the ladder and comes to stand in front of Alex. She now has full control over what she allows him to see or feel from her. He crinkles his brow and takes in her neutral stance. "What are you thinking, Alex?"

"I've been thinking about our strategy, and I propose only some of us should go to Alars." Rick looks at her, surprised.

"What do you mean? You think we should split up?"

"Yes, I need to find my Stones. The more my powers grow, the stronger my connection to them gets." For the past ten days, Alex has felt her Stones calling to her. With every lesson learned and every stride taken, Alex is pulled to them.

"OK, so Veela will go down to the surface of Alars and research war strategies, and you and I will go find your Stones. I assume you know exactly where they are?"

"I do, but you cannot come with me." As Alex says this, Rick's face falls. Alex knew her friend would feel betrayed by her decision to proceed alone, but the Stones call to her and only her. This is when she starts to separate herself from the safety of her friends and her protectors. "Rick, I'm sorry, but I need to do this alone. The Stones are calling to me. I have studied the ship's controls, and I can get to them on my own." Seeing his desperation, she adds something to soften the separation, "Please."

Veela watches the exchange with her breath held. She knew the moment would come when Alexia needed to step away from them, to proceed along her journey as the Defender. "Rick, 'a Defender must choose her own path,' you told me that. Well, Alexia is choosing, and we must listen."

Rick sighs and looks at Alex with watery eyes. "Fine, I will go with Veela to Alars, but you must be careful. As you know, the Stones are on Solax, the home of the PPC. If you are seen without a disguise, you will be recognized and immediately taken into custody. I will not be able to rescue you a second time."

Alex nods, "I understand."

"No, I don't think you do. Your disguise may not be enough; you may need your powers as well. If you come across any beings, you will need to listen to their emotions, to their minds, and feel when they start to grow suspicious. As a last resort, you may use your telepathic powers. Put ideas into the minds of those who may suspect you are disguised. Make suggestions that they think are their own. You would be surprised what an untrained mind will do under the intrusion of someone with strong telepathic control. Use that skill cautiously as it will not work on all beings, especially if they have a high degree of telepathic control as I do."

"OK, Rick, I've got this," Alex responds with confidence in her statement.

Rick looks at her forlornly but shows her a caring smile. "Good luck, my friend." Giving a small hug to Veela and Rick, Alex watches them depart the ship.

CHAPTER

Brookstone starts his experiment by releasing one low-level creature into a lightly populated area. He used one of his stolen ships from Zeya to transport the Shreiker through space. He has been slowly collecting ships to transport his army. It's taken years, but good things come to those who wait, and now he has what he requires to move his entire army.

Taking the Shreiker from Zeya to the surface of Trayton, Brookstone stood back and released the creature. It wreaked mild havoc before it was put down by a group of lumber yard security guards with sophisticated wood chopping weapons.

Next, he released three Shreikers onto a busy street on Lillon. These ones were more successful. A member of the PPC was dispatched to the location to assess the situation and enact a plan. It was only a few seconds before the creatures sensed his Stone Set and converged on him. They used their light and heat dampening powers to disable his Stone Set and kill him. His Stone Set immediately disappeared. The entire exchange took less than fifteen seconds. Brookstone was extremely impressed with the results.

The creatures were then put down by a series of guards that had been dispatched from Barter. The heavy fire from their prison-issued weapons was enough to eventually kill the creatures. This irritated Brookstone as he thought their armor was thicker than that. *I know Dru will be able to withstand their fire.* He thinks fondly of his prized possession awaiting him back on Zeya.

For each experiment, Brookstone watched as his creatures ran through the streets and buildings while being careful to stay a safe distance away. He was mindful to ensure that no one saw him in the area. He made notes in his holoscroll and changed his deployment strategy based on the creatures results and the PPC's response.

Brookstone, now back in his office, goes over his notes. These experiments provided him two necessary insights to ensure his army's success. First, he studied how his creatures fared in the real world. Second, he gained more information on how the PPC would respond. Most importantly, he established that the PPC will fall to his army. *They are so easily manipulated.* He chuckles to himself. Part of him is disgusted to be a member of a Council that is so weak, but another part of him is incredibly proud of himself for being able to manipulate this group of 'leaders'. *Just a few more random attacks, and they will surely declare war.*

CHAPTER

38

Alex sits down at the spaceship controls and enters her coordinates. With tentative fingers, she reaches out and places her hand on the gel control pad. Wires leap forward and wrap painlessly around her fingers. She has studied the Knowledge Computer and watched as Rick learned how to control the ship. She is confident that she is capable of flying the ship, but she is still nervous about venturing through space by herself. With a deep breath, she wills the ship to take off from the landing pad on Alars. In seconds she is airborne and rising toward the atmosphere of the planet. The darkness of space zooms toward her as she pushes the ship forward.

It will take Alex roughly two weeks to reach the far side of Solax. With every passing moment she moves deeper into outer space, putting more and more distance between herself and her friends. The old Alex would have feared the intense loneliness and been scared that she would fall into a deep depression as her mind struggled to find things to distract herself with. Now, thoughts of her family flow freely in her mind, but they don't cripple her. They leave her feeling sad but not distraught. She works through her coping mechanisms and focuses on the things in her control. Alex tells herself that she will see them again. She smiles at her newfound strength, the mental discipline to control her emotions and work through the depression and anxiety.

She works to pass the time by training her physical self. Now that she is truly alone, it is harder to train her mental powers. Still, she focuses her physical senses on different things, testing them. She sits in silence and works to expand and contract her hearing, listening for the light hum of the ship or turning on music as loud as possible and restricting her ears until the noise is barely a whisper to her. She turns the lights on and off to test her eyes, demanding they adjust quickly. She spends time watching the rapid food warming device, turning it on and off, looking for the variations in the heat signatures.

She has also been practicing reaching out to Rickert, who is now millions of miles away.

"We have a base connection," his voice rings through her head one day while she sits alone on the ship. *"Once you have an established connection with someone, you become tuned into their mental frequency, and it becomes easier to communicate with them over long distances. The more we practice, the easier it will get. Eventually, we should be able to talk to each other even if we are galaxies away!"* He sounds overly excited about that, Alex chuckles to herself.

"I'm not sure I want a permanent phone line to you, Rickert," she responds mentally to him.

The duo shares a laugh before ending their mental connection, and Alex is left to busy herself on the ship once more.

After twelve days of isolation on the ship, Alex moves to the control panel and looks down at the navigation screen. Solax is now in the middle of the screen. The small dot that is her ship zips towards it.

"Almost there," she says aloud to herself. She gets up from her seated position and moves to the bathroom on the second level. Her muscles glide past each other under her skin, and the aches and pains she once felt are long gone. Her body is a thing of impeccable engineering. There are no flaws in her system; everything about her is perfectly structured to produce the highest possible outcome. She truly is built for combat.

She moves smoothly to the bathroom and takes in her appearance once more. She still struggles with what stares back at her. The twinkle of her eyes, the shape of her face, her muscular body, and the faint scars that now mark her neck and forehead. *In time I suppose I will grow used to you,* she says to her reflection. *But for now, you are still an alien to me.*

CHAPTER

39

inally, after his fifth experiment, the PPC called an emergency meeting. All members of the Council have gathered. Brookstone entered the room second to last, only shadowed by Rickert, who used his Stone Set to travel in from some unknown location. *He looks tired,* Brookstone thinks to himself, taking pity on him for a moment. He lets the emotion slide out of his mind, only to be replaced by a forced feeling of hate. *You cannot pity him; you must hate him, hate them all. That's the only way this is going to work.*

"Rickert, you are looking well," Brookstone addresses him, a sarcastic tinge in his voice.

"Not at all, my friend. Haven't you heard, creatures run amuck on our planets, civilians are dying. I am plagued with grief, unable to sleep."

Brookstone doesn't believe that is the reason for his fatigue, but he plays along. "I agree, the news is terrible; hopefully, we can come up with a plan of defense against these terrible monsters."

Returning his skeptical look, Rickert looks Brookstone in the eye. Brookstone simply stares back, not moving an inch. The duo steps further into the room and turn in opposite directions, seeking seats on different sides of the room.

Here comes the exciting part, Brookstone thinks to himself. *Here comes the moment where these fools declare war and put me in command.*

CHAPTER

40

On day fifteen, Alex arrives on the darkened side of Solax. As she closes the final bit of distance, she feels her Stone Set call to her, guiding her to their location.

Alex has done her homework on the Stone Sets. She now understands why the Stones left her and where they went. The Stones are sentient beings; they think and react just like other beings. Interestingly, the Stones have a unique ability to know someone's potential. Apparently, Alex has a lot of potential. Hence, the reason the Stone Set chose her. After all the work Veela put into Alex, she is starting to see the potential for herself. Her confidence continues to grow. She now spends hours a day visualizing herself as the Defender and putting herself in that role.

She is ready; she can feel it, the Stones can feel it. They are ready to connect with her, ready to unleash her full potential.

As she readies herself to disembark the ship, she feels the familiar mental knock inside her head. She opens her mind to the incoming connection from Rick. Immediately, her mind is flooded with his panicked voice.

"Things have started happening, Alex. Creatures are starting to roam the streets of the galaxy cities. At first, we thought they were smuggled creatures breaking free of their transport carriers, but now we aren't so sure. The PPC is growing concerned, and I am worried about our future. We need you, Alex, and we need you to be ready."

Alex sends him calming vibes through their mental connection. *"Calm down, Rick. I have arrived at Solax. I'm less than a day away from having the Stones in my possession. I'm in control of my powers, and I'm physically as strong as I am ever going to be. I'm ready."*

She can feel Rick start to calm down. *"OK, that's good to hear. But there is more; we found the Factions. While you were in surgery, I tried to find them, but there was no hint of them anywhere. Amazingly, we found the information here, on Alars. We found tons of references to them in one of the main libraries. There are two Factions on Valyrn, one on Trayton, and one on Lillon."*

"So, what does that mean? While I may be in the best shape of my life, I still need an army; I don't think I can fight those creatures on my own."

"I think you need to go to Valyrn and speak with the Faction leaders. They may still rally behind you and give you the support you need. Only a true Defender can bring the outcasts together."

Alex considers this, trying to wrap her mind around the task of rallying a group of outcasts. Ultimately, she knows that she needs their support. It's more than simply the fear of fighting the enemy by herself. Alex has a deep intuition that she needs them, and they have something that will help her win the war. She turns back to her conversation with Rick, *"Good idea. But first, I need to find my Stone Set. And every second I stay on this ship is a second I lose. I have to go, Rick; the future is coming at us fast."*

"Alexia, wait," she pulls up short at the use of her full name. *"The PPC held an emergency meeting to decide how to approach the growing threat of the creatures."* He pauses, allowing dread to creep into Alex's mind. *"The PPC has declared war. They are panicking; they aren't prepared for this. I tried to lead them toward the prophecy. I showed them everything I had, but I played right into Brookstone's hand. He was relying on me to be the one that sold them the prophecy. He knew what I would do, and he played me like a card. What I didn't see coming was his willingness to back me up. He reinforced everything I said. He supported everything about the prophecy being true, about the civilizations facing doom, even about the Defender."*

"Then he threw me for a loop. He pulled rank on me and used his influence to brainwash the others. Alex. . . he has everyone believing that he is the Defender, and that you are the leader of this new species. . . everyone is now hunting for you."

CHAPTER

41

"OK," Alex takes a moment to collect her thoughts and maintain the telepathic connection to Rick. *"Here are the problems: I have no army, my control over my powers is growing but not one hundred percent there yet. Furthermore, Brookstone has convinced everyone he is the Defender, and I am the one responsible for the creatures; and to top it off, I still don't have my Stone Set. I gotta say, that's a lot of problems."* Alex's mind starts to hurt as she processes all the information.

Silence fills her head, like static filling the space between her and Rick. Alex can feel him relaying parts of their conversation to Veela, who must still be with him. *"Rick, where are you?"*

"I'm back on Alars with Veela. I had to travel to Solax for the PPC meeting but came back here as soon as I could. Alex, I think you need to focus on one problem at a time. I can feel your indecision leaking through."

Forgetting for a moment that Rick can't see her, she nods, then remembers herself, *"You're right, one thing at a time. I need my Stone Set. It will all get easier once I have that. I can ditch the spaceship travel and save a ton of time."* She pauses for a moment. *"The plan will remain the same. My Stone Set is here on Solax. I should be heading into an unpopulated portion of the planet, which means I should be able to retrieve the Set and travel away from here."*

"And don't worry about my ship," Rick assures her. *"I can retrieve it anytime or hire someone to transport it back to me."*

"To be honest, I wasn't really worried about your ship, Rick. We have so much else going on that your ship didn't quite make my list. I'll connect with you when I have my Stone Set, and we can make our next plan of attack," Alex sighs as she signs off from their conversation.

The ship ramp lowers, and she steps down onto the rough soil of Solax. Just like when she landed on Muskoux for the first time, she is overtaken by the sights around her. Oddly, this time it reminds her more of home. Tall green trees grow around her. Rocks and sand scatter around her feet. The only distinguishing factor between Earth and Solax is the distinct shape of the rocks that are all either perfectly round or rectangular. *This is definitely the home of the Stone Sets,* Alex thinks to herself. The wind moves through her hair, lifting it slightly off of her shoulders. She has landed her ship at the base of a mountain. A tall cliff rises up the side and casts a shadow over her. There are no signs of life here.

Rick has told her about Solax and that this planet is the origin of the Stones, but he also told her that when Perma removed the Stones and gave them to their Holders, the land turned on itself. The creatures stopped thriving, and only the current organisms could survive; nothing new existed or evolved here.

The PPC made this their home as penance for the gifts they were given. The founding members claimed this soil as their own and promised to protect it as it was now unable to protect itself. Eventually, the species native to the land died out, leaving only the members of the PPC and those that arrived by ship left to walk the land of Solax. This makes it easy for Alex to travel without worrying about coming across any wildlife, but it also causes her great sorrow to understand the cost of Perma's actions. Another example of a dominant species coming in and ruining the beauty that nature tries to create.

With a heavy sigh, she looks up the jagged cliff and spots a large cave opening roughly one thousand feet up. As her eyes land on it, she feels the increasingly familiar call of her Stones; they lie somewhere in that cave.

The Stones were originally found in a large open field, but Rick believes that after they were all taken from the surface, the land changed. The planet created a more private place to protect its most valuable assets. If the Stones ever returned, they would be protected from those deemed unworthy.

Alex looks around and sees no straightforward way up the cliffside. *Time to test this body in the real world.* She walks to the base of the cliff and places a hand on the jagged rocks, and begins to climb. At first, she struggles to find a rhythm with her artificially enhanced muscles throwing her farther than she intends or not far enough, causing her to grapple at the side of the cliff as she slides down toward the ground.

Gradually, as she ascends, she adapts to the needs and wants of her body, listening to her muscles and finding a rhythm. With only ten feet to go, she gathers her courage and gives herself one final swing, launching herself upward and rolling gracefully to a standing position. Giving a loud, celebratory cheer, she throws her arms up in joy; then flinches, surprised by the sound of her own voice echoing out at her from the cave. She continues to laugh lightly to herself but makes a mental note to try and keep quiet. *There may be no wild species running around trying to kill me, but there may be civilized ones.*

Gathering her wits, she moves into the mouth of the cave. Her enhanced eyes adjust to the lack of light around her and take only a millisecond to put her in a place where she can comfortably see her surroundings. The cave is dark, but small lights refract off the walls leaving her feeling warm and comfortable. There is no threat in this cave; she feels almost as if she has been called home.

She makes her way through the cave, tuning her ears to listen for sounds, making sure no species walk the cave alongside her. She uses her lean body to slide between thin cave walls and duck under and over large boulders. The walls are jagged and often catch her clothes and skin, causing small trails of blood to run down her arms and legs.

She travels forward and upward for a long time before the cave walls open around her, and she walks into a large, round chamber. The chamber has a lone source of light through the roof, spilling in from the outside world. The edges of the chamber are cast in shadows, but Alex has no time to spare for them as her eyes are drawn to the centre of the room. Sitting on a small pedestal designed by nature are her Stones, waiting for their rightful Holder to come and claim them.

A wide smile spreads across her face. *Everything I have worked for, been waiting for, is just ahead of me, only thirty more feet, and I'm there.* She steps forward out of the cave tunnel and further into the chamber.

With her eyes focused entirely on her Stone Set, she nearly misses the other Set in the room. All around her, she can see pedestals, ready and waiting to receive the Stone Sets, should they decide to come home. Only one of them is occupied. Alex stops moving and stares at the second Stone Set. She knows in her heart that those are not her Stones; the other Set clearly calls to her. For some reason, she does pause to wonder whom they belong to. *If that Set is here, that means that a PPC member must have died.* She thinks back to the recent attacks and wonders if that could be the cause of the death. *I wonder if this Set has chosen a new recipient or if it has returned here?* Alex makes a note to ask Rick about the mysterious Set but turns her attention back to her own Set.

Moving her feet once more, she approaches her Stone Set. With only three feet to go, she stops abruptly as the ground beneath her foot makes a sudden shift. She feels her outstretched foot depress into the ground and looks around frantically as the feelings of a trap rise around her.

CHAPTER

42

"**A**lexia Harmon, do not move," a loud voice rings out around the room. Alex restricts her ears to avoid the noise damaging her eardrums. It now filters through her ears as a soft whisper. "By the laws enacted and enforced by the Planetary Peace Council, you are under arrest. You are formally charged with conspiracy to do harm, illegal experiments resulting in the creation of a mutant species, and the murders of eighteen civilians and one Council member."

Alex grows cold as her charges are read, "No, you don't understand, I'm trying to help. Those mutants, they aren't mine. I am not the creator of anything."

A figure steps out from the shadows, and Brookstone leers down at her. "If not you, then who?" He smiles mischievously at her, and his emotions flood her mind. Alex is shocked to find him radiating with pride and joy, all focused around his vast intelligence. She can feel his own ego swell as his mind focuses on his own ability to pull off a scheme like this. *It's him; he is the creator of the army!* The sudden realization rocks Alex to the core, but before she can get any words out, Brookstone addresses someone else in the room. "Guards, seize her, and remember, we need her alive."

Six figures step out of the shadows, and Alex recognizes them as the guards from Barter. She makes another step toward her Stone Set. As her foot lifts off the soft piece of ground, a large cage slams down, covering her Stone Set, making it impossible for her to get to them. Alex jumps back as Brookstone's laugh rings throughout the room. "You thought you would really get your hands on a Stone Set? You foolish being, we weren't born yesterday."

Alex looks around, and her eyes land on the other Set. As her mind considers dashing for them, she feels her body become repulsed at the idea, as if grabbing a Stone Set not meant for her could potentially kill her. *Damn it!* She curses to herself. *I need my Stones!*

Brookstone continues to laugh, "No, those aren't meant for you, Alexia, but you know that. Those were ripped from the hands of my poor fallen comrade, a result of your creatures killing him on Lillon." His voice drips with fake remorse. Alex works to tune out what he is saying and turns her telepathic powers on him, trying to listen into his mind. She is surprised to find his confusion around the other Stone Set. *He doesn't know why they are here either; he is just as confused about their presence as I am.*

As she uses her mental powers, she nearly misses the movement of the guards. They circle around her, bringing out advanced-looking weapons that Alex has never seen before. Coming back to the physical world, she pushes her back against the bars that now surround her Stone Set. She has no real combat experience, only what she has learned from the Knowledge Computers. Her last fight was with Molly T. in second grade. She looks longingly behind her at the Stones, which are only inches from her grasp.

With a slow and measured breath, she leaps at the two nearest guards and swings her legs around in a circle, catching them at the knees and knocking them down. They fall with a heavy thud. As they work to regain their footing, Alex points her feet at their heads and sends two hard kicks out at them. With a fast one-two, the guards go down again in an unconscious heap. *Two down, four to go.*

She scampers back and puts as much space between her and her assailants. Looking around, her eyes land on a pile of rocks to the far right. Quickly she dives for them and launches two well-aimed stones at a guard's head. His head whips backward as the rocks make contact, and he falls to the ground, dropping his weapon.

Without thinking, Alex lunges for the gun and hoists it up, and steadies it to take aim at the remaining three guards. Before she can get a steady shot, the guard closest to her knocks the gun from her hand just as another guard strikes her in the side of the head with the butt of his weapon.

The shock sends Alex flying into the wall of the chamber. Despite her throbbing head, she is pleased to learn that instead of caving in her skull, it only left her dazed. She stumbles away from the wall, holding her head in an effort to appear more wounded than she is. The ploy works, and the two guards that struck her lower their weapons and advance on her. One of them begins reaching for their handcuffs. The third guard stands behind them with his weapon aimed at her chest. Soon, the two guards are within striking distance. Dropping to the ground to get herself out of the aim of the gun, she lashes out with a strong arm. Her fist makes contact with the first guard's abdomen sending him flying. As he jars backward, Alex spins on the ground and kicks her foot up at his head, causing it to snap backward; he drops to the ground. The second guard draws his weapon up, but he is too slow. Alex is on top of him in one leap and tackles him to the ground. She wrestles his weapon out of his hands and smacks it down onto his face.

Her movements were too fast for the third and final guard to follow. He stands dumbly behind her and watches as her maneuvers take out all his comrades. With one deliberate swing, she aims the weapon at his chest and fires. The strong pulse of the weapon jolts her arm backward, but her muscles absorb the thrust. She stands still, her feet rooted in place. The guard's chest explodes, and blood pours out from his alien body. He drops to the ground. Alex stares in horror at her actions. She pulls the emotion into her body and shoves it down. *Something to feel for later, but not now.*

Standing among the five unconscious guards and one dead one, she swings the weapon around wildly, looking for Brookstone. Seeing the losing battle unfold in front of him, he has backed himself toward the Stones, blocking her access to them.

"You have changed, Alexia. It seems the doctor has worked her talents in your favour. But you can't have the Stones; I'll kill you before you lay a hand on them." As the words escape his lips, Alex can see the Stones behind him start to absorb light from the room, sucking it in and refracting it back into each other. Without warning, a flash of light emits from inside the cage, leaving Alex and Brookstone blinded.

Alex feels the Stones slide into her hand, pushing between her palms and the gun. They glide in with the same mysterious powers that brought them to her in the first place. Thanks to her medically enhanced eyes, her sight returns faster than Brookstone's, ultimately giving her the advantage. She steps away from him and the now-empty cage and levels her weapon at him. "I guess that wasn't for you to decide," she fires her weapon at his chest.

CHAPTER

Her aim is true, but Brookstone feels it coming and vanishes before her eyes, using his Stone Set to escape. Alex looks around the cave, at the guards on the ground, and then finally to her Stone Set, now nestled safely in her palms.

"Best be leaving before these beings wake up," she says aloud. Dropping the gun to the ground, she steadies herself. *OK, the way Rick described this, I should simply think of where I want to go.* Focusing on the Pillar Stone, used for space travel, she thinks of her spaceship outside at the bottom of the cliff, and imagines herself standing there.

With a slight whoosh, Alex finds herself standing exactly where she pictured. The ship just behind her and the large cliff towering above her once more. With a small laugh, she opens the telepathic connection to Rick, mentally knocking on his door.

"Alex, are you alright? Did you find your Stone Set?" his voice rings through in her head.

She smiles broadly and responds in her mind, *"I sure did, but you'll never guess who was there."*

Quickly, she fills Rick in on her encounter with Brookstone and how she had to fight for her Stones. She can feel him relaying her story to Veela on the other side. He is impressed to hear of her hand-to-hand combat skills but not surprised, *"You showed potential in the Cataloguing. That's when I knew you were meant for something. No one else has displayed physical combat skills in over a century. So, Brookstone escaped?"* Alex can hear the mixed emotions in his voice. A part of him feeling conflicted by the fact that his old friend has become so dark but also relieved that he escaped.

"He did, I'm not sure where he disappeared to, but he knows I have the Stone Set. There was also another Stone Set in the cave. Brookstone was just as confused about its presence as I was. He said it was from the fallen PPC member. He didn't know why it was on Solax, why it didn't go to the next worthy being. Any ideas?"

Rick takes a moment before responding. *"I have a theory...it may have something to do with the planets, that they may be the worthiest right now. I'll need to do some more research into that theory, though."*

She pauses for a moment, concerned about how her friend will react to the next piece of information. *"There's more. When Brookstone challenged me in the cave, I was able to get a read on his thoughts. Rick, he is the creator of the army; he is the being behind our destruction."*

Rick is silent for a long moment, but his emotions flood through their open pathway. Alex can feel his despair as he processes the information, and then it moves to acceptance.

"That actually makes sense," he finally replies. *"It's time for us to gather back together, and we will fill you in on what we have learned. Come meet us on Alars. Go to the ship, I will send you the coordinates, and you can use your Stone Set to travel here. We will be waiting for you."*

* * *

As promised, Rick and Veela are waiting for Alex in a small library on the vast knowledge planet of Alars. The galaxies' most intelligent beings live and work here, collecting information and storing it in holoscrolls. Some of the information is still in books, collected thousands of years ago, and stored in the libraries that are scattered across the surface of the planet.

Rick and Veela have spent the past two weeks searching the libraries and speaking to many beings. All of these efforts are in hopes of trying to help Alex develop a war strategy that might be effective against the new enemy.

As Alex's feet find solid ground on the wood floor of the library, she glances around, taking in her new surroundings. Only seconds ago, she was standing on the fresh ground of Solax, and now she is inside a library on Alars. She smiles down at her Stone Set and then tucks them safely into her pocket.

"We will need to get you a holder for those!" Rick says, giving her a broad smile. Veela stands behind him, smiling gingerly at her.

"It's good to see you two," She smiles back and looks around for a seat. "Fill me in on what you have found."

Rick, Veela, and Alex spend the next several hours going over holoscrolls and books, pulling out maps, and examining historical times from when the galaxies were racked with war. They even study some historical war strategies from Earth. Alex never was much of a history person. She has always been more focused on the here and now, but with the thought of war being in her near future, she focuses on all the details.

"The prophecy tells us the destruction must happen, right?" she asks, lifting her head up from a dusty, old book.

"Correct. It also tells us it can end, but it's unfortunately vague on the how part," Rick responds, his face also buried in a book.

Alex contemplates the history she has read versus the future she knows is coming. "A lot of these wars always end with one army winning over the other, but destruction always lies in its wake. The winning army kills off the remainder of the forces and works to rebuild what they destroyed. In this situation, our armies aren't evenly stacked. One side is incredibly strong, while the other is weaker than anything in these history books. We don't stand a chance if we try to stand up to them in our current state. We will be demolished, and there will be nothing left to save," Alex shakes her head as she realizes how devastating this battle will be without an advantage.

"We need to find their weak spot. If Brookstone is their creator, he must have an insurance plan, some way to control or stop them. Rick, you know him best, what do you think he would have done?" Alex asks him.

Rick looks up and gives a heavy sigh, sad to have to reminisce about his old friend this way. "Well, I suppose he would have engineered a way to control them, he is a scientist after all. Veela, is there a way, scientifically speaking, that he could control an army of that size?"

"Absolutely, the problem is that there are a thousand different ways and unless he tells us exactly what way he chose, we can't leverage that theory. Unless..." she pauses, her mind running away from her as she follows an idea down a rabbit hole. "Unless we capture one of the creatures and I study it, find the weak point, find what controls them."

The trio looks around at each other, eyeing one another to see who is going to volunteer for that job.

"I agree," Alex finally says. "But even with my advanced skills and body, I can't capture one of the creatures, not while also battling in the middle of a war. I'm also assuming you would like it alive?" she asks Veela.

"Yes, please," Veela responds.

"Right, so we are back to the original problem of needing more support, an army. I think our next move is clear." She closes her book with a loud thud, and dust flies out. "We can't fight these creatures, not in the sense of classic war, but we can try and outsmart them. If we can outmaneuver them and bring Brookstone down in the process, we may have a chance." Alex feels herself step into a role of command; it feels natural, like a jacket that was made just for her.

"Veela, you need to set up a lab somewhere here on Alars. Somewhere that we can bring a creature for you to study if we need to. We might luck out and find Brookstone's lab, but in case we don't, we need you to be ready with our own space. Privacy is key."

"Rick, you need to find out where Brookstone is hiding. As I said, if we can find his lab, we may be able to get ahead of all of this and take the army down before it gets out of control." Rickert looks at her tentatively as Alex continues detailing their plan, "I know this may make you uncomfortable, but you know him best. Step into his mind Rick, use your knowledge of him."

Rick and Veela nod back at her, taking her words as commands they must follow. "What will you do?" Veela asks her.

"I'm going to focus on defenses. I know we can't win this war the traditional way, but we can do everything in our power to limit the catastrophic outcomes." She looks each of them in the eyes and stands, her confidence growing by the second. "I'm going to find myself an army."

CHAPTER

44

age boils through his veins. "I DON'T FAIL!" he screams into the open space around him. He is back in his home on Solax; it was the first place that popped into Brookstone's mind when Alex shot at him.

Her strength was beyond what he imagined. The way she moved, it just shouldn't be this way. Doctor Veela has transformed her, and she is only just beginning to grow. The longer he waits, the stronger she gets, especially now that she has her Stone Set.

Brookstone thinks back to the cave. He was surprised to find two Stone Sets there. However, he didn't have much time to investigate. The guards only had moments to set up the trap around Alex's Set, which was thankfully engraved with her name, giving them the guidance needed to ensure the trap was deployed on the right Set.

He couldn't have predicted that there would be two sets in that cave. It's highly irregular for Stone Sets to come back to Solax. When studying Alexia's Set, he figured out that the Stones were waiting for her. When he saw the Set clearly etched with her name, he confirmed that they were firmly bonded to her. However, the second Set didn't have any etchings on it. They were blank with no identifiers. He has never come across a blank Set. He doesn't know what it means yet, but it is something he plans to study after his war.

The battle comes first, and no matter how strong Alexia gets, she cannot stop him. He alone is in control of his army. The galaxy needs him; he is the only one that can stop what he has started.

Brookstone is afraid that he gave away more than he intended. He underestimated her powers, and he could feel her prodding around in his mind. If she saw what he was thinking, felt what he was feeling, then she would certainly know that he was in control of the army. She might know everything, or just enough to be even more dangerous to his plan. He lets out an angry growl and works to control his rattled mind.

Walking over to his hologram TV, he flips it on and tries to clear the rage from his body. An image of a small green alien flickers through and speaks of the creature attacks on Lillon and Trayton. Everyone is terrified and unsure of what to make of these creatures, these demons that run free in the streets.

The PPC did exactly as he expected, even better, actually. It was so easy to manipulate them to think that this big bad human was responsible for it all. That she was some evil mastermind. It's enough to make him laugh out loud.

Fools, they have no idea what a true mastermind looks like, what it takes to be a true genius. For crying out loud,

I have been sitting under their noses for two hundred and fifty years! He chuckles to himself.

He has now been given the official title of General in this war, and Alexia has been labelled as the enemy. "Perfect," he chuckles to himself.

He turns back to the hologram and turns it off, taking a seat at his table. His home on Solax is the biggest one on the planet. *Rightfully so*, he thinks to himself, *I am the longest-standing member of the PPC.* Just like everything else in his life, he had to fight for this home. The previous owner was a cranky old being. So stuck in his ways that he couldn't see past his own nose. At the time, it was the old being living in the home with his three sons; he was also a long-standing Stone Set Holder.

It took Brookstone nearly fifty years to build up the courage to kill the being and then another twenty-five to actually put the plan in motion. He needed what the old being had—the power, the prestige, and let's be honest, the house. So, he manipulated him into handing down his Stone Set to his middle son, a man hand-picked by Brookstone as the best successor. The old being was easy to manipulate, just as naïve as the rest of the PPC members. Typically, the Stone Set would go to the eldest child. Brookstone knew the eldest, knew he was just as weak as his father. So, he got to know the middle child, learned his strengths, and sold him as the best option for the Stone Set, as the next natural heir. Once the transfer was made, Brookstone gathered his courage and planned out the murder.

Brookstone does not like messes. No, a gory murder was not for him; poison was more his style. Something that had grace and elegance. A slip of a poisonous flower into the old man's breakfast and then served by the eldest son was the perfect plan. As the being died on the medical planet Meera, the eldest son was carted off to Barter on murder charges.

The middle child, now the Holder of the Stone Set, was too devastated to continue living in the house. As a gift to Brookstone for his friendship during this grim time, he gave his new friend the house while taking himself and his younger brother to a smaller home on Solax.

That was the beginning of a beautiful friendship between Rickert and Brookstone.

CHAPTER

45

lex walks across the surface of Valyrn. Before she used her Stone Set to travel from Alars, she gathered as much information about the Factions as she could. Rick and Veela were right; the two biggest Factions appear to be in the north and south poles of Valyrn. "That is where I will start," she told them while studying the map so that she could transport herself there.

She also took time to learn as much about their customs as possible.

"They may know you are a fugitive but based on what I have learned about them, they likely won't care," Rick tells her as she readies herself to make the space jump. "They don't honour the ruling or laws of the PPC. They may even welcome you more warmly because you have been cast out by the PPC. Still be cautious because if they believe that you are the creator of the army, their hospitality may be sorely lacking."

The trio says their goodbyes, and Rick and Alex space jump to their assigned destinations, leaving Veela to her mission on Alars.

Upon arriving on Valyrn, Alex does a quick scan of her surroundings. Her landing spot is ideal for a covert arrival. She chose somewhere that would be unpopulated but still within walking distance to the first Faction. At least, that is what she hopes. Because she doesn't know exactly where the Factions are, she is really hoping that her new, enhanced senses will guide her.

The land around her is filled with rolling hills and dense treetops. It is nothing like the desolate part of Valyrn she first found herself on so many months ago. This new terrain is perfect for large civilizations to go unnoticed. Using her ears, she closes her eyes and focuses, listening for any noise that isn't created by nature. Her hearing drifts farther and farther out, the noises dancing in her eardrums. At first, she is greeted by nothing but the sound of trees, wind, and wild species roaming the lands. As she extends farther out, she starts to pick up on the noise of something else. She can't quite place what the sound is, so she opens her eyes and trains them in the right direction. Using her enhanced sight, she looks for signs of heat coming from the wilderness and is surprised to see a strong heat signature coming from a valley roughly one hundred miles away.

Unsure if it is a herd of wild beings or a civilization, Alex starts to walk in that direction. Soon, she remembers that her body is built for high-speed running and opens her legs up into a jog, then a run, then a sprint. Her legs move at incredible speed as she bounces over the terrain and lands down softly, only to bounce back up again. Her body is no longer weighed down by the increased gravity of the planet. Rather, her muscles adapt and produce a stronger push with extraordinarily little effort from her. As she propels forward, her enhanced lungs work to give her oxygen, but Alex is surprised to find that they don't need to work very hard. *Nice work, Veela*, she thinks to herself as she sprints forward and leaps over a fallen tree.

It takes her just over two hours to close the distance between her landing spot and the heat signature. Alex only pauses to listen for signs of danger or to ensure she is heading in the right direction. Growing more confident that she is indeed moving toward a civilization, Alex slows down to a walk once more. At this point, her body is shaking slightly from muscle fatigue, and her new lungs burn as they try to process oxygen to feed her body.

She comes to a stop and listens once more, working to hear over the sound of her own laboured breathing. As her control returns, she becomes aware of sounds in the treetops, shuffling around her in near silence. Trying to act as if she has not detected them, she walks to the base of a large fallen tree. The tree spans roughly eight feet wide, and the centre has been hollowed out by creatures and time. She braces her hands against the edge of the tree and pretends to catch her breath. Trying to be discreet, she scans the treetops, careful not to alert the occupants to her awareness. As her eyes glide over the lowest hanging branches, she can make out shapes moving, sliding through the trees. Unable to tell if they are wild or civilized, she ducks into the tree to hide herself from view.

As her body makes the sudden movement, something cracks into the side of the tree directly where her head had been moments ago.

"I come in peace!" she yells out, but unsure if she is speaking the right dialect, she calls it out repeatedly, cycling through all the different languages she knows are native to this galaxy. On her fifth attempt, she hears a being start to speak, followed by the thump of a weapon being fired at her tree stump and then the sounds of someone being berated. "I told you not to shoot," the angry whisper floats down from the treetops.

Confused, Alex waits for someone to start speaking again. Cautiously, she raises one hand out from the tree and then another. "I come in peace," she repeats in the last dialect she tried.

Slowly, with her hands held above her head, she exits the protection of the tree and stands upright. She looks up to the treetops and is surprised to find a dozen sets of eyes staring back at her. One of the beings drops down and lands softly on the fallen tree before her, putting it eight feet higher than Alex/s head. It keeps a weapon pointed at her chest but eyes her with curiosity rather than the hostility that Alex expected.

She takes in the being's physical state and worn clothes. It is tall and muscular, the strongest being Alex has yet to come across in this galaxy, besides herself and the creature from her future vision. The being has pale yellow skin that appears darker under the shadows of the trees. It has two arms and two legs and a short midsection, making it appear stunted in growth. Everything else about the being screams 'leader'. It stands tall, confidence exuding outward. Its face is set with a strong determination with eyes hard from years of experience to back up their knowledge of life. The being appears hard and emotionless, but yet Alex is overwhelmed with a feeling of trust towards them.

Alex looks at the leader and slowly lowers her hands, careful to keep her eye on the weapon, which is still pointed at her. The being does not do anything that suggests they may shoot.

"My name is Alex; I am from planet Earth. Are you from one of the Factions?" inquires Alex in a calm voice.

The being looks at her and takes a firmer grip on the weapon, "Alex? As in Alexia Harmon? The human that was declared an enemy by the PPC and is now being hunted like an animal?"

"Yes, that's me," Alex's voice is nervous.

At the confirmation, the being drops her weapon to her hip and gives a wild smile, laughing out loud, "Welcome, Alexia! We were so hoping you would come to us." She makes a sharp whistle with her mouth. The remaining eleven beings drop down to the ground around her.

The beings are from all different walks of life, and only two of them look the same. *Relatives possibly?* Alex thinks to herself. She feels the tension leave her body as they crowd around, smiling and waving at her.

"My name is Everly, I am the Commander of this Faction, and this is our welcoming party," she motions to those around her. All the beings carry high-powered weapons that look more powerful than those equipped by the Barter guards. "Come with me; I'll take you to the main community."

Everly motions one of the beings over to her and gives some gruff orders. The being nods to her and turns back to the clan, motioning for them to follow. The beings all nod to Everly and Alexia. With quick movements, they climb back up to the treetops and disappear. "Security," Everly comments to her, "Can't have just anyone walking in here. Come, this way."

Alex follows her and comments, "I'm surprised you know who I am, yet you aren't afraid of me." She looks at Everly, still cautious that the Faction Commander may be taking her straight into a trap.

"We know who you are. We know you didn't create the creatures that threaten the civilizations. If that is what the PPC honestly believes, then they are fools." She scoffs at the mention of the PPC, as if it leaves a foul taste in her mouth.

Alex wonders what Everly means when she says, *they know who she is.* She turns her attention back to simply following the leader, who seems content to travel the rest of the distance in silence.

Alex follows Everly for another few miles until they reach a large stream. Alex steps forward, preparing to walk through the fast-flowing water when Everly roughly grabs her and pulls her back. "Not so fast; this section of the water is booby-trapped. Another security measure to keep prying eyes at bay. Listen, can you hear it?"

Alex stands still and turns her hearing toward the rushing water. Over the normal sounds of nature, Alex hears a soft hum, the sound of electricity coursing through the water. Everly walks to a large boulder and pops open a secret compartment to reveal a small control panel. As she pushes a button, the humming stops, and the water becomes harmless. "Normally, we would just swing over it," she says, motioning to the treetops, "but I'm guessing you aren't so good in the trees." She laughs to herself, not waiting for an answer.

Leading Alex through the water, she activates the energy field once more on the other side. The two women walk up the alternate side of the hill and come to rest at the top. Below them, Alex can make out an entire civilization the size of a small Earthly city. She stares in awe as beings swing through trees and run across the ground. Every being moves with a relaxed purpose, a sense of ease about them that does not come with city life. The beings look happy, content with their place in life. It makes Alex overjoyed to see.

Noticing her appreciative stare, Everly laughs once more, "Quite the sight, isn't it? Welcome to Haldree."

CHAPTER

46

L ater that night, Alex finds herself seated around a small campfire directly outside of the tent they have provided her. The quiet night air fills her lungs, bringing her into a rare moment of true peace. She reaches out to Rick, anxious to share with him what she has found and to learn about his progress.

"Hello, Alex," Rick's voice rings through as the connection is made. *"How are you faring on your adventure?"*

"Things are going better than planned. I found the northern Faction, it's a settlement called Haldree. The leader, Everly, has been very accommodating. I think she suspects I am here to seek refuge from the PPC," Alex tells Rick.

"And let me guess, you haven't had the heart to tell her the real reason? That you're there to ask them to join an army?" Rick's comments.

Alex hesitates, feeling his judgment come through, *"No...not exactly. They have been so kind, Rick! The people here are truly at peace. Their society functions like none I have seen before. Everyone has a place, and everyone contributes. It's incredible. How can I ask them to give up everything to go to war for me? A war that will surely destroy everything they have built, all to protect the very thing they are trying to escape?"*

"That's a tough one, but you said it yourself, we can't do this without them. If you don't get them to stand behind you, then we don't have a chance," Rick counters with the reality of the situation they are in.

"I know that. But that doesn't make it any easier. What if we don't need them, Rick? What if this is the future?" She looks around at the happy beings that surround her, all of them unaware of the conversation she is having in her head.

"Do you think that's possible? You are our Defender, Alex; do you think we are meant to live like them?" Rick's thought comes through.

Alex sighs, *"No, while this is a beautiful way of life, it can't exist for everyone, not at the expense of killing millions of beings to achieve it. That is too high a price to pay. You're right, Rick, we do need them, but I think I need to change my strategy. I can't ask them to sacrifice so much. I'll come up with a better plan. Hopefully, Everly will be willing to hear me out. Enough about me, how are things going with you? Any luck finding Brookstone?"*

"So far he hasn't left his home on Solax. I was able to nab some high-tech security gear from Barter, and now I can watch him through the walls of his mansion. So far, he just seems to be pacing his living room, gesturing wildly at no one." Alex can hear the concern in his voice.

"What if he uses his Stone Set to travel? Will you be able to follow him?" Alex's question comes with a worried undertone.

"No, but I will be able to use my own Stone Set to enter his house. My current plan is to wait for him to leave and sneak in. Hopefully, he has left some clues behind indicating where he is keeping the creatures."

"What if he's hidden the clues somewhere? You said he lives in a mansion; that could be a lot of searching."

"Don't worry about that; I have a lot of experience with that house, and I know where all the good hiding places are." Rick's reply has Alex wondering how he would know the mansion layout so well but leaves the question for another time.

Confident in Rick's ability, she changes the subject once more, *"Any word from Veela?"*

"Not yet. When we left her, she was going to start asking the locals about any vacant spaces. She has a colleague from Alars that she was going to reach out to, Elbee, I believe. Honestly, I have been so preoccupied with my own stakeout that I haven't had a chance to check in with her. But I trust her; she will do as she needs." Rick's trust in Veela puts Alex at ease.

"Well, then everything is going according to the plan. I'll check back in with you tomorrow; good luck."

She cuts the connection off and moves to her tent. The space is small and reminds her fondly of camping back on Earth. She sits down on the small cot, and her memory takes her to a happy place. She goes back to when she used to camp with her husband, snuggled together for warmth against the cold nights. Alex feels the warmth of his hug and lays down on the bed. As her imagination plays with the memory, she drifts off to sleep.

* * *

Alex awakens to the soft sound of beings chattering outside her tent. The sound flows through the thin walls and pulls her from her slumber. Stretching out on the cot, Alex listens contentedly to the sounds around her and smiles, taking in a deep breath of fresh air.

She pushes herself up and moves to the doorway. As she pulls at the door to step outside, she finds her path blocked by a group of small alien children. Screaming because they have been caught outside her tent, they turn to run, all except one. A small boy remains behind, and Alex assumes he is too nervous to run away. Alex takes in the alien boy; he looks oddly familiar to her, but she can't place it. While he is small, he is also strong, both physically and mentally. Alex can feel the leadership skills in his mind; he didn't stay because he was too afraid to run. He stayed to allow his friends time to escape. *Brave boy.* Alex immediately likes him.

"Hello, I'm Alex." She kneels in front of the small boy while peering into his deep blue eyes and pushes back the urge to pinch his pudgy cheeks. "What is your name?"

"Evar," he replies in a small, but strong voice.

"Hello, Evar, were you and your friends playing outside my tent?" He gives her a small nod and starts to back away, afraid he is going to get in trouble. "Oh no, don't worry, little one. You won't get in trouble with me." She smiles at him, and his little body relaxes.

"My mom says we aren't to play around the visitors, that we should give them their privacy, but we heard that Alexia Harmon had come to our Faction. We just had to see for ourselves." He looks at her nervously, like he wants to ask her a question.

"Well, go on, little one, spit it out," Alex urges him.

"Are you really the one from the prophecy?" Surprised by his question, Alex looks at him questioningly.

"What do you know about the prophecy?" She asks him.

"Our elders teach it to us. They say it's the main reason we live outside of the PPC, to keep us safe from them, from the doom they are creating for themselves. So, is it true? Are you the Defender?"

Alex continues to stare at this boy, his innocence and boldness reminding her of her daughter back on Earth. "Yes," she replies confidently. "I am the Defender. Now, tell me, little one, where is your Commander? If I'm going to be the Defender, I'm going to need her help." *That explains why Everly said she knew who I was, why she wasn't worried that I had created the creatures. She already thinks I'm the Defender.*

Evar runs ahead, leading her to the largest structure in the community. He runs inside and jumps on Everly's lap. "Mommy, she is the Defender, she said so herself." Smiling down on her son, she pats him on the head. Alex chuckles inwardly. *That's why he looks so familiar— mother and son.*

"Hush now, my son. It seems Alexia and I have business to attend to." She nudges him off her lap, "Run along and play with your friends." He scampers past Alex, throwing her a small wave, and then disappears out the door.

"That is a very sweet boy you have there," Alex calls to Everly as she approaches the seated woman.

"Yes, he is my pride and joy. Tell me, Alexia, do you have children?"

"Please, call me Alex, and yes, I do, a daughter back on Earth."

"How your heart must ache for her. How long has it been since you have seen her, held her?"

"A little over seven months now." Alex feels tears well in her eyes and a sob rise in her throat. She envies this woman for being able to be a mother to her child; she envies her ability to live a life that includes him. Alex's own life has taken her so far from her daughter.

"That is truly terrible, Alex. Family is everything here. Everything we do is in the interest of the next generations. All my decisions as Commander centre around what will be best for my son and his generation. This is why we separated from the PPC so long ago. You see, the PPC is selfish and broken. They think only of their own power and wealth with no consideration of the future. I know that you are aware of the prophecy, and I know that the PPC believes it to be fake, but you and I know better, don't we?"

"Yes, that is why I have come."

"While I am sad to hear this, I am not surprised. It was naïve of me to think you simply wanted to escape the beings that hunted you." She sighs deeply. "The prophecy is happening, isn't it? That is why foreign creatures run freely through their cities, why members of the PPC are falling."

"Yes," replies Alex

"And you believe you are the Defender?" Everly raises one eyebrow in question.

"Yes," Alex says with conviction.

Everly eyes her with a heavy gaze, as if measuring her value, her worth. After a long moment, she finally speaks. "Yes, I can see that. You have power, that much is clear, but only someone that is truly on the outside could be our Defender. You know, for a while I thought I could be the Defender." She chuckles at the idea. "Then I realized even I was not far enough on the outside. Even I was still too close to the problem to be the solution. But you, you are different, and I can see that."

Alex is humbled by her words. *How many beings in this galaxy have believed they are the Defender? Why do I believe that I am, more importantly, why do others believe in me?*

"Everly, I need your support. We have a plan to stop the incoming war, but the greater Gatlin population is not set up to defend themselves, whereas I believe you are. Am I right in thinking that you are well defended?"

Everly considers her answer carefully. "We are...but you have to understand, Alex, I will not send my people into a war that is not theirs. Even if you are the Defender."

Alex is not surprised; in fact, she respects Everly even more for honouring her people. The PPC has done nothing to help this civilization. Rather they have sidelined them, even hunted them to the point where they had to go into hiding. She can hardly blame Everly for not wanting to fight for them.

"That being said," Everly continues, "we can help you defend yourself. As you said, we are well defended, probably too well given that the threat against us is now facing its own extinction. Here is my commitment to you and your cause; we will give you weapons, everything that we can spare. What you do with them is up to you."

Alex looks at her gratefully, "Thank you, it's honestly more than I expected. I respect your life here, and I understand why you are choosing to not throw your people into a war."

"Thank you, and you should know that the support for your cause will spread beyond just my Faction. The Factions have ways of communicating. If you would like, I can send a message on your behalf asking for their support." Everly's offer is one Alex deeply appreciates.

Alex had planned to travel to all the Factions asking for their individual support, but this poses a new opportunity for her. "Everly, that would be amazing. I imagine that the other Commanders will feel the same as you, unwilling to risk their own beings, and I respect that. However, we will take any resources they are willing to spare."

"I will reach out to them and see what they can do. Here, take this." She hands Alex a small box. "This is how the Factions communicate; it's a holobox. It is tuned in to the other four Factions, plus ours. If you need us, simply click this button, and it will ring through. If we call you, the box will shake; press this button to answer."

"Thank you so much. Is there anything you need from me to help gain their support?"

Everly considers the question, and then a small smile shows across her face, "Can you tell a story to our children? They would be thrilled to say they were the generation that heard a story from the Defender. Plus, the tales of your generosity to our younger population will spread faster than your tales of need. We support each other here, Alex, and as far as I am concerned, you are one of us. Welcome to being an outcast."

CHAPTER

47

ickert has laid in wait outside of Brookstone's home for hours. He is not a patient being, so this is a challenge for him. Part of him wants to simply knock on the door and ask his old friend to let him in, both to his house and his life.

Truth be told, he misses his friend. They have had many great years together, but he could no longer stand by and watch his friend deteriorate his mind. He tried to get him to stop jumping throughout the timelines, but Brookstone was obsessed. He would not hear anything that Rickert told him. *How can I blame him?* Rickert thinks to himself. *I am exactly the same. I didn't quit even after it ruined my relationship with Veela, even when it drove Brookstone and I apart.*

Throughout his life, Rickert has accumulated a fair amount of guilt, for so many things—the death of his father, the imprisonment of his brother, the ruining of his relationship with Veela, for standing by while Brookstone destroyed himself. Sometimes, he wishes the Stone Set had never made its way into his life, that his father had never handed it down to him. He is certain that jealousy is what drove his brother to poison his father. He knows it's why his younger brother abandoned him so many years ago.

Rickert takes a shaky breath. All this time sitting still isn't doing anything good for his mind. He sighs deeply and adjusts his body, getting ready to stand up and quit. He glances through his high-tech lenses one more time and sees Brookstone start to stir. For hours, he was simply sitting in one place, perfectly motionless. It was quite an eerie thing to watch, but now he is moving. Rickert watches as Brookstone stands up and moves across the room to grab something, and then suddenly, he is gone, leaving only a slow fading heat signature in his place.

"Finally," Rickert mumbles to himself. Using his own Stone Set, he pictures the inside of the house and wills himself to travel there. With a whoosh, he finds himself inside the living room of the home.

The mansion is exactly as he remembers; Brookstone has changed little of the interior. The smooth floors shine like they were freshly washed, but Rickert knows that is a part of the design as they will always appear clean. The walls are covered in artwork, reminiscences of his father. *Strange that Brookstone kept all of this.* On the far wall is a hologram. He can picture Brookstone sitting before it, watching the Gatlin News. A long couch takes up a sizable part of the floor space, and next to it is a comfortable-looking chair. On the far side of the room is a large rectangular desk with a series of drawers. The desk is the only thing in the room that is new. The rest is exactly the same as when Rickert lived here.

The colours of the room are quite bland, which is another byproduct of Rickert's father. Staring around, Rickert is reminded of how much he disliked his father; how bland and cranky the being truly was. He regrets his death, but he does not miss him.

Shaking off the feelings of his father, he quickly moves about the living room, searching through papers on the desk and in the drawers.

Finding nothing, he moves to the main study just to the left of the room. He is careful to listen for the familiar whooshing of Brookstone returning. This room has changed substantially. His father was a tidy man, but Brookstone is not. Papers are scattered around the room, covering the walls and the floor. Rickert stares at the mess, worry for the state of his friend's mind creeping over him. There are multiple desks in this space, as if Brookstone needed one for each of his moods. Each desk is completely different from the next. One is pristine, while another is a disaster. *It's like he is a different being for each desk.* Sadness overcomes Rickert as he stares into the life of a mad man.

Rickert begins moving through the various desks, looking through all the obvious places. Next, he moves to the more secret ones. As a young being living in this house, he had many hiding spots, a few of which he had shared with Brookstone in the early parts of their friendship.

He remembers those days fondly. Brookstone was the first being to really take an interest in Rickert. Rickert was awkward as a young being, and he never had many friends. When Brookstone started speaking to him regularly, Rickert was thrilled. He craved the company, and to have a member of the PPC interested in him was beyond complimentary. The two beings spent hours together at Rickert's home. In that time, Rickert showed him all the spaces where he would hide things from his controlling father.

Snapping out of his reminiscing, he moves out of the office, through the living room, and into the entryway of the home. A large staircase flows from the main door to the second level. He climbs the stairs and moves to the third bedroom down the hall, his old room.

As Rickert opens the door, he is surprised to find that Brookstone has converted it into a second office. This one is as full of files as the main office. He moves to the lone desk and takes in all the papers strewn about. His heart drops as he finds drawings of the creatures from the future. He was still holding out hope that his friend was just simply fascinated by the creatures, but that hope is quickly vanishing. He continues to move through the files, picking up a holoscroll and rolling it open. In front of him, a series of scientific reports pop up, files on genealogy for a variety of species and their associated compatibilities.

"No, no, no! Brookstone, please tell me you didn't do this," Rickert is deeply troubled by what he sees. He moves to a small table opposite of the desk, and lifts another holoscroll; this one is definitive and with it, his hope is gone. This holoscroll holds the experimental data that Brookstone has been collecting during his trials. The trials where he watched as innocent beings were slaughtered by his creations. "Brookstone, why? Why did you do this?"

Throwing out his ideas of inconspicuousness, he stuffs the scrolls into his pockets. *This may be just the thing to clear Alex's name and put her back in control. Plus, Veela may be able to make more sense of these schematics than I can.*

Rickert feels numb as he continues to look through the office space. There is no doubt in his mind now that Brookstone is indeed the creator of their destruction. He still doesn't understand why, but he doesn't need to figure that out right now. He still needs to focus on finding the location of the creatures, where Brookstone has been hiding them.

Moving across the room, he spots his old hiding space at the back of the walk-in closet. The space is cleared out, but there are marks on the floor suggesting that someone has frequently used the space. Moving inside the closet, he pushes on the blank section of wall and feels it depress under his fingers, and hears the familiar click as the latch inside releases. The door swings open, and a small hidden compartment reveals itself. Inside are more papers and holoscrolls. Rickert pulls them out and sifts through them. His eyes land on a bill of sale for a piece of land on Zeya. "Now, why would you be buying land on Zeya?" Rickert says aloud, but before he has time to think about an answer, he hears a whooshing sound from downstairs. Quickly, he closes the hidden door behind him and uses his own Stone Set to escape.

Rickert takes himself back to Alars in hopes of finding Veela. He looks around the library space and isn't surprised to find that she is not there. They planned for this though, he knows to wait for her to return.

He sits himself down on one of the uncomfortable chairs and takes a moment to collect himself. While he has not been close with Brookstone for many years, he still finds himself feeling the familiar pull of heartbreak. The feelings of guilt and despair rock through his body. *If I hadn't left you, hadn't pushed you away, would you still have ended up on this path? Is this my fault?* Rickert breathes deeply and tries to centre himself.

He turns inward and reaches out to Alex, eager to hear a friendly voice. The connection is formed, and he feels Alex's confidence flooding his mind.

"Hello, Rick, how are things going on your end?"

"Well, I was able to get into his house, and I found what we need, but you were right, Alex, he has created an army, he is the one that will lead us to our destruction," replies Rick with distress.

Alex pauses before replying; he can feel her pity coming across the connection, *"I'm sorry, Rick, I know he was once your friend, but that man is gone. This version of Brookstone is dark, twisted."*

"I know that now. I also grabbed a few things for Veela to look over. Hopefully, she can make sense of the work Brookstone has done and find us a way to stop the army. I'm waiting for her now. How are things going for you?" Rick steers the conversation away from the painful topic that is Brookstone.

Alex fills him in on the progress she has made in Haldree, the commitment that she has gained, and the promise to spread her message.

"That's wonderful news, and I think I have collected the evidence we need to clear your name. With that, we should be able to shine the light on Brookstone and open the PPC's eyes to the menace that he has become." Rick says, feeling confident about the path they are on.

"Perfect, then I will be able to step forward as the Defender. I'll be done there soon; I just have one more thing to do. See you shortly." The connection cuts off, and Rickert is left sitting alone in the library.

CHAPTER

48

Alex sat with the young ones of Haldree for hours. She told them of adventures back on Earth, stories that she once told to her own daughter. Her heart is filled with joy as their happy faces stared up at her. The mother inside her feels the ache for her own child. As the stories finished, the children walked away smiling, but her own heart broke. *Soon*, she thinks to herself.

When she picked up her Stones on Solax, her first thought was to leave this crazy world behind and simply return to Earth. What she would have given to sneak back into her home, a home that looks exactly the way she left it nearly seven months ago, and crawl into bed beside her husband. To wake him with kisses and whisper sweet things in his ears, things to make him laugh. Then she would walk to her daughter's room and open the door on her still sleeping baby. She would tiptoe in and gently rub her back until she awakes from her slumber. Then she would embrace her and never let her go.

Yes, all these things went through her mind the moment she grasped her Stone Set. But she knew that if she left here, she would never return. She knows that every moment in this galaxy is precious because every moment takes it closer to its doom.

While Alex longs for her family, she could never live with herself knowing that she let an entire galaxy fall because of her selfishness. It was another moment when she chose her destiny over her own wants. This was another act of a Defender; the willingness to sacrifice her own life to save the lives of others, to save beings that she has no real connection to.

Alex says her goodbyes to the beings of Haldree and transports herself back to the library on Alars.

Glancing around, she finds Rick asleep in an uncomfortable-looking chair, his head lolling off to the side. She walks up to a chair next to him and sits down. She smiles as he snores lightly and decides to let him sleep. She slept last night, so her need for sleep won't arise again for another few days.

While she waits for Veela to arrive, or for Rick to wake up, she picks up a book on historical wars and flips through the pages. A chapter on civilian warfare catches her eye. She reads about a time in the galaxy when civil wars threatened the civilizations on Lillon, a planet now known for its party lifestyle.

She reads about how the members of the PPC at the time were facing a rebellion from the beings of the civilization due to the PPC meddling too much in the affairs of the planet. The civilization felt that the Stone Holders should not be allowed to come and go as they please, but they should be held to the same laws of the universe as the rest of them.

Alex finds this interesting; it is the first time she has seen anything that shows resentment toward the PPC. *Well, that does make sense. Most of the beings that I have been exposed to are either a member of the PPC or someone who works for them, besides the Factions, of course.* She thinks back to her first encounters with Stellie and Androx, servants of the PPC processes. Only Veela seems to have some hesitancy when it comes to the Stones. The idea that the civilizations once rebelled intrigues her. *Is there a potential future beyond this war where Stone Holders no longer exist?* Banking the idea for later, she moves further into the book, looking for other examples of civil wars. In the history of the Gatlin Galaxy, she comes across three more instances of civil war that centre around discontent with the PPC. *Interesting, maybe things aren't as happy and civilized as I originally thought. That explains the existence of the Factions; they likely split off after one of these civil wars and distanced themselves.*

She puts the book down and picks up another, this one featuring war-time strategies. She absentmindedly flips through the book as Rick snores beside her. Her eyes scan the pages, and her advanced mind absorbs the information at an incredible rate. Once again, a page catches her eye and she pauses, taking an extra moment to reread the content.

The book tells her of a strategy used during a war between two planets in another galaxy. One planet was highly underdefended, and a neighbouring planet felt it was their right to invade and take over their weaker neighbour.

The defenseless planet, against all odds, defeated the incoming invaders by the simple fact that they outnumbered the invaders three to one. The leaders of the planet used the civilians to build blockades and fortify homes. Then when the invaders arrived, the civilians used the objects in their homes to beat the invaders back. They threw literally everything they had at the enemy. The weapons of the invaders dropped from their hands, and the civilians charged the streets and turned their own weapons on them. Millions died, but the planet remained in the hands of its occupants. The neighbouring army retreated and never tried to invade again.

Alex reads the passage a third time and tries to picture someone as unprepared as Androx facing off against the creatures from the future. The idea makes her shiver as the real possibility of him being torn apart runs through her mind. Then she imagines the scenario where Androx is warned about his doom, where he has time to prepare and fight back. Additionally, if he has a weapon, say a weapon from the Factions, then his chances of survival increase even further.

Turning to Rick, she lightly taps him on the shoulder. He wakes with a startled snort. "Oh, my goodness, Alexia, you scared me! How long have you been here?"

Ignoring the question, she taps on the pages of the book. "I think we need to warn the people about what is coming."

"The PPC has already decided that isn't a good idea…" Rick pauses, "But keeping it a secret was our new General's idea; Brookstone was the one who was adamant that we keep the war quiet for as long as we can."

"Exactly! I think that is because he is afraid of the defenses the civilizations could put in place."

"Defenses?" Rick laughs an unhumorous laugh, "What defenses? That's the whole reason we are where we are. We have nothing."

"Not necessarily, not anymore. The Factions are going to give us everything they can to build up our defenses, but we have been underestimating the power of the civilians. We have multiple worlds of people that are sitting by unaware, waiting for slaughter. If we can reach out to them, we can rally them to protect themselves. At least until we have a chance to eliminate the army through Brookstone," says Alex excitedly.

Rick considers this for a moment, "You're right, and we have the evidence we need to remove Brookstone from his seat as General. He should be imprisoned as well, but it is awfully hard to catch a Stone Holder when they don't want to be caught, especially one that has gone insane." Alex knows that all too well from her last encounter with him. "I say we approach the PPC and show them what we have found. They already believe the prophecy is real, and when they see that Brookstone is behind their inevitable destruction, they will crumble. That's where you come in. We will rip their 'Defender' away from them and then present them with a new one. If I'm correct, they will be tripping over themselves to bow at your feet," Rickert rolls his eyes at their weakness.

"Can you call a meeting, but one that excludes Brookstone?" asks Alex.

"Yes, but word travels fast among the PPC members; he will likely find out before the meeting is done," Rickert knows how gossipy the members are.

"That's OK. As long as we have time to present our findings and put the blame where it belongs. I don't want him there, not when his mental state is so fragile. Who knows how he will react. He very well could release his army earlier than he planned," Alex rationalizes. She glances around the library one more time, ensuring that Veela isn't about to walk through the door. Following her gaze, Rick picks up on what she is thinking.

"Don't worry, she will be fine. She is a smart and capable being. I will reach out telepathically and send a message to the PPC members asking for an immediate audience." He turns inward for a moment and sends out a message. He then walks across the library and pulls out a map of Solax. "The primary meeting place of the PPC is here." He points to a location on the map.

Alex studies the map and pulls out her Stone Set. Focusing on this location, she feels herself pull away from Alars.

CHAPTER

49

Alex lands softly in the centre of a large room. The room is circular and features seats on all sides, roughly 300 chairs, enough for the entire PPC to assemble. Rick appears next to her seconds later.

"The call has been answered; I suggest you take a seat while the others arrive," Rick says to her. "I will stay here and address the crowd first."

Alex moves off to the side as beings start whooshing in, each finding their own seat. The first few members to appear notice her right away and eye her with extreme fear, but Rick reaches out to them telepathically and soothes their worried minds. As more beings filter in, Alex becomes lost in the crowd. Although all the seats around her remain open, no one is willing to sit next to her. The last few to arrive choose to stand rather than sit next to her.

Rick clears his throat loudly, his voice is amplified in the same way that Stellie's was during Alex's Cataloguing. "Thank you for joining us on such short notice."

"Where is Brookstone? He is our General, he should be here, should he not?" a yellow alien speaks out from the far side of the room.

"Not for this, my friend," Rick replies. A murmur moves through the crowd. "Brookstone has led us astray. He has made us believe that Alexia Harmon is the creator of a new army and the leader of our destruction. That is not true." The crowd around her grows more restless. "Please hear me out. I have evidence, proof that Alexia is not our enemy. Brace yourselves." Rickert pulls out the holoscroll and puts it inside a machine to his left. The holoscroll is amplified large enough for the entire room to read, and Brookstone's species notes appear. The crowd gasps as they read what has been put in front of them. "These are schematics I personally pulled from Brookstone's home. Here, we can clearly see that he has been the one engineering the new species. He is the creator of the army."

He pulls out the holoscroll and puts in another one; this time Brookstone's experiment notes flash up. The crowd roars in anger and betrayal. "Yes, here you can see that it is Brookstone who has been releasing the creatures into our civilizations. He is not our Defender; he is our destroyer."

The crowd roars, and just as Rick predicted, they begin to crumble. All around her, Alex can feel their panic rising. Her powers are bombarded with their emotions and thoughts. She covers her ears and closes her eyes, trying to block out the steady flow, but it is too much. With one last desperate thought, she telepathically screams out to them all, "*QUIET!*" she shouts into their heads. Immediately, the room goes silent. The beings in the room look around confused, and then their eyes focus on her.

"Ladies and gentlemen," Rick's voice pulls through the silence. "I present to you our true Defender."

He motions for her to come stand next to him. She stands and moves to the centre of the room, conscious that all eyes follow her. As she approaches Rick, he moves off to the side and lets her take the main stage.

Looking around nervously, she focuses her attention within; *I was made to do this.* With one final deep breath, she moves to speak. "Hello…" it comes out so much weaker than she intended.

"My name is Alex, and as you know, I am from Earth." She stops again to gather her thoughts. "I am an outsider." The crowd murmurs in agreement. "I know nothing of your worlds, of your cultures or your beliefs. Well, I only know as much as I could find in the Knowledge Computers. But that hardly shows how things really work. It gives you facts, but it will never give you feeling. Yet I have feelings, feelings about this galaxy, about the outcome of your well-being, about your future." She pauses, her confidence growing with every word.

"I also know of your prophecy." She recites it to them.

"The future holds a dark age.
The lights will dim and leave the
civilizations in darkness.
This dark age will bring death and destruction to
the galaxies, unlike any that time has seen before.

At the head of this destruction stands one being, a being that cannot be stopped by their peers, cannot be sated by power, and will not be controlled by morals. Only one being can end the destruction, only one being is powerful enough to kill that which is created and end the tyranny. They alone, this unseen warrior, are the Defender of man."

She lets the room fall to silence as her words ring around the circular space. Each being holds completely still as they soak in her words. *Rick was right, they are desperate for a Defender.*

"We have shown you who the true enemy is, Brookstone. He is the creator of your destruction. He will be the one to tear you apart, but only if you let him. I am here to tell you there is a way to stop him, to end his destruction before it rips the worlds apart. I stand before you, as an outsider, as a human. More importantly, I will stand as your Defender."

Silence follows her words. Then one by one, the beings around her stand and raise their hands to her. The gesture is silent but powerful. Open hands thrust up into the air move up and down, in what Alex assumes is a form of applause; a signal that they accept her for what she claims to be.

The silent applause carries on for several moments as Rick and Alex look around the room. Alex stares around her in shock; she didn't believe for a second that she could really pull this crowd to her side. Rick, on the other hand, stares at Alex, never having doubted her for a second.

"What will you have us do? How can we defend ourselves against an army that is beyond anything we have seen or faced before?" The same yellow alien calls out, ending the applause and shifting the crowd back into a panicked feeling.

"I have a plan, but you may not like it." She looks around at them and pushes a calming feeling out, telepathically maneuvering them into a more receptive state. Most of them respond, and she watches as they visibly relax; others are aware of her intrusion and block her, choosing to remain panicked. "I have spoken with the Factions." An unhappy murmur moves through the crowd; even those she has mentally sedated react to the word. "Hear me out. I have spoken with the Factions, and they are willing to support our defense efforts. They will be arming us with the technology and gear we need to build a strong defense. This alone won't be enough. Even if we pull all the guards from Barter and place them on all the planets, it won't be enough to stop the creatures from destroying everything. We need the civilians to fight too."

"We don't fight, Outsider." The yellow alien pushes her again. "You are new here, but we solve our problems with the Stones as we always have."

"And yet you haven't found a solution to your problem, have you?" Alex cuts him off. Not waiting for an answer, she continues, "That's because there is no answer to this problem that involves the Stones. For some reason, every path we explore, every future we see," she pauses momentarily, realizing her small slip at admitting that some members have been jumping through time. She works to remember what she was saying.

"No matter where we look, it's always the same thing. If you do what you have always done, you will be destroyed. There is no future for you unless you take a different path. That is why I am here. These Stones," she holds up her Set for them to see, "they are nothing more than a natural element to me. They are not a weapon, they are not a way of life, they are nothing but a way for the galaxies to continue moving forward. Devices that are supposed to be one with nature, not manipulated by beings like us." She lowers her arms and makes eye contact with the aliens around her. Knowing that this is the part they aren't going to like, she braces herself.

"The future does not have the Stones in it." The crowd bristles all around her. Some shout out in defiance and some move their hands protectively over their Stones, as if she is going to try and steal them away. Once again, she pushes on them mentally, willing them to calm. It takes more effort this time but eventually the crowd settles. Alex feels a dull headache forming. "For thousands of years, the Stones have been pulled from their natural intention and manipulated by beings that were never meant to hold them. When Pillar and Perma removed the Stones from their natural habitat on Solax, the entire planet rebelled. Its ability to support naturally occurring life was stripped away. Well, my new prediction is that if you don't change the way the Stones are used, then all the planets will react the same way."

"Dr. Veela has been filling me in on her research of the Stones. She has concluded that the ripple effects caused by jumping are spreading well beyond just the

Holder. It is affecting the beings around the Holder too, and eventually the effects will spread to the planets. The consequences of altering the intention of nature will catch up with you. With or without this war, you are doomed; unless we separate ourselves from the Stones."

Once again, the room is silent.

"I have a plan to ensure the civilizations are still allowed to thrive. First, we must make it through this war. There is something about the Stones that calls to our enemy; we can see that in Brookstone's notes," she motions to the holoscroll still up in front of them. "As a Stone Set Holder, you need to shift your view of them. They are no longer your tools because they are now your ending. Can you separate yourself from them? Even if you don't think the separation is meant to be forever, can you separate from them long enough to win this war?"

The crowd around her looks incredibly nervous. Some aliens nod to her, while others shake their heads. *About half are buying in; that will have to do, I guess.* Rick gives her a small nod seeing the same thing as her. Half is as good as they could hope for.

Turning back to the crowd, she addresses them one more time. "We need to rally the civilians. We cannot leave them in the dark any longer. War is coming, and we need them to be able to defend themselves. I have a plan, but I need you to communicate it."

"What do we tell them? Why would they believe us?" an unknown voice calls from the crowd.

Alex considers this for a moment, how will she convince billions of beings to rally together?

"Tell them the truth, all of it. Tell them about the enemies, about the corruption in the PPC, about how the Stones are affecting them all. Tell them everything. The civilizations are tired. Your own history shows that they have disagreed with the PPC in the past. Validate them, admit you were wrong, but tell them that you are still on their side. Tell them that you face a greater enemy that threatens you all." She pauses for a moment, letting the message sink in. She knows she is asking for a lot. After all, it's hard for anyone to admit they were wrong when there are thousands of years of history telling them that they were right.

"You need them, and you will not survive without them. If the civilizations feel that need is respected, they will rally."

Heads nod around her. Alex opens herself to the emotions in the room once more and is surprised to find how many of them feel guilty. It is as if they are hearing something they suspected to be true.

Rick moves to stand directly next to her and looks at her with admiration. "Well, friends, our Defender has spoken; now it is our duty to do as she wills us to. It's time to save the galaxy."

CHAPTER

50

eela waits nervously in her new lab on Alars. She is a scientist; war is no place for her. When word of Alex's success with the PPC reached her, she felt a sense of pride knowing her part in making Alex what she is today.

Twelve hours after their rousing speech on Solax, Rick and Alex finally met her in the library on Alars. She took them to her new lab and sat by patiently as they each filled her in on what had happened in her absence.

When it was her turn, she underwhelmed them by waving to the lab around her. "Well, finding a lab was my only responsibility, and I would say I did quite well. This is a shared space with my friend Elbee. He technically owns this space, but he is letting us borrow it for now...." Her explanation trails off in disappointment. She put in a lot of work to find this lab, but in the end, Rick will likely find Brookstone's lab first. This means that they will likely perform the required explorations there. Fortunately, the lab is still here, just in case. But her face still shows unhappiness at her lack of contribution.

"Well, now I have something for you to work on." Rick hands her the holoscrolls from Brookstone's office. "These are much too scientific for my brain, but we are hoping you can figure out a weakness in this army."

Veela looks up at him, more conflicting emotions spreading through her; war is no place for a scientist. She was not meant to look at a creature with the intention of destroying it; she was meant to save lives. Regardless, as she glances at the holoscroll she becomes aware of her role in this war. They need her to stop the creatures. Without her knowledge, they will all die. *Maybe I'm the Defender.* She laughs to herself at the idea.

She turns back to Alex and Rick and nods to them, "Leave it with me; I will find you something."

And find something she did. It took her two days, but at the end of the second day she knew everything there was to know about the creatures. Most of all she discovered their weak points. She knew that their bellies were the most likely to be penetrated by weapons, and their pincers were encased in a hard outer shell. This armour would withstand anything their weapons threw at them. Most importantly, she knew that they were all linked telepathically. An implant in their spines controls their minds, forcing their actions.

From what she can tell, the creatures are controlled by two external sources, but she was unable to pinpoint exactly what they are. Brookstone's notes are erratic. He bounces back and forth between referring to the creatures by label numbers and then names. It's hard for her to tell which ones he means.

From what she can decipher, Brookstone holds one of the controllers, and one of the creatures holds the other.

She shares this news with Rickert and Alex, pleased with herself as they react to her news.

"We can use this," Alex says to the two of them. "Rickert, have you had any more luck finding Brookstone's office on Zeya?"

"I'm getting close to a location. I've narrowed it down to a shipping yard on the far side of the planet, but the shipping yard is nearly two thousand miles long. It's taking me time to find the exact location of his lab. Somehow, he has managed to hide an entire army from detection. I'm not surprised I am having a challenging time trying to find it right away."

"Good, keep looking. Great work, Veela; if we find the lab, we can stop Brookstone and the other controlling creature before the army is released." Alex feels immense pride in her team.

"But that will leave the army uncontrolled?" Rick looks at her with concern.

"I have a solution for that," Veela cuts in excitedly. "I have been studying the technology Brookstone used to telepathically connect the beings, and I think he stole a lot of my work in the process." She furrows her brow; *How dare he use my work and research for something so dark.* "A lot of what he based his work on is what I used to enhance Alex. Essentially, the telepathic powers that connect the creatures are the same ones that Alex has in her mind. With a bit of tweaking, I can alter Alex's mind to match the frequency of the creatures thus putting her in control."

Rick and Alex look at her optimistically. "Does that mean you don't need us to capture one of the creatures?" Alex asks, hoping that part of their mission is about to change.

"Maybe, if we can find one of the sources, I can study it and then match Alexia to it. But to put her truly in control, we have to eliminate both of the other control sources. Regardless, Alexia you will still have to destroy the lead creature. As for the other controller..." She looks carefully at Rick. "I don't know how Brookstone has maintained his telepathic control over the creatures, but I fear he may have inserted a control chip into his own mind. The only way to sever that connection, I'm sorry to say, is to kill him."

* * *

Alex watches Rick carefully in the days following the report from Veela. The three of them developed a plan to find Brookstone and eliminate him, but it puts Rick in a terrible position. Alex has been looking for signs of him deviating from the plan, but so far, he hasn't shown any.

Can he really kill his best friend? Alex has wondered this question repeatedly for several days. *I have to trust him, trust that he will do what he has to.*

The plan was a mixture of all their minds: Alex lending the practical and impartial part, Rick giving them the best options when it came to the civilizations and the behaviours of Brookstone, and Veela adding a factual base to all their decisions.

The plan hinges on their ability to find Brookstone, which is why Rick is at the centre of it all. He knows the mind of that man, even if it has been twisted and torn. He is the only one that can find and stop him.

Alex is responsible for fighting on the front lines. Supporting the war efforts as it spreads across the galaxy is key to survival. She will fight alongside the civilians and the PPC members. Her goal is to find the main creature that controls the army, the one that Brookstone mentions in his notes. She needs to take this creature out to ensure she has full control of the army. Once Brookstone and the lead creature are eliminated, she will be able to assume control of the army. The last portion requires the magic hands of Veela; she will study the telepathic controller that Brookstone or the lead creature are using to control the army and find a way to transfer the control to Alex.

The three of them will meet at Brookstone's lab, and Veela will perform the surgery that is required on Alex's mind. The surgery will alter her telepathic frequency and allow her to take control to end the war.

Easy peasy, Alex says to herself. In her thoughts, there are so many things that can go wrong, so many moving parts that could fall apart and end the civilizations as she knows it. In her gut, she feels the power of her decisions, like a force is guiding her, telling her what is right and wrong. The voice of a Defender rings out in her mind.

She spends the days readying herself mentally and physically. She can feel the war approaching in her bones; she knows it is just around the corner. Brookstone surely knows what they are up to by now. It explains why he has suddenly disappeared. *Rick will find him. He has to.*

CHAPTER

51

News of the secret PPC meeting soon reaches Brookstone. He is very displeased to hear that he has been removed as General and labeled as the new enemy.

He can no longer go to his own home or any of the locations he once could have, not when his face and story of betrayal are being spread across the galaxy. He has spent the last few days living and sleeping in his office on Zeya.

He has no idea how they found the evidence to point them toward him as the guilty party, but he is grateful that he hid the location of his lab in the secret compartment at his home. He is confident that no one will look there.

"I should have been more careful, Dru, but it doesn't matter, not really. I will still be their Defender; they just can't see it right now. What do you think, Dru? Are we ready to release the army?"

Dru clicks back at him.

"I know, but every day we wait, the more defenses they put in place." Brookstone is very frustrated by the message coming from the PPC. When he built his plan, he did not consider that they would be able to look past their own vanity and reach out for help. That is not something they have ever done, so why would they do it now? *Because of her,* his own voice sneers in his head.

She was the one variability he didn't plan for, that he couldn't have seen coming. Her strategy is pathetic, though. She will do nothing but slow his army down. *I really should have put her through the jarring process sooner,* he sighs the absent thought to himself. Regardless of her efforts, the PPC will still be destroyed. They will still rely heavily on their Stones, and because of that, they will fall to their own arrogance.

He sighs at Dru and considers his options, the voices in his head telling him a million different things. One stands apart from the rest, louder; *Do it, do it now.*

Brookstone steadies himself and looks at Dru. "We do it today. Today is the day we start a war."

* * *

Alex has been impressed with the way the PPC and the civilians have reacted. Weapons have started to arrive on the different planets, graciously sent to her by the Factions. The civilians took the news surprisingly well. Many responded to the admission of guilt from the PPC with their heads held high as if to say, 'We told you so.'

"The galaxy civilizations were ready for this," Alex says to Rick as they watch the PPC members pop in and out around them. Roughly half of them have abandoned their Stones immediately after her speech, now aware of the effects that the jumping was having on their minds, regardless of when or where they jumped to.

Veela's research helped convince the others. When they finally met back up on Alars, Rick had her record a scientific message outlining her research and the results. The remaining stubborn group of PPC members were shocked to hear the terrifying news confirmed by such a respected doctor, and they too abandoned their Stones. Teleportation stations were set up at the heart of Solax to allow members to transport in and out, moving among the planets.

It was a new sensation to move through the teleportation stations, with the members having become so used to jumping and the ability to control time and space. Losing this gave them the feeling of travelling in an uncontrolled manner, like they were at the mercy of the transport lines. However, the members adapted quickly. For a few members, Alex urged them to hold onto their Stones for now so that they could spread her message more quickly and move to places that require their attention. She still reminds them constantly that when the fighting starts, they need to abandon both Stones entirely.

Alex has delegated a lot of work to the beings that know this galaxy best. The PPC members have worked tirelessly to move the guards off Barter and station them on all the occupied planets. They are now at the heart of the civilizations. They have dispersed the weapons that have arrived from the Factions and helped the civilians prepare their homes for war.

As Alex watches, she feels a vibration coming from one of her pockets. Her mind immediately flashes back to her cell phone. Remembering herself, she reaches into her pocket and pulls out the small holocube. With the click of a button, Everly appears in holographic form in front of her.

"Alex! Good to see you. I trust the weapons are arriving as promised?" Everly's smiling face and booming voice come from the holocube.

"Yes, we are working to distribute them now. Thank you, we might stand a chance. Are you sure you won't join us when it comes time to fight?" Alex tries to sway Everly one last time.

"No, Alex, this is not our battle. We will remain in our Factions and protect them if necessary. When all is said and done, come find us. We will gladly help you rebuild," Everly smiles one last time before her face disappears from the holocube.

The connection cuts out. Rick looks at Alex, "Rebuild. Funny, I have been so wrapped up in the prophecy that the future beyond it has never occurred to me. Scary to think that the life we have known for the last three thousand years is about to crash down around us."

"Scary and exhilarating," Alex says with a smile. "I see so much potential in your future, Rick. It's not scary to look forward."

"How can you see our future?" He looks at her, confused. "My Stones never take me anywhere beyond the war."

She laughs and points to her head, "This kind of seeing, Rick, my imagination."

As Rick continues to stare at her with confusion, a large gray alien hurries through the room, dodging incoming aliens and moving around chairs. He hurries up to Alex and stops just short of her with a panicked look on his face.

"Defender, reports are coming in of attacks all around the galaxy. Entire civilizations are under attack," he delivers his report anxiously.

The room around them grows quiet, and all eyes turn to Alex.

She looks at them and, in a calm voice, says, "Welcome to the war."

CHAPTER

52

The room around her erupts into motion at the word 'war.' Alex has been prepping them for this moment; she watches the members of the room drop their Stones and leave the room, readying themselves to defend Solax. Other members across the galaxy will be doing the same thing. They are all leaving behind the safety of their Stones to walk into the unknown. Or at least Alex hopes they are. She places her own Stone Set into her pocket as she will need hers to jump to Zeya once Rickert signals her. She looks at Rickert, they know their roles, and he is the only other being who will keep his Stone Set.

She watches as he grasps his Stones. Giving her one last look, he whooshes away to Zeya. He claims to have found Brookstone's office and should be headed there now. The faster he moves, the sooner this war may be over.

Alex takes a deep breath and moves to exit the room. During their planning, Rick came to the theory that Brookstone would try and destroy the PPC first. This place would be his main target. So, Alex has placed herself purposefully on Solax to help defend what she can. However, if the main creature that controls the army does not appear here, she will travel to the other planets to find it.

The Factions' weapons are of incredible quality and design. With the supplies sent to her, the cities were able to outfit the boundaries with laser fields that will electrocute any beings that make contact, but Alex realized that this barrier also traps everyone in the cities. In the three days of preparation time they had, they spent time evacuating those that could not fight, and then fortifying the homes and shops of those who could. Large bombs were placed in central locations, and civilians were given guns with instructions to aim for the creature's bellies.

Alex has her own set of special weaponry and armour. Physical armour is rare in this galaxy as there has been no need for it, but one of the Factions on Lillon had been studying ancient wars and recreated a high-tech assassin's suit made entirely out of alien material. The suit glides with Alex's skin and gives her one hundred percent mobility. If it is damaged, it has the ability to repair itself. If she takes a direct hit, the suit can absorb roughly fifty percent of the damage before Alex is injured.

The weapons she received were also tailored just for her. The news of her double-headed blade that she used during the Cataloguing process spread, and a blacksmith on Trayton was able to recreate it for her. She now stands with the dual-action blade attached to her forearm. The bomb launcher that helped her kill the spider creature during her Cataloguing is now slung over her shoulder.

Strapped to her leg is a pistol with a triangular barrel and an internal crystal that will harness the atmospheric energy and concentrate it into a deadly ball of power. Lastly, there are two small knives sheathed between her shoulder blades. Between the weapons and the armour, Alex certainly looks the role of a Defender. No being in this galaxy has ever seen someone outfitted for the purpose of war.

Stay alive, find the creature, kill it, and then get to Rick. Easy. Her thoughts run through the steps she needs to take, repeating them to herself as she exits the building.

As she steps out into the cooling air of Solax, she is surprised to find it is quiet. They don't know exactly how the creatures are being moved between the planets. Since they are originating from Zeya, the planet of transportation, it's likely they will teleport in using the established lines or arrive by carrier ship.

To plan for both scenarios, Alex had each planet build up reinforcements in those areas, using the guards from Barter as the primary supporters.

She steps further out and away from the building, waiting for the sounds of war to greet her, but from what she can see, nothing is happening. She turns to one of the PPC members next to her, "Any word on how they have been arriving?"

He checks his holoscroll, "Most have been through carrier ships that seem to be landing directly into the middle of the cities."

"That makes sense, but why aren't they here yet? I thought this would be the first place they hit." As the last word leaves her mouth, she feels a rumbling beneath her feet. Looking down, panic races through her, "What is beneath us?" she shouts at the PPC member.

"Just an empty cave, it's rumoured to hold the Stones, but no one has explored it in ages."

Alex immediately realizes her mistake, *Brookstone knows about that cave, and he knows that it opens up right under the heart of Solax.* "Everyone, run!"

The crowd around her looks confused, but they take her advice and run in opposite directions. Alex turns to run back toward the building as the ground beneath her collapses, and she is sucked down into the ground. Rocks and concrete crush her body as she tumbles down fifty feet into the cave. Around her she can hear the whooping sounds of the creatures as they move past the debris and flood up to the surface, ready to start their hunt.

She gasps and coughs for air, dust filling her lungs. Scanning her body, she feels that her left leg is trapped under a large boulder. She uses her strong arms to try and shift the boulder, but it is not enough. As she continues to struggle, another PPC member comes rushing down to her aid. As he reaches her, he gives her a brief smile, "Look at me, saving the Defender!" Before he can do more than place his hands on the rock, a large pincer erupts through the centre of his chest. Blood runs down his body and bubbles out of his mouth as he tries to breathe. The creature lifts him into the air and throws his dying form against the wall. Alex looks up in terror as her leg pinches under the large boulder that still traps her in place. She is now at the mercy of this creature.

The creature looks down at her and lifts its bloodied pincer, ready to skewer her. She scrambles for either of her guns, but they are trapped against her pinned body. As the creature swings down to contact her chest, Alex throws her arms out and the blades on her forearm spring forward. The protective shell on the pincers is too thick for the blades to do any real damage, but it does throw the creature off balance. As the creature lunges forward, its belly exposed, and Alex thrusts her blades up into it. The heavy being flops down on top of her.

Great, now there are two heavy things crushing me.

All around her, Alex can hear weapon fire, the screaming of beings as they are slaughtered, and the whooping of the creatures as they run around the land as if it is a giant playground built just for them. Smoke drifts towards her as the city of Solax starts to burn.

Alex continues to struggle to free herself from the weight until she finally remembers the Stones in her pockets. Cursing herself for being so slow, she pulls them out and transports herself to the more stable surface of Solax once more.

She was right; the city around her burns. The members of the PPC stand by as their homes burn to the ground. Far off, Alex can hear the electrical fields zapping and stinging as beings try to flee through it. She can only hope that the creatures pursuing them are also destroyed.

On the battlefield in front of her, a close combat war rages on, but it is heavily one-sided. She scans the ground and sees the yellow alien that was so outspoken at the PPC meeting. He is on his knees with his back turned to her, seeming to look for something. Alex looks for danger and then approaches him. As she rounds to face him, she has to fight to not scream. Most of the alien's face has been obliterated, and his one remaining ear is dripping a steady stream of blood. His left arm is missing as well. *That must be what he is looking for.*

Alex looks at him with pity. "Help me?" he says up to her, the sound coming out as a gurgle, blood spewing from his mouth.

"Yes, I will help you." Alex walks around behind the alien, levels her gun at the back of his head, and pulls the trigger.

* * *

Rickert lands in the large shipping yard on Zeya. He knows that Brookstone's lab is here. He has been studying the layout exclusively for the past three days. Reports are coming in that majority of the creatures are arriving by aircraft carrier. This means that there is a location here somewhere that suddenly has fewer ships. Rick pulls out his holoscroll and scans through the information he pulled on this location.

"Aha," he says out loud. According to his notes, there should be eighteen shipping freighters in the northern dock, but from what he is looking at right now, there are only five.

Rick searches for the building that manages the north dock. Finding it, he makes note of the sign on the door that says 'Vacant' and then another sign that says 'Danger, do not enter.' *If it's empty, why is it dangerous? This is it; it has to be.*

Rick opens the door and steps inside. The front office is very plain, nothing that would suggest something sinister is happening. Moving farther into the space, he notices a door behind the desk. The doorway leads to a set of stairs taking him down into an underground cavern. Stepping down the stairs Rick hears movement below.

He makes a quick connection to Alex, *"I have found Brookstone's office space. It is in shipping yard G on Zeya, far left corner. Come when you have found and killed the other controlling creature."* He doesn't wait for a response before cutting off the connection.

Taking care to move quietly, he walks down the stairs, and he can hear the movement of a single being in the room below.

"Brookstone? It's me, Rickert. I'm going to come into the room, OK, I just want to talk."

The shuffling stops, and Rick can hear Brookstone breathing. Cautiously, he steps out into the open room. On one side, he sees a desk that is littered with papers; on the other side, he finds a wall covered with the prophecy. He turns to his friend. Brookstone looks tired and old, which is exactly the way Rickert feels.

"What has happened to us?" he asks. Brookstone looks at him with a confused look on his face. "Was it the Stone travel? Was it the prophecy itself? We were so close."

Brookstone considers the questions for a moment and then begins to laugh. "Oh, Rickert, this was always our destiny; I am the Defender. I had to be on the outskirts. You were merely a stepping stone to my final role."

"I don't believe that. Two hundred years ago, you sought me out; you wanted to be my friend. You found me. If I was just a means to an end, then why put in all the effort?"

"I needed things from you. I needed the social standing that your father offered, and you were so desperate for a friend, and your father was so easy to manipulate. Yes, I will admit that you did grow on me. My feelings for you grew beyond what I expected them to. It nearly cost me everything." He pauses and looks Rickert in the eye, his face growing softer. "I loved you, you know. Truly and deeply, but you were a fool, and I could see that from a million miles away. I thought for sure that killing your father would push you into my arms, but instead, you ran to that stupid doctor."

"What?" Rickert's face goes pale, and he stares at Brookstone. "What do you mean 'killing my father'?"

"Oops, I guess that secret is out. I killed your father. It simply had to be done. Like I said, I needed what he had, and you were so much easier to manipulate than him. While he was old, he was still determined to live for a thousand more years. As long as he was alive, he would always be the primary leader of the PPC, and that was supposed to be my role. He had to be eliminated. Plus, I really wanted his house."

Rickert cannot speak; he cannot breathe. All these years, he has blamed himself, his brother for the death of his father. To find out it was his best friend; there is no recovering from this.

Without thinking, Rickert pulls a concealed weapon from his sleeve and lunges for Brookstone. The being doesn't expect the quick movement, and the blade strikes deeply into his abdomen. As Brookstone tumbles back and Rickert breathes with rage while ripping the weapon from Brookstone's stomach and tearing open a substantial portion of flesh. As the two grapple, a bracelet that was concealed under Brookstone's robe becomes dislodged and falls to the ground.

As the being grasps at his bleeding stomach, he stumbles back against the wall, looking horrified at Rickert. Rickert stares at him as he watches the brown alien that he has known all his life transform into something else. The distinguishing features that made Brookstone into the alien he was disappeared, leaving a human standing in his place.

"NO!" Brookstone howls and lunges for the bracelet.

Rickert is stunned into silence and unable to move. He watches the wounded human shuffle across the ground, trying to grasp the bracelet and get it out back on. Coming to his senses, Rickert moves across the room and kicks the bracelet out of Brookstone's reach.

The man lies on the ground in a sad ball, terrified to have his secret revealed like this. Rickert looks around the room and locates Brookstone's Stone Set. They are safely across the room, well out of the reach of the injured human.

"Brookstone...what is going on?"

Brookstone whimpers from the pain in his belly, blood steadily rushing out of the wound. He looks up at Rickert, seeking pity in the eyes of the being he once loved. Finding none, his head flops back down toward the ground. He begins to cry softly, all the fight leaving his body.

"Two hundred and fifty years ago, I was a junior scientist on Earth. Our technology was laughable, and it made the study of space challenging. My entire family was full of scientists; something in our bloodline called us to the stars. I had spent so much of my life wanting more but never having the opportunity. I was out one night studying the sky as I had done a million times before, but something about this time was different. As I watched the stars, a light flashed across the sky and blinded me. That's when I found the Stone Set. They came to me. They chose me. At first, I didn't understand them. They told me that I was supposed to protect them. Their communications danced in my head every time I was near them. They were urging me to keep them safe and to keep them on Earth."

"For many years, I did nothing with the Stones. Eventually, I grew too curious, and I started to study them. I was trying to understand how they worked and what they did. One evening, after a long day of studying a far-off galaxy through a telescope, I returned to the Stones and placed them in my hands. My mind was still thinking of this galaxy, and without warning, I was suddenly transported away from Earth and brought to a foreign land."

"As you can imagine, I almost lost my mind. I was an undefended human moving about this desolate planet. I quickly transported back to Earth and shoved the stones away, terrified of their potential. Fortunately, my fear didn't last long. It was only a few weeks before I was out exploring the galaxies once more. With every jump I made, I would spend weeks in the new location, studying the planet and the space that surrounded it. For months, I kept landing on places that hosted no life, until I found Gatlin."

"Gatlin was the first time I came across another living species, the first time I was exposed to an alien. Luckily, I had been preparing myself for this. I knew that there had to be more than just humans out there. I landed myself on Solax, and that's when I met your father. He found me in the cave of the Stones and took me under his wing. He kept me hidden from the rest of the PPC members, knowing that they would never accept a human as one of their own. He helped me learn their mannerisms, gave me access to the technology to change my appearance. Then he introduced me to the PPC, and the rest is history."

While Brookstone tells his story, his complexion grows pale from blood loss. His body has started to sag, and his breathing now sounds laboured. Rickert just stares at him. He remembers a time when his father seemed to distance himself from the family. He thought it was just something to do with his responsibilities to the PPC; never could he have imagined that he was harbouring a human.

"I don't understand, Brookstone. Why would my father help you?"

"Don't you get it? He was the one who introduced me to the prophecy. He is the one who knew what was coming. Because of him, I knew my role as the Defender."

"My father is the one who told you that you were destined to be the Defender? Then why did you kill him?" Rickert's entire life is being turned upside down during one conversation.

"As time went on, your father changed. He became weak with old age, not truly supporting the prophecy. He was no longer an asset in my plan. I was sorry to do it since he was like a father figure to me as well, but it had to be done." He pauses, "Did you know my real name is Allan? No, of course you don't." He laughs lightly to himself, then winces from the pain. "I haven't told anyone my first name in nearly two hundred and fifty years. Well, it's only fitting that it is you that knows." His face grows sad, "I wish things had been different between us. I wish you had loved me the way I loved you. Part of me wants to simply jump back and start all over again, but I know it doesn't work that way. I know the damage I have caused." Brookstone is now lying on the ground in a puddle of his own blood. Rickert comes to stand over him.

"I think I'm dying, and to be honest, I think it's what I deserve. Something went wrong in my destiny. I was supposed to be the Defender, but I think I did something wrong." His voice is trailing off, and his eyes now look through Rickert rather than at him. "Can you forgive me?"

Rickert looks down at his old friend and kneels on the ground beside him, tears streaming down his face. He takes Brookstone's dying face in his hands and strokes his cheek.

Brookstone closes his eyes at the comforting sensation and lets out a rattling breath.

Rickert continues to stroke his old friend's face and then moves his head to look him in the eyes. "Brookstone, Allan, you were my oldest friend. You were the one I leaned on when my life was the hardest. You were the one that brought me into the prophecy and showed me just how powerful I could be. You were everything, but no, I can never forgive you." And with that, Rickert lets Brookstone's head fall to the ground and walks away from the dying man.

CHAPTER

53

A lex feels nothing as she moves through the war scene in front of her. Her mind has become robotic, moving into survival mode to get her through this time. *Don't feel, don't let it in.*

So far, all the creatures Alex has gone up against seem to be just another member of the army. Nothing makes them stand out; nothing makes them special. Alex moves her body through the destruction with a gracefulness that she didn't know she had. She slices through the bellies of creatures while dodging around razor-sharp pincers. She watches as most of the fighters around her fall to the loud whooping sound of the creatures, but her superior ears reduce the noise to nothing more than an annoying sound.

She has seen the killing power of these creatures up close. She is pleased to find that they were right about Brookstone, that his main target was the PPC members. At first, she watched in terror as one of the creatures circled a PPC member, hunting him. As it moved within three feet of the member, a large black bubble snapped up around them, plunging them into complete darkness. Alex couldn't see anything within the blackness, it was as if the light had been pushed from the space. Then the cold started to radiate from the space, like the heat was being sucked out. At first, Alex didn't understand what was happening, but then she realized that the creatures were neutralizing the Stone's capabilities.

All the Stone Holders that did not take her advice and leave their Stones behind have fallen to the creatures. All the beings that dropped their Stones and replaced them with weapons have survived. So far, only about a third of the PPC members have truly left their Stones behind. This means that the PPC is falling, just as Brookstone planned.

Alex moves into a quick run and uses her body mass to slam into the back of a creature that is currently devouring the body of a dying PPC member. As the creature stumbles forward, she dives below its stomach and fires her pistol upward. The creature splits in two and green fluid splashes over Alex. *Disgusting,* she thinks to herself as she moves to stand and looks for her next target. The army is never-ending; they seem to keep coming from within the depths of the cave, now skittering over the surface like a swarm of bugs.

Alex stops for a moment and realizes that none of them are flying. She recalls the vision that Rick had shown her so many months ago and recalls the being, that one was definitely flying.

Quickly, she reaches out to Rick. *"Rick, where was that image you showed me? The first image of the creatures? Where were you when you were confronted with it?"*

Rick's voice comes across distant and sad, *"It was on Valyrn; why?"*

"I think we got it wrong. I think the leader of the creatures is on Valyrn, not Solax." She curses to herself; all that time wasted here. She is about to break off the connection when Rick's sad voice comes through again.

"Brookstone is dead. He was controlling the beings via remote, but I don't know where he has hidden it. I'm reaching out to Veela now to get her to Brookstone's lab. If we are going to figure out the exact frequency that we need to take control of the army, she will need the main creature. Alex, we need the creature alive. Can you do that?"

Alex's thoughts spin in her mind. Killing the creature was one thing, but taking it alive, that's a whole different problem. *"I can try, but how will I knock it out? From what I can tell, these creatures can't be simply knocked unconscious from impact."*

Rick is silent for a moment, his sadness radiating through their connection. *"Did the Factions send anything for sedation?"*

"Not that I saw. Does Brookstone have anything in his office?" Alex can feel Rick become distracted as he looks around the office.

"Yes, he has a tranquilizer gun here with a heavy sedation serum in it. Where are you? I'll bring it to you."

Alex rushes away from the main battlefield and enters a small house, one that is not yet on fire. She sends a mental image of the home through to Rick, and with a whoosh, he appears in front of her. He hands her the dart gun and then disappears back to Zeya, mumbling something about needing to meet Veela.

Alex spends a brief moment worried about her friend; about what he must have gone through to ensure that Brookstone was killed, but she has no more than a moment to spare. She tucks the new gun into her armoured pockets. Grabbing her Stones, she makes the space jump to the centre of the main city on Valyrn.

The scene she jumps into is exactly what Rick had shown her so many months ago. The large light that shone over the city has collapsed, leaving fires blazing all around. The city burns as creatures roam freely. Civilians run through the street, some armed with weapons gifted to them by the Factions. Others run with nothing but items found in their homes: pots, pans, shoes. Nothing that will kill a creature, but it may slow them down. That is all Alex expects, slow them down.

She winds herself through the streets and looks up toward the sky, trying to find the flying creature. Every corner she takes, every alley she walks down, she is faced with more creatures. They swarm through the city. As she travels, she does what she can to kill the ones that stand in her way. Slaying the beasts with her large guns where she can but relying on close combat if she must. She has found the beasts lack skill when it comes to fighting up close. They seem to rely mostly on the loud whooping sound that they can emanate to incapacitate their victims. When the noises don't work on Alex, they wave their pincers around wildly, hoping for contact. She can easily evade these erratic movements and slip underneath them to strike for their hearts.

She moves farther out from the centre of the city where the defenses set up by the PPC are less, and this is where she finds it.

The tallest creature Alex has yet to see stands roughly thirty feet in front of her. Its wings spread wide, having just landed on the ground, looking for its next target. The creature is facing away from Alex as she ducks behind an overturned vehicle on the side of the street and hides herself from view. Peering through the broken windows, she watches the creature as it folds its wings in and looks around, calculating its next move. The being turns, and Alex is once again struck by the humanness of its eyes. Although Alex is hidden, it becomes obvious the being can sense her. The creature moves toward the car that Alex is hiding behind, using its tall legs to take large, strong steps.

Suddenly, it stops moving and trains its eyes on her exact position behind the car. It crouches down and clicks in her direction. Then Alex feels something calling her telepathically. It's not a sound that she recognizes; it's definitely not Rick. Cautiously, she opens herself to the incoming call.

"Hello, Alexia Harmon," the creature's thoughts come through in a raspy alien voice.

Alex's heart goes cold, and she braces herself against the car for support.

"I see you have increased your powers beyond what Brookstone knew them to be. How exciting. I always knew he would misjudge you, underestimate you. He was a fool. While I am grateful to him for creating me, that is the extent of my feelings for the being. His weakness is

more than I care for. He has too much emotion in his deteriorating mind. I could sense it; he loves." The way the creature says 'loves' makes Alex feel dirty, like it's incredibly weak to love. Her heart seems to beat slower as she listens to the voice in her head.

"*But you, Alexia Harmon, you are stronger; I can feel that. While you have similar weaknesses to Brookstone, you are not blinded by them. You are not shattered like he was. No, I think you are rather cold, like me. If given the choice, you would give it all up, just for the power. That family you have, the one that floats in the back of your mind, you don't really care for them. You know your future isn't with them. It's here, in this galaxy.*"

Alex feels herself jumpstart back into action. At the mention of her family, her mind starts working again. Blocking herself off from the alien's telepathy, she pulls out her tranquilizer gun and readies herself.

She opens the connection back up, "*What exactly are you?*" This part is about stalling and distracting.

"*Well, I think I am many things. From what I gathered, Brookstone has pieced me together from a variety of species, taking the strongest parts of them. Do you like my eyes? They are based on his own, which are human, I believe. My sight comes with upgrades, of course, so maybe they are more like yours.*"

Alex doesn't have time to process what the creature is telling her. She is shifting her body weight back and forth to test how sensitive the creature's hearing is. As she watches the creature through the broken car windows she sees its eyes shift, following her every movement. There will be no way to sneak past the creature, so all of the combat must be head-on.

Alex turns back to her weapons and makes sure everything is set up. She forms her plan of attack in her mind, working through the motions. With her mind distracted, she nearly misses that the creature has stopped talking. Alex glances back to where it was standing, going cold as she realizes it is gone. Frantically, she looks around, desperately to find where the creature has gone. Her eyes glance up to the sky and find the creature circling her like a hawk, its eyes trained on her.

Alex aims her gun up to the sky and fires. The tranquilizer dart soars by harmlessly, and the creature whoops at her in laughter. *"Alexia Harmon, we are at an impasse. You believe you are the Defender, and I believe you are right. But you also believe that Brookstone was the destroyer in your prophecy and that is where you are wrong. I am your destroyer, Alexia. I will be the one to end your worlds, to turn out the lights in this galaxy, and make the civilizations crumble."*

With that final thought still floating in her mind, the creature dives at her. It comes down spinning through the air, wings tucked in tight, its body in a missile position. Alex makes a split-second decision and jumps sideways, rolling out of the way. The creature predicts her movements and slams into the ground feet first, moving immediately into a charge toward her.

Alex rolls away and works to find her footing. Jumping to her feet, she leaps backward as the creature barrels toward her. Using the momentum from the creature, she grasps it by the wings and pulls it down on top of her. The two beings crash down together, and Alex wraps her legs and arms around it while using her muscles to pin the pincers and wings down. Unfortunately, from this position Alex is exposed to its wide mouth and many teeth. She tries desperately to stay clear of the teeth. The creature's long nose wraps around the back of Alex's head and pulls her in, the razor-sharp teeth latch onto her neck.

Alex screams as teeth dig into her flesh and tear away the skin. Blood shoots from her neck and runs down to the ground, a pool forming below her. Quickly her pain turns to rage. She uses her heavy mass to roll the creature to the ground so that she is on top. With a roar that alarms even Alex, she rips her neck away from the creature's mouth and smashes her head back into the creature's face.

The motion leaves them both dazed. Alex now has a new cut across the top of her forehead, and the creature's nose is split open.

They stumble apart, and Alex reaches for her tranquilizer weapon once more, but before she can bring it up and fire, the creature takes flight. She feels the mental call from the creature, but this time the creature is angry, *"There is no point in fighting, Alexia Harmon. I am your end. While you may be the Defender, I was created to be the destroyer. You cannot stop me, despite how strongly you believe. I will not be put down by you."*

"You know, you talk a lot," Alex responds. "If we are going to keep doing this dance all day, I should at least know your name?" Alex looks up at the creature and watches it circle.

"Name? Well, Brookstone called me Dru. I suppose you could say that is my name, but it doesn't matter, not really. I was not built to have a name; I was built for a purpose, and right now, you are standing in the way of my purpose." The creature dives at her again, her positions and motions exactly the same as before.

This time Alex is expecting it, and instead of jumping to the side, she flops to the ground and throws her feet up into the sky. As the creature slams into her outstretched legs, Alex feels her reinforced bones start to bend as the alien metal strains against the force. The plan works; Dru is thrown to the side, and the wings that were wrapped around her body are shredded by the jagged pavement as she skids along the ground.

Dru stands up and stretches out her wings. Realizing the extent of her damage, she roars in anger. Letting out a massive whoop, she lunges for Alex. Alex pulls her tranquilizer weapon up and lets loose a series of shots. Dru throws her wing up to protect against the incoming bullets, but a large hole lets one tranquilizer through. It sinks into her neck. Dru stumbles backward and uses her nose to pull it out. Looking at the tranquilizer with confusion, she continues toward Alex. Her feet begin moving with unstable wobbles as the tranquilizer works into her system.

Quickly, Alex pulls the trigger again, but no shots fire. Realizing she has run out of ammo, she changes tactics and moves to hand combat. She releases the blades from her forearms and plants her feet on the ground. *Don't kill it, Alex; we need it alive. But alive doesn't mean completely unharmed.*

Alex slashes out at the creature's pincers and feels her blades lock against its thick armour. The two beings struggle against each other, finding they are equal in strength. Alex has studied combat, an area where Dru and all the creatures seem to be sorely lacking. *Your mistake Brookstone; an army kept in cages is a sloppy army in the field.*

She feigns left, and as Dru moves to follow her, Alex ducks down and pulls the blades free. With the creature's pincers no longer restricted, Dru's momentum plunges her forward. Alex side steps and forces the blade up under Dru's pincers, making contact with the soft side of her body.

Dru wails in pain and stumbles away. Alex feels the creature trying to make a mental connection with her once more. As the creature knocks on her mind's door, Alex takes the time to reload her weapon.

"No, I'm done with talking. Your time's up, bitch." Alex lifts her newly loaded weapon and fires three rounds of tranquilizers into the creature's stomach.

Dru stumbles back and looks down to where the tranquilizers stick out. Her feet stumble under her, and she crashes down, her pincers splaying out at awkward angles.

As the dust settles, Alex approaches the creature with caution and taps its leg with her foot. Then she uses the barrel of her weapon to poke it in the eye. *No one can fake being asleep when they are poked in the eye.* Satisfied that the creature is indeed unconscious, she reaches out to Rick to tell him the good news.

"Rick, I've neutralized the main creature. I'm ready to transport her to you. Where is the nearest transport

station?" She gives him a brief description of where she is on Valyrn.

"Just a few blocks from you, you'll have to drag the creature and then use its pincer to press the destination button for Zeya. It will then be transported here, where we are ready to receive it." Rick replies, relieved that Alex has found the leader.

Alex sighs at the effort before her. *"Is Veela with you?"*

"Yes, she is ready with the cart to move the creature from the transport station to the lab. Everything is set up for your surgery." Rick replies.

"OK, I'll see you in ten minutes." Alex cuts the conversation off and turns back to the creature. The scene around her is morbid. All around her, buildings are on fire. Beings run and scream in terror as creatures chase after them. The air is filled with smoke and harsh lights flickering from the flames. Alex glances up at the infrastructure that maintains the ecosystem for the planet. It, too, is on fire. *It's only a matter of time until it stops functioning and the life support that we all depend on is gone.* The thought terrifies her, forcing her mind to run wild as she imagines herself, and all the others, suffocating to death.

Quickly, she grasps her prey by the feet and starts dragging the heavy thing down the block. She doesn't make it far before she encounters another creature. This one looks from her to the leader on the ground. With a loud whoop, it lunges after her. Alex lifts her weapon and fires. The creature drops to the ground as the tranquilizer knocks it unconscious.

Alex takes a moment to reload her weapon with bullets that are meant to kill and walks over to the creature, firing a round between its eyes.

She jogs back to Dru and continues dragging her down the street. She closes the gap to the transport station, only stopping to kill creatures as they confront her. As she gets closer to the station, she notices the creatures are starting to get denser, causing her to stop more often and fight to defend herself and her captive.

After fifteen minutes of fighting and dragging, she feels Rick knocking. Killing a creature by sliding her arm blades into its head, she answers the call. *"A little busy here, Rick."* She yells to him mentally, turning her attention back to dragging Dru.

"Well, you need to speed it up. I'm getting reports from the remaining PPC members that the creatures are starting to converge on the transport stations, all of them heading to Valyrn. They know you have their leader, and they are coming to rescue it."

CHAPTER

54

A lex feels the panic rise in her chest. Dru must have sent out a distress call before she was knocked unconscious, and now all the creatures are about to converge on her. She looks around, desperately planning the fastest route to the teleportation station.

The station is only two blocks away, but at the pace she is moving, it could take nearly thirty minutes to cover the distance. Her eyes land on one of the hovercrafts she once saw the beings of Valyrn travelling on. Quickly, she runs over to it and picks it up. The thing sparks and spits at her, clearly damaged. She finds the on switch and flips. With a shutter and shake, the hovercraft hums to life. Placing it on the ground, she is pleased to find that it floats six inches above the ground. She darts back to the unconscious Dru and forces the machine under the shoulders of the creature. Then she grabs its feet and takes off at a fast run. With the assistance of the hovercraft, Alex is able to cover a full block without needing to slow down.

As she approaches her final block, she skids to a halt. Coming through the transportation station are hundreds of beings. They flock through the station and begin to sprint straight for her. Alex turns hard on her heels. Still dragging Dru behind her, she sprints in the opposite direction.

"Rick!" she screams out telepathically for him.

"What is it?" his voice mirrors the panic in hers.

"There are too many creatures coming through the teleportation station. I need another way off this planet." There is silence from the other side of the connection while Rick talks with Veela to develop a plan. *"Now, Rick!"* she screams at him.

The army behind her is closing in fast. Even without dragging Dru, she won't be able to outrun them; their legs move with incredible speed and strength.

"Alexia, you need to get the creature back to the centre of the city. There are Barter Guards there that have been defending the central transport station. They can provide cover fire for you while you get the creature to the station and teleport it here."

"But they will all be slaughtered!" Panic races through her body as she realizes the weight of what she must do.

"It's the only option we have. It's either them or everyone in the galaxy," Rick states the reality of the situation. Alex agrees, even though it goes against every one of her instincts.

Alex continues to sprint forward but changes her direction slightly, pointing her toward the city centre. She feels the tears running down her cheeks as she brings the mass of the army straight into the unsuspecting guards and civilians. *I'm sorry. I am so sorry,* she thinks to herself as she rounds the final corner. Her lungs and legs burn from exertion. The back of Dru's head is leaving a trail of thick green blood; the back of her scalp has been sheared off as it bounces along the ground. An unfortunate by-product of being dragged across the concrete at high speeds.

The armed forces that have been holding the city centre are shocked to see her sprinting toward them at full speed, dragging one of the creatures behind her. They start to cheer and applaud her as they see their Defender approach, but then their shouts turn to screams of terror as they see what follows her.

Alex feels her heart break as she watches the crowd around her start to scream and run. Most of the civilians do not try and fight; they simply turn and flee in the opposite direction. It is only the guards of Barter that stand their ground, aiming their weapons past her at the incoming army. They open fire, and Alex feels the wind around her jump and shift as the bullets fire around her.

She charges through the wall of guards and heads straight for the still secure teleportation station. She skids to a halt, and Dru smashes into the wall of the station. Alex looks around and realizes this is the same station that brought her to the centre of Valyrn so many months ago.

With hurried motions, she grabs Dru and hauls her off the hoverboard then lifts one of her heavy pincers up to the transportation button for Zeya. With a whoosh, Dru disappears before her eyes.

Alex looks around at the war scene and watches as the army around her collides with the few beings left standing. They are annihilated instantly. The front of the army uses their pincers to slice the guards' bodies and cut the beings in half. Those that run are chased down and slaughtered like animals. The army barely slows as it heads for their final target, her.

Turning back to the transport station, she levels her weapon at the control panel. She doesn't want the army to follow her through, so she pulls the trigger, and the panel explodes. Stepping outside the station, she turns her bomb weapon on the remaining two stations. With an impressive explosion, the stations erupt and burn before her eyes. Turning one final time, she faces the army head-on. Fire rages all around her as the enemy surges towards her. The sky is dark, the light over Valyrn having fallen, casting the city into dark shadows. The stars of the foreign galaxy beyond the planet dance in the dark sky. An intense feeling of rage washes over Alex. She raises her arms and screams at the large mass as they converge toward her. Suddenly, the image on Rick's wall flashes before her mind. *This was always the prophecy. It wasn't my army I stood in front of, it was the army of the enemy.* She takes one more second and then the army is on her. Pincers and mouths fly toward her as she grabs her Stone Set and teleports to Zeya, leaving the entire civilization of Valyrn to be destroyed.

CHAPTER

55

A lex lands on Zeya, her heart still races from the battle she left behind on Valyrn. Her current landing location is entirely different from what she just escaped. Rick told her where to find Brookstone's office, but the teleportation station that she used to send Dru through is nowhere near this location. This means that Rick and Veela are not here to greet her.

Alex takes a moment to absorb her surroundings and catch her breath. She reaches out to Rick, *"Did you get her?"*

"Yes, Veela is giving it another round of sedatives to keep it unconscious. There are no signs of the army coming this way, so it must not be able to communicate with them in its current state. Best to keep it that way."

"Agreed..." Alex pauses, remorse washing over her, *"Rick, I left them to die. They will all be slaughtered. I think the entire army has converged on Valyrn, all trying to get back to save her."* Alex's anguish at the massacre is almost too much to bear.

"There is nothing you could have done. We need you alive, and escaping was the best thing you could have done." Rick pauses for a moment to help Veela with something. *"We have the creature loaded onto the cart. We are heading your direction now. I suggest you go down into Brookstone's office and wait for us. We shouldn't be long."*

The connection breaks off, and Alex is left standing alone, feeling a million miles away from everything. The thoughts in her mind swirl in and out, her vision beginning to blur. For the first time in months, Alex is overwhelmed by the feelings of a panic attack. She crouches down to the ground and places her head between her knees. *An entire planet is going to fall because of my actions. I am responsible for the death of millions.* Her heart races, and her lungs seem to collapse as she struggles to catch a breath. Her mind is out of control, taking her beyond anything she has felt before.

She lies down on the ground as her body shakes with spent adrenaline and terror. As the panic races through her, a vision of her family dances behind her eyes. Suddenly, Alex can clearly see them in her mind. Her daughter laughs vibrantly as she plays in the backyard, and her husband chases after her, in a vigorous game of tag. She lets her mind stay with them, allowing her memories to overtake her and pull her to a happier place. *Once this is all over, I can go back to them, I can leave this all behind.* As she works to reassure herself, Dru's words echo in her mind.

"I think you are rather cold, like me. If given the choice, you would give it all up, just for the power. That

family you have, the one that floats in the back of your mind, you don't really care for them. You know your future isn't with them. It's here, in this galaxy."

Alex shudders at the memory. When Dru first spoke the words into her mind, Alex pushed against them, she rebelled. *That's not me, I love my family.* But another part of her resonated with the words. *Can I really step away from all this and go back to Earth to live a normal life, after everything I know?* Part of her does crave the power, the strength that comes with being the Defender. She was weak on Earth, constantly plagued by fear and anxiety, but here she is so much more. *What if Dru is right? What if my future is here?*

Her heart splits apart again. Could she really be the type of person that walks away from her family for fame and glory? *No, they are my world, without them, there is no reason.* Her mind circles back to them again, and her heart begins to repair itself. She knows her priorities; it's them. Dru was wrong, she is not cold, and love does not equal weakness. Love is strength; it is her strength.

Slowly she picks herself up, pushing herself to stand. Her legs shake under the weight of her panic attack, and her breath waivers. She pushes forward and makes her way to the office, each step helping to clear her mind. She enters the building and goes down the narrow staircase and enters Brookstone's office. On the ground in the centre of the room is a body covered by a sheet. *Brookstone.*

She moves past him and takes the second flight of stairs down to the lab, where she takes in the space that Veela has set up. The medical table in the middle of the room has been set up for Dru. There is another temporary table next to it; this one is set up for Alex. She shudders at the idea of more brain surgery, but she knows it is necessary.

Alex moves to a small chair and sits down; her legs continue to shake, now with the spent exertion from the battle. She rests her guns on the table and rubs her hands together. Doing a quick inventory of her injuries, she is surprised to find that her neck injury is the only significant one, followed by the gash across her forehead. The rest of her wounds are merely bruises, the majority of the damage having been absorbed by her armour.

She moves to a mirror and looks at her neck. Her skin is pale, and blood trickles from the open gash. Alex feels faint as she looks closely at the teeth marks on her skin and the depth of the wound. She can see muscle and bone. Finally, as the adrenaline wears off, the pain hits her. She staggers back to the chair and sits down shakily.

She takes some medical cloth and places it over the wound in an attempt to stop the bleeding. The pain sends her into a tailspin, and she blacks out for a moment. Waking up with her head on the desk, she feels a new bruise forming in the middle of her forehead from where she smacked it on the desk. Being more cautious, she places the cloth back over her neck and applies light pressure.

She sits still and allows her thoughts to wander back to her family. Roughly five minutes later, she hears the door of the upper office open. She jumps up and grabs her weapons. Crouching behind the edge of the table, she aims at the base of the staircase.

Veela enters first, guiding the hovering medical bed down the stairs with Rick trailing after it. Alex lowers her weapon and steps out from behind the table, making both Rick and Veela jump with surprise.

Recovering first, Rick rushes over to her and hugs her. "I'm so glad to see you, alive and mostly well." He makes note of her still bleeding neck wound.

Veela eyes it as well, "I can fix that."

"First, let's figure out exactly what makes her tick," Alex says, brushing Rick and Veela away from her neck and motioning to Dru.

The trio loads Dru onto the table and fastens the restraints that Brookstone had installed. Veela sets to work immediately, cutting into the creature's spine and digging around. Finally, she finds a small chip and works to remove it. With a bone-cracking sound, the chip is ripped free, and Veela holds it up in triumph. She takes it across the room to the lab workbench and puts it under a microscope for closer observation. With a series of explorative murmurs, Veela finally gives off triumphant '*aha!*'

She motions for Rick and Alex to come closer. "I have figured it out. We were right; the technology is remarkably similar to that in Alexia's mind, almost identical. A simple tweak to her frequency and range will put her in control of the army." She smiles broadly, happy to be playing her role in this war perfectly.

"OK, so what does that look like for me?" Alex asks warily.

"Well, normally I would suggest we sedate you, but time is not on our side. Every second we spend down here, the army rages across the galaxy. We need to get it in control and quickly. So, if you're up for it, I can perform the surgery with you awake. That way, you can immediately use the powers and bring the army to a halt," Veela replies clinically.

Sighing deeply, Alex gives her a nod. "This is going to hurt, isn't it?"

Veela is already moving to ready herself, "Yes," she responds curtly, forgetting her interaction skills. She winces at how harsh she sounded and adds, "Sorry."

Alex lies down on the table and takes long breaths to steady herself. Veela moves over to her and motions for Alex to roll over so that she is face down on the table. "You have to stay very still, Alexia. I'll be working directly in the base of your brain, where your spine and brain connect. Any movement at all could leave you paralyzed or dead."

"Excellent," Alex adds sarcastically, but the tone is lost on Veela.

"That most certainly would not be excellent," Veela responds with a confused look.

Sighing again, Alex looks to Rick, "Rick, would you mind holding my hand, and if necessary, holding me still?"

"Sure," Rick smiles encouragingly. He moves from across the room and takes a spot opposite Veela. He firmly grips Alex's hand and begins to tell her a story to distract her. His voice is full of sorrow, and Alex can feel his pain. He has endured so much today, so much loss and pain. He will need time to grieve, but that time is not now.

As Rick talks, Veela moves her hands over the base of Alex's head and feels for the soft spot that joins her skull and spine. "OK, here we go." Using a small knife, Veela cuts into Alex's skin, a long thin line, big enough for Veela to insert three fingers. Alex gasps in pain and grips Rick's hand, surely crushing his fingers with her immense strength, but he says nothing. He merely continues telling his story in hopes of distracting her.

Veela puts her knife down and inserts a finger into the open cut, feeling around for something. Alex feels the edges of her vision start to darken as her body threatens to pass out. "Breathe, Alexia, the worst is over," Veela tries to reassure her, but Alex knows she is lying.

With one finger still touching Alex's spine, Veela inserts a small tool and pushes around to alter the hardware already inside her mind. The bile in Alex's stomach rises, and she works to keep herself from throwing up. Doing her best to stay still, she begs Veela to finish. "Almost done, Alexia, almost…." With one final hard push, Veela pulls out of Alex's body and leaves Alex to breathe shakily as her body tries to move through the pain.

"Alexia, I need you to try and reach out. Connect with the army, even with just one being. Can you find them?" Veela asks tentatively.

Still shaking, Alex opens her mind and tries to locate the army. Like an overwhelming tidal wave, they come crashing into her mind. Thousands of them pop into existence, and her mind works to place them into categories. She can feel each of the beings, but none of them are as sentient as Dru. She truly was one of a kind.

The army itself cannot communicate. It can only receive orders and destroy. It has no further purpose beyond that. Alex shudders as she takes in the immense power of the army, an army designed solely for destruction.

"Yes, I can feel them," she replies through gritted teeth. Veela and Rick smile widely next to her.

"Time for the final test," Rick gives her hand a squeeze as he hopes for the best. "Can you tell them to stand down? Can you control them?"

Alex reaches out once more and connects with the creatures of the army. "Yes."

She gives a solid command that she feels ripple through the mass. *Stand down, stop fighting.* Alex feels the creatures respond. Immediately, they stop fighting, their collective mind changes its goal from destroying to retreating.

Alex can feel parts of her connection being severed as creatures are killed. She assumes that what is left of the civilians are continuing to fight even as the creatures turn away from them. She can hardly blame them. She too would kill the terrifying creatures, even if they seemingly stopped attacking.

Alex holds the connection to the army to ensure they continue to stand down, but she brings the conversation back to Rick and Veela. "They have stopped. It's working."

Both Veela and Rick laugh and smile, each of them immensely proud of the role they have played. Veela ends the celebrations first as she turns back to Alex and starts to apply a new layer of skin to the new gash on her neck. Once finished, she turns her attention to the injury caused by Dru. "This one will need some aftercare, but we can at least stop the bleeding."

Grateful for the care, Alex remains on the table until Veela is finished. Rick doesn't move from her side; she can feel the pride radiating off of him. "It's over, Alex. The war is over. You saved us."

Alex takes a deep breath, finally feeling like there is hope for them.

CHAPTER

The next few weeks move in a blur for Alex. The destruction caused by the army was more than she could have imagined. All the civilized parts of Valyrn were lost to the enemy. Majority of the civilians were killed, and all the PPC members that were on the planet at the time of the invasion are gone. The only remaining populace on the planet are the north and south Factions. They alone were able to keep the army back and defend their lands.

Solax was hit hard as well. Most of the homes were destroyed, leaving nothing but the main square behind. There were a few members of the PPC that managed to hide while the army rampaged. These members have retrieved their Stone Sets and are now seeking refuge on Zeya.

Zeya was the only planet left virtually untouched. It seems that Brookstone wanted to keep the fighting away from him and distributed his army to every location but Zeya.

Lillon, Trayton, and Alars saw minor destruction. The civilians there were well-armed and managed to hold the army off. The buildings remain standing, and the casualties were minimal. Even so, there are still years of repairs ahead of them.

Thankfully, the medical planets Aya and Meera were also virtually untouched. Now they are overrun with beings as they teleport in for medical help. The hospitals are full, and the doctors will be overworked for months as the full extent of the damage is revealed.

After taking control of the army, Alex had them return to their carrier ships on each of the planets. From there, bombs were laid in the ships, and the army was destroyed. Alex will always remember the feeling of loss as her connection to the army was severed.

The only remaining creature is Dru. Veela insisted on keeping her for research purposes. "It is our scientific duty to study her and understand what makes her superior. If we understand, we can defend ourselves against it in the future. Besides, she is a sentient being. She thinks and feels so we cannot simply kill her without first understanding her," Veela's words ring true, and her logic is sound, and the remaining PPC members all agree they need to know how to prevent attacks like this for the future.

Alex is not convinced; she feels that leaving Dru alive is an unnecessary risk. When they removed Dru's chip for studying, Alex's ability to control Dru was also removed. She has no control over this creature which means it is free to make its own decisions now. Veela tried to reinsert the chip, but too much damage was done during its removal.

Regardless of the failed attempt, Dru's mind is so advanced that she likely would have outgrown Brookstone's control in a matter of months.

Regardless of the threat, Veela is determined to keep Dru. She had the main cage transported to her home office on Aya and then had Dru transported under the watchful eye of the few remaining Barter guards.

Veela left shortly after Dru, her curiosity too great to keep her from the creature for long.

Rick and Alex were left to clean up the rest of the mess. Most of the PPC was destroyed by the army. What remains of it has gathered on Zeya and are looking to Rick and Alex for guidance.

The duo feels greatly unprepared for this portion of the war; the aftermath.

It is Rick that comes up with the first order of business. He gathers the remaining members of the PPC and gives them orders to help return the civilizations to some semblance of their old lives. Even with the best efforts put forward, Alex knows their old lives are gone.

"Rick, we need to disconnect the members from their Stones. I stand by what I said to them, the Stones are poisoning the civilizations, causing ripple effects that are catastrophic. You need to be the one who helps them; you need to lead them," Alex implores Rick to guide the PPC into a new era.

"I can't be their leader; I am not the Defender." Rick looks incredibly nervous at the idea of leading.

"Rick, I *was* their Defender; I did my part. But my time here is coming to an end. I can feel it, and I know you can too," Alex says with a slight bit of guilt.

Rick nods sadly to her, confirming her suspicions, "You're right, they need a leader, and I suppose that leader can be me. I'll call the Council together, what remains of them at least."

***

The next day the Council gathers. There are only twenty-four remaining members: twenty-four of three hundred. Rick looks sadly out at the small crowd, his eyes falling on all the empty spaces around them. They are gathered in a small shipping warehouse on Zeya, seeing as this is the only place left untouched.

The group looks tired and sad. They have lost over two hundred of their comrades, their close friends. Most of them have also lost family to the war. This galaxy has never experienced loss like this, and Alex's heart breaks for them.

Rick clears his throat and looks nervously at Alex. Only weeks before it was her that stood before them, trying to get them to work together to save themselves. Now it is Rick who stands before them, trying to put the broken pieces back together.

"My friends," he addresses them with a somber voice, "Our losses have been great. Our cities have fallen. Valyrn is gone to us. Solax is uninhabitable. Our friends and family have been killed or wounded. Our civilizations have been ravaged, and our way of life is gone."

Alex worries about Ricks' ability to bring his speech back around.

"But *we* are not gone," he motions to the beings standing around him. "We still stand, whether that is because we stood and fought or because we hid, it doesn't matter. The point is we are not gone." He takes a moment to look each of them in the eyes.

"And as long as we stand, our future has hope. I think you already know that we cannot act as we have in the past. We had too much corruption in our ranks, too much selfishness, and we turned a blind eye to it all. Our Stones are our weakness." He looks down at his own Set in his hands, and with a motion of saying goodbye, he sets his Stones down into a box by his side.

"We must return the Stones to where they came from. When the first PPC member was killed during Brookstone's experiments, his Stone Set returned to their natural habitat on Solax. Alexia and Brookstone found them there. We believe the Stones are no longer transferring themselves to beings that are best suited for them, rather they are returning to the planets that need them most. All of those that fell during the war lost their Stone Sets, and from what we can deduce, with the help of Dr. Veela, is that they have also moved to various planets to support the timelines and return life to their surfaces. The Stones are trying to right the wrong that was done by our Council.

"We have been passing the Stones down for too long, holding them hostage and keeping them from fulfilling their destinies. That time is over. Please stand with me, follow me. Together we can start repairing the damage we, and our generations before us, have done."

One by one, the members come forward and place the Stones in the box along with Rickert's. Some take a moment to say a formal goodbye while others simply drop theirs in the box, unable to find the words.

Alex watches as an entire way of life ends before her eyes. Once all the Stones have been separated from their former Holders, they form a circle around Rick once again.

"Excellent, the Stones will be transported back to their home on Solax, where we hope they will find their final destinations as they see fit." He closes the lid on the box. "Now it's time to talk about our future. I am not a man that is used to looking forward, not without the help of my Stone Set anyways." He gives a light chuckle as he admits to breaking their rules for time travel. "But Alex has reminded me of the power of our minds, our imaginations. We have a unique opportunity set before us to shape the way we manage ourselves going forward. I believe the PPC is still needed and that the Galaxy of Gatlin still needs leadership, but that leadership needs to look different. The purpose of that leadership needs to be renewed." The crowd around him looks nervous. Without their Stones, they feel a loss of power, a loss of confidence.

"Rick, I hear what you are saying, but how can this group be the leader of a galaxy? There is nothing that separates us from the basic beings now," a large orange alien steps forward.

"I think that is the point. We need to be basic beings, to be just like everyone else. We have led the galaxy from a point of superiority, separated from them by an entire planet, living in isolation on Solax. I think it's time to step out of the shell we have created and rejoin the civilizations. To help us with, that I have called in a friend."

This is Alex's cue. She steps to the middle of the room and sets the holocube down, giving the outgoing button a click. Everly flashes up before them.

The remaining members of the PPC recognize her immediately as a Faction member and their old biases cause them to sneer at her. Everly lets the reaction roll over her, leaving her unfazed and smiling back at them.

"I know you don't like me or what I stand for," Everly speaks to the crowd around her. Her voice rings through strong and with the authority of a true leader, something this group hasn't heard in a long time. "But the truth is you need me. I have spent my entire life living outside your reign, outside your influence. My community, along with the other Factions, has thrived without you or your Stones." As she continues to speak, the crowd around her leans in to listen, attracted to her confidence.

"I can offer you a new future, a new goal. I come before you to offer a truce between the Factions and the PPC. I recommend that the leaders of the five Factions join what remains of the PPC. Together, we can rebuild what has fallen and reshape what remains. A new future is in front of us. This is a future that is beyond the manipulation of the Stones, functioning as things were designed to be." She lets her voice trail off, and the members nod along with her.

Rick steps beside her holographic image and addresses the crowd. "This is it, my friends, this is my proposal. Join with the Factions, be the leaders of this new time! What do you say?" Rick's voice rises in bravado in an effort to rally the remaining PPC members. The crowd cheers in earnest for a new beginning.

CHAPTER

57

Her time has come, the time for her to go home. Her Stones nestle themselves in her pocket. Here they will stay until she is ready to make her final jump back to Earth, back to her family. The new Council has determined that she should keep her Stones and carry them back to Earth to set its timeline back in motion once again.

Veela believes the Stones would choose to stay with her anyways since they selected her as the worthiest being in the first place. The Stones from the remaining members were returned to Solax. From there, they whooshed themselves away to some foreign location or to another being, if they so chose. Either way, the balance would be returned between nature and being. The Stones would see to a new future.

Alex stands in the centre of Veela's large living room back on Aya for what she secretly hopes is the last time. Veela has been here since the war ended, studying the sedated Dru and trying to unlock her secrets. She was happy to hear the remaining Council members handed over their Stone Sets. She believes that any future enemies they may face would try to attack them through their Stones. "Being rid of those things was a desirable choice," Veela pats Rick on the forearm as she makes the comment. He still clearly feels naked without his Stone Set. He had to travel through the transportation stations for the first time in two hundred and twenty-five years and then take public transit to Veela's home. It was terribly humbling for him. Both Alex and Veela laughed at the small brown alien.

Rick has taken a seat next to Everly and the other Faction leaders on the new Council. They have set up their main headquarters on Trayton. This resourceful planet was deemed the best to help coordinate the rebuilding process. The cities of Valyrn still remain uninhabitable, and all the old PPC members agreed they should not go back to Solax. "The planet needs time to heal from our damage. Let's leave it be," Rick told the group.

Other key members from the civilizations have also been selected to help organize the process to rebuild. An entirely new Council is being formed, but they still haven't agreed on a new name. "Progress takes time," Everly told Rick as the group kindly debated what they should be calling themselves.

Rick is a patient leader, having taken on the role with grace. He does not seem to be too tainted by the old ways, but he does have a hesitancy in his actions. He was so badly burned by the betrayal from Brookstone that he has vowed to never let that kind of deception into his life again. He maintains a watchful eye over each new and old Council member.

Both he and Veela seem to be coming closer together, rekindling the lost love they once had. It makes Alex happy to see the two beings drawn back to each other.

Alex paces around the living room and smiles as her friends enter the room. Veela looks tired but happy to have such a scientific wonder lying on the table in her lab. Rick also looks tired but equally happy. They stride in holding hands, the tall orange alien towering over the stout brown being. *A perfect pair*, Alex thinks to herself with a smile.

"Are you sure you must go? There is so much left for us to do here." Rick has spent most of his free time trying to convince Alex to stay, but her family calls to her.

"My time here is done, Rick," Alex replies with a tinge of sadness.

"We can find a way to bring your family to us," Veela tries weakly to back up Rick's pleas for her to stay.

Alex just smiles at them and reaches out to hug each of them in turn.

"If you ever need me, you know where to find me." She pulls out her Stone Set and places them in her hands. "But please knock first." She gives a wink to Rick and taps her forehead. They aren't sure how far their connection will carry, but it is possible she will still be able to communicate with Rick from Earth.

She takes a breath to steady herself and looks around the room once more. With one final smile, she grips her Stones and imagines her home in her mind. With the whoosh that is becoming so familiar, she is transported away from Aya, out of the Galaxy of Gatlin, and lands on the soft ground of Earth.

CHAPTER

58

lex takes in the sights around her. Everything is exactly as she left it. As promised, time has stood still here. At the return of her and her Stone Set, time is once again pushed forward, ready to resume its natural pattern.

Alex stands in her backyard with the cloudy sky overhead. The day is exactly as she remembers it. The sun is starting to peek through the clouds, and the rays touch her face. She closes her eyes and absorbs the heat, listening to the sounds of the birds and the children in her neighbourhood.

Alex still has all her powers, but Veela did a bit of work on her to return her physical appearance to that of her old ones. Her eyes no longer sparkle so intensely, her scars are hidden under new skin, and the shape of her face is the same as it once was. Veela wasn't able to change much about her body shape though, she is still as muscular as she was back in Gatlin. She decided that she could wear baggy clothes for a while and tell people she had just been working out. *No need to tell anyone that I have alien muscle tissue and metals running through my body.* Alex laughs at the idea of uttering those words to someone here, on Earth. Doctors would never let her out of the small, padded cell they put her in. Mind you, she could probably break out easily enough.

Opening her eyes once more, she steps through the back door of her house and looks lovingly at the home before her; the toys scattered on the ground, the dishes in the sink. *Perfection,* she thinks to herself. Quietly, she tiptoes through the house to the base of the stairs. She is about to climb up to seek the comforting arms of her husband when a noise makes her draw up short. Crouching down slightly, her new instincts kick in, and she looks around for danger.

A ruffling noise floats down to her. She climbs slowly up the stairs and rounds the corner to the hallway, where the doors to her sleeping husband and daughter sit. Her heart grows cold as she notices the door to her daughter's bedroom is ajar. Alex crouches down and steps toward the door. Suddenly, it swings open, and a small creature comes flying out at her.

"Mommy!" her daughter screams as she collides into her arms.

THE END

EPILOGUE

Dru has been in and out of consciousness for months. The doctor that works on her keeps her sedated majority of the time, but occasionally she is brought to consciousness.

This time Dru can feel the doctor hovering over her. She toes the fine line between unconscious and awake. With a sudden rush, she feels the adrenaline pump into her body through the thin IV as the doctor attempts to wake her up.

Dru's eyes flash open and land on the doctor. Taking a moment to centre herself, Dru reaches out telepathically to the doctor. Dru can tell that the doctor's mind is weak. She is intelligent but has no telepathic control. Dru sees everything the moment she opens the mental connection between them.

"Where am I?" Dru asks Veela.

The doctor stares at her with wild eyes. "You can communicate?" she speaks out loud in response.

"I feel like that is obvious at this point. Brookstone created me to lead his army. I need to be able to communicate, even with those that are far inferior to me."

The insult seems to snap the doctor out of her trance. "I am not inferior. After all, you are the one strapped to my table."

"*For now,*" Dru responds in a bored tone. "*How long have I been here, and why can I no longer feel my army?*"

"It's been six months since we captured you and destroyed your army. The war is over; you lost," the doctor replies triumphantly.

"*Hmm, that's disappointing. Was it Alexia Harmon who saved the day? Was she the Defender you were all hoping for?*" Dru's curiosity about Alexia is piqued.

"Yes, she was. She is the one who took control of the army and ended the destruction. She is gone now, back to Earth." The doctor looks pleased with herself, like she is lording a win over Dru's head. But Dru never really expected to win. Brookstone's plan was pathetic, his reasoning was simplistic and short-sighted.

"*So, your Defender is gone then. Interesting.*" Dru's response makes the doctor's face falls slack as she realizes she has revealed something she probably shouldn't have.

"Yes, she is. But we are rebuilding that which Brookstone destroyed." She scrambles to cover up what she revealed, but Dru has stopped listening, her mind moving quickly to plan her escape. The doctor has been making mistakes this entire time. Each time she woke Dru to conduct more tests, Dru's system worked to clear itself of the tranquilizers coursing through her system. Now Dru can process a full dose of tranquilizers in under fifteen minutes, but the doctor still expects the tranquilizers to last days.

But Dru couldn't escape, not yet. Something in her own mind was holding her back, and now she knows. She was waiting to find out if the galaxy was still protected. It's not that she fears Alexia Harmon, but things would be a lot easier if she were gone.

Finally, Veela stops rambling, and Dru finds space in her mind to plant an idea. It's a subtle form of telepathy that Dru was working to master back when Brookstone still stood outside her cage. She simply reaches out and inserts something. At first, she started with images, making Brookstone remember things that weren't real, but then she was able to insert voices. It drove Brookstone mad, hearing so many voices inside his head. It makes Dru laugh at his stupidity. He thought he controlled her, but it was always the other way around.

Dru suggests to the doctor that she should sedate Dru once again and place her back in the cage. *It's time for lunch, doctor, you are hungry. You will be back after lunch, so you only need a small amount of tranquilizer.*

The doctor stops fidgeting and looks at her watch. "Time for you to go back to sleep. I'll see you after lunch." She reaches to the lab bench behind her and pulls out the sedatives, measuring out half a dose.

Dru slips off to sleep as the doctor rolls her back into the cage, leaving her attached to the bed frame. Dru can feel the doctor exit the cage and leave for lunch.

Dru peeks out from behind her sedated eyelids. The tranquilizers are heavy in her system, but they are not strong enough to put her completely to sleep. With a slight flex to her pincers, the restraints around her body snap.

Stretching her pincers out to the sides, she moves to a seated position and unfurls her wings behind her back.

Taking a heavy pincer, she reaches down to the far corner of the cage and pulls back a loose tile in the floor. Dru has spent months hollowing out this space, creating a small hole to hide her most valuable treasure. This is the moment Dru has been waiting for, a moment that presented itself to her months ago, but Dru needed to be sure she could escape successfully. She needed to know that after she escaped, she could roam freely in the galaxy, and fulfill her purpose.

Dru reaches down and pulls out a Stone Set. She clicks manically as she holds them against her body. With a single thought, Dru is pulled from the cage and transported away.

CHARACTER DESCRIPTIONS

Shown in order of appearance

Alex - A tall, lean human that hails from Earth. She is a wife and mother. She has lean legs, long blonde hair, and a strong upper body. She suffers from chronic anxiety and depression, often affecting her physically and emotionally. She is a mid-level employee on Earth and the newest Stone Set Holder. She enjoys running and physical activity. She has been enhanced past her basic human form to possess emotion-sensing, mind reading, and telepathic control.

Androx - A green-skinned alien with a slight body frame. His height does not exceed five feet. His round head features thin lips that mirror those of a human, and two deep-set eyes that hide a depth of knowledge. He is not built for manual labour, but rather relies on his intelligence. Unlike the 'traditional human body,' he has three legs and four arms. He works at the Embassy of Valyrn as a Cataloguer and originally hails from Lillon.

Stellie - A tall, purple alien with a single small eye and a small round mouth. She has advanced alien hands with two extra fingers. She is just over six feet tall but has a very thin body frame. Her arms are thin and spindly, legs long and lean. She has a high-pitched voice and is the Lead Cataloguer at the Embassy of Valyrn.

Rickert - A short, brown alien with a body shaped like an ice cream cone. He has a small head on top of extremely broad shoulders that extend down to narrow hips and small feet. His eyes are startlingly blue and wise, while his smile is bright. He has four-fingered hands. He is one of three brothers, his eldest is in jail for murdering his father, who was a previous Stone Set Holder. He has a romantic relationship with Veela. He was once best friends with Brookstone.

Brookstone - A brown-skinned alien with a stern face. His face features round eyes set heavily into his large head, a small cat-like nose, and a pencil-thin mouth. He exclusively wears a long robe that hides the shape of his body. His voice is a low baritone. He is roughly the same height as a human. He hails from the planet Earth, but currently resides on Solax. He was once best friends with Rickert.

Dru - She is a member of the unique species called a Shreikers, and she closely resembles a large insect. Huge pincers jut from her body, and she can emit a loud whooping sound that will kill all those standing within range. She has two legs and human-like eyes. Her nose is that of a small elephant. Her mouth opens horizontally and holds thousands of small teeth. She has wings that curl around her back, allowing her to fly. She is the creation of Brookstone and the leader of the Shreiker army. She communicates telepathically.

Kody - A small black creature, commonly known as a dog on Earth. Kept as a pet by Rickert, he lives on Muskoux and is fondly referred to as a Floofin.

Veela - A tall, orange alien with soft, smooth skin. Her hair is a vibrant orange and flows down the side of her head and her back. She has full lips and three eyes set on an oval face. She has four arms and two legs. She is a doctor who lives and works on planet Aya. She lacks people skills but is a famous doctor throughout the entire galaxy. The PPC holds her in high regard. She is in a romantic relationship with Rickert.

Everly - She is a tall and muscular alien that holds an air of authority. She has pale yellow skin, two arms, two legs, and a short mid-section. She is incredibly confident, a natural-born leader. Her face is set in a permanent state of strong determination, and her eyes are hard with years of experience. She lives in Haldree on the planet Valyrn and leads the civilization of the northern Faction as their Commander. She is the mother of one son, Evar.

Evar - Son to the Commander of Haldree (Everly), about seven years old. He is a brave boy who has the makings of a leader. He is small, but he is also strong, both physically and mentally. He has deep blue eyes and pudgy round cheeks.

CONTRIBUTORS

**A special thank you to all those
who contributed funds to
assist in the publication of this book**

Savannah Noel

Jennifer and Darryl Low

Mona Johnston

Adam Brown

Andrea Williamson

Kelsey Hamill

Amy Richards

Teresa Vander

Meer-Chasse

Scarlett Noel

Zinnia and Doug Johnston

Jordanna Rowat

Samantha Hannah

Al Johnston

Karen Soehn

Erin Dentzien

Inez Goodwin

Kyle Soehn

Heather Harper

Sheri Gagne

Kailey McLeod

Ashley Regner

Michael Clark

Michael Green

Caitlin Brown

Jody Blackmore

Chris Johnston

CPSIA information can be obtained
at www.ICGtesting.com
Printed in the USA
LVHW092028280122
709434LV00009B/228

9 780228 866046